Danielle,

Best Wishes,

Janet R Freed

W9-CYA-764

Six Feet from Impact

by

Janet K. Roof

Bloomington, IN authorHOUSE Milton Keynes, UK

AuthorHouse™
1663 Liberty Drive, Suite 200
Bloomington, IN 47403
www.authorhouse.com
Phone: 1-800-839-8640

AuthorHouse™ UK Ltd.
500 Avebury Boulevard
Central Milton Keynes, MK9 2BE
www.authorhouse.co.uk
Phone: 08001974150

*This book is a work of fiction. People, places, events, and situations
are the product of the author's imagination. Any resemblance to actual
persons, living or dead, or historical events, is purely coincidental.*

© 2006 Janet K. Roof. All rights reserved.

*No part of this book may be reproduced, stored in a retrieval system, or
transmitted by any means without the written permission of the author.*

First published by AuthorHouse 4/18/2006

ISBN: 1-4259-2995-8 (sc)

Library of Congress Control Number: 2006903110

Printed in the United States of America
Bloomington, Indiana

This book is printed on acid-free paper.

I would like to dedicate this book to the beautiful coast of the New Jersey Shore. For without its inspiration my vision would not have been possible.

Chapter One

*T*he intense glow of brilliant light was so concentrated you would think that your eyes would melt and trickle down your face just looking at it. Your first thought would be to hurry and hide, cover up your body, and get out of the light! The impulse to hide in the darkness, as a vampire would run from the sunlight, would run surging through your veins. However, it was not like that at all. I, too, was marked like one of the so-called vampires who wanted to run from its treacherous grasp and wished I had not done what I had done to have been thrown into this line of work.

Maybe they did not deem themselves deserving of the job that they had, the job we were all damned to have for all of eternity. I myself hadn't heard of anyone who ever got to leave. I guess I was one of the true risk-takers, one who longed for true death. I tried to laugh in the face of it, but it just laughed at me instead.

I have been roaming this earth for a few hundred years; in that time the world has changed before my very eyes. Over the years, I have become a master at my work. I can tell you at first, I was inexperienced and clumsy, making many mistakes in my given trade. As time went on, things became second nature to me. My speed and agility and my ability to manipulate the elements all became an obsession to me. Hope seemed to be the only thing I had to assist me in my work. I made many mistakes in the process, and my heart was the price I had to pay for all of them.

My soul, on the other hand, was in question. I wasn't sure if I even had one anymore or ever did for that matter. My name is John Davis. Well, it was John Davis before that dreadful day so many years ago. The last time my ears heard my name called out by another mortal being, I was the center of attention only minutes away from being hanged.

Who could have thought when my body was bound to that massive oak tree that my life that day wouldn't end? Only my life as I knew it was over. As I stood tethered up there on that hill overlooking the meadow where we played as children, a million things flashed through my mind: My first horse, hiding from my pa after I crashed the wagon, my wedding day, the day my son was born, and the most recent, the day I took another man's life. I would rather have been left swinging from that wretched tree as a snack for the scavenger birds to feast upon than be cursed for all of eternity.

Why didn't someone else come for me that day? Why did it have to be her? With the face of an angel, she had a bright orange light radiating from around her body. The innocent eyes of a child spoke to me as she gazed upon me on that very day. I didn't know who she was, but there was something very calming about her. But instead of feeling overwhelmed with peace and serenity, I felt a calm sense of fear, an emotion that as a mortal man wasn't available to me. I would exist to know this feeling well, know it to be the only feeling offered to me, something I just wasn't able to put my finger on...

It was an extremely hot day. The tourists were still arriving. It would be one of the most lucrative Fourth of July holidays the Jersey Shore had seen in years. I had ranged my territory beginning at Sunset Island and crossing over Barnegat Bay to Seaside Heights through Seaside Park and extending down to the three thousand acres that filled what was left of Island Beach State Park. More people vacationing on my turf would mean that I'd be working double time to keep life's balance in order. It's funny to me how if I had never done the dirty deed so long ago that got me into this line of work, I would have never known that people like me even existed. It's funny what things in life we take for granted, how every day we almost come face-to-face with death. Who would have thought that walking down the street or in many cases, going for a pit stop in your own bathroom would be such a high risk?

I grew to love my work over time, so much so, that I sometimes spent more time than I was allotted on my acquaintances. Intervening with death is hard work, and on occasion, I would come across a person that I was sure deserved to be amongst the living. I would do whatever I could within my power to protect that gift of life. It would work sometimes, and on one particular occasion, it worked for about a week. Nevertheless, as many times as I tried and as many times as I would save them from their fate of death, they would always find that glowing spot under their feet; the green light always came back eventually.

That dreaded green light sucked them in and took their lives. I think not knowing where they went was the most crippling of all. If only I was sure it was a pleasant environment, a place of peace and love, it would have put my mind at ease. I always hoped that their fate had been one better than I had received. What if their fate was worse than the fate I had made for myself? Where and what could they be doing to fulfill their destinies? Maybe no one has the answer.

You see, everyone has a final breath that they take before they pass on. The only thing that is different about each breath is that your final breath is taken in a place of its own, a place where the light is the crisp color of life. Not everyone dies in the same place. As one man may die in his bed while he is sleeping, another will go by being hit by a bus on Main Street. My job is to distract destiny long enough to get mortals out of its way, out of the way of the harmful light that can come to them at any time in any place. Sometimes, the diversion would be as easy as dropping an acorn on one's head. It was long enough to distract them, long enough for the light to disappear.

Others took a bit more ingenuity. I saved a family from total devastation reducing the number for whom the bell tolls by four.

"Come on, kids, settle down back there," a father shouted into the back seat of a late model wagon.

"He started it," a little girl squealed and kicked the back of her father's seat.

"Did not. Mom, she's pulling my hair!" the boy exclaimed.

3

"Billy's getting sand in my ice cream. Dad, will you tell him to stop?" the furious sister replied.

As the family's car began to depart the parking lot on the corner of Hamilton Avenue and Ocean Terrace, I could see the bright green space grow larger as they approached the intersection. You see, a terrible light that radiates for multiple victims is far brighter and larger than the light that comes for a single victim.

Thinking briefly and rushing with speed that was far faster than any mortal man, I ran as fast as I could headfirst into a traffic sign, forcing it to buckle over, topple into the street, and block the family's path over the horrible light that was waiting for them in the intersection. The man slammed on his brakes, and the car came to an abrupt stop, shaking the passengers around and causing them to stop fighting and take notice of the situation.

"Harold, what are you doing?" the mother screamed.

"Now that I have all of your attention, buckle up and keep your mouths shut. I want quiet for the remainder of the trip." He smiled to himself and proceeded on his way, safe and out of the way of the deadly green light.

I'm not sure if everyone would have died that day, but what I can tell you is those children didn't have to see their father die. He would live for another day, just long enough to tuck them into bed and tell his children he loved them and make love to his wife just one last time. This, in turn, was long enough to satisfy me with the job that I had done.

It was just another typical day of work at my own private patch of the Jersey Shore. I figured if I hung out around at the beach in Seaside Heights, maybe I could have a few laughs or maybe get an eyeful of the girls who loved to tan their bodies with practically nothing on.

Looking around the beach at everyone laughing and having a good time, I found that the light was totally out of sight. Being so pleased that the light was dormant, I couldn't do anything but smile about it. Something like this happened so seldom that I didn't let it worry me; in fact, I didn't worry about it at all, and I just enjoyed the day.

I watched the people with their families, friends, and loved ones frolicking about on the coast and wondered with jealousy if I had done things differently, would I have been as happy in my life as they were in theirs?

There was a Spanish couple kissing under a red and white umbrella. Their children were playing in the sand around them. I watched them as they began to smile at one another.

"I love you, Poppy," the woman smiled and said.

"I love you, too, Mommy," the man said and continued to kiss his beloved.

Their children giggled at the sight of their parents kissing on the beach and huddled together laughing quietly with their hands cupped over their mouths. *So much love,* I thought to myself. How I longed for the love of another human being.

A preppy couple was bickering about who should get up early and make the coffee. The woman reached into her bag and opened up a date planner.

"See my schedule, Tim? When do I have the time? I'm too busy taking care of the business to make the damn coffee. Forget it. I'll buy a damn coffeemaker that has a timer; it serves a better purpose than you do. You can kiss my ass."

There were many people sitting in beach chairs reading books, only looking over top of them whenever a lifeguard blew his whistle. Most were just relaxing, enjoying the cool summer breeze. The part of the beach that I enjoyed the most spanned between Casino Pier on Sherman Avenue and Funtown Pier on Porter Avenue. Tourists would flock to this part of the beach being that it was centered in the heart of this exciting summer town. Every time I would hear the pop of a flip-top can, my mouth would water for the cool, refreshing taste of a cold beer, or any beverage for that matter.

Things were easier to come by in this day and age, and people seemed to waste more than they could consume. Daily life now was not at all as it was when I lived on this earth. Back then, we had to struggle to get what we had and fight to keep it. It was a more difficult time to live in. Today's hardships seemed like tripe compared to the daily obstacles one would have to overcome when I was a mortal on this earth.

I took my time looking over all who were on the beach that day. My eyes panned over the crowd, wondering if the dreaded light would come and disrupt my peaceful day by ruining the lives of the people that it laid its deadly grip upon. I could see flashes of the light out in the water, but they were far away from all human life. I was sure the flashes of light were just for the small fish that were about to be eaten by some much larger, hungrier fish. This light was different. It was green with a dark blue ring around it, the same way the light looked when it came for someone who was about to be murdered by another man's hand, two lights connecting into one, the victim and their killer. Whether it be for food or for some other ungodly reason, the murderous light was distinguished by the dark blue haze that circled its green counterpart.

I had been told that the only lives that couldn't be interfered with were those which were to be taken by the hand of another, murders. Under no circumstances was I to intervene with the mortals who were to be murdered. If only I was able to tell the murdering party that their fate would be one of total damnation, maybe they wouldn't kill and be destined to roam this earth like me. However, knowing their simple minds, at the time, I knew they wouldn't listen anyway. I knew for sure if I had been forewarned, I would have never been in that situation of putting out the lights and taking another man's life. I found it funny, how, as I turned off those lights, my eternity was to be spent protecting others from that same light.

I walked the beach admiring the girls in their skimpy beachwear, skin as far as the eye could see. There were many beautiful women relaxing out on the beach that day, but when I strolled up to the next blanket, I never expected that I would come across the most beautiful female that ever adorned the Atlantic Ocean. My heart sank. She was gorgeous, with long brown hair that seemed to go on forever; the sun, in some places, lightened it, and the way it lay against her tan skin, it was spectacular. Her legs were solid and muscular. She had jowls of native descent. She had a sexy little dimple in her chin with an elegant neck and shoulder combo.

I had never been more captivated by the sight of a woman before. This woman was like no ordinary woman; she was a sex kitten. Everything about her spewed sex, from her modestly painted fingernails down to her perfectly painted pedicure; she was flawless. Her skin had a radiant glow from the sun, and she had teeth as white as new-fallen snow. If I could have just seen the eyes that were covered by her amber specs, my day would have been complete. Why did she have to be wearing those sunglasses? I was sure that her eyes were more beautiful than I could have ever imagined.

The wind gusted gently around me, and I could smell a strong scent of wildflowers in the air. That was strange to smell on the beach. I looked around to see what was causing the sweet scent but couldn't pinpoint where it was coming from. I continued to gaze at the beautiful Kitten as she ran her fingers through the sand beside her chair. Her lips were plump and pouty and looked delicious as they wrapped around the straw protruding from her Coke can.

In the distance, I could see the light out of the corner of my eye. "Crap!" I had to go fulfill my destiny, assisting the mortals in despair. Never taking another look at the sexy Kitten, I darted down the beach. I could see the people looking with dismay out at a splashing sight in the water. Someone was in trouble. I ran down the beach, gaining on the glowing light. I could see the flailing figure struggling to keep its head above the waterline. It sank down for an instant and then bobbed back up again. I ran harder and seemed to be there in a flash. The lifeguard was just getting off his post and on his way into the water when I first got to the swimmer.

She was frantically trying to keep her head above the water, but her strength gave out, and she began to sink. The guard dove down to retrieve the woman and pulled her up, keeping her head out of the water. He wrapped his arm around her and started swimming back to shore. Knowing where he was headed, I knew that if he pulled out the victim and brought her to the part of the beach that was glowing green, the girl would be a goner. I needed to distract him long enough in the crashing waves so that the current would take him a little farther down the shore, just far enough away from the glowing green light, and then he could attempt to revive her.

I pushed the water current hard around his feet and even tried pulling the lifeguard and the victim out of the harmful path leading to the light, but nothing I did made any difference. When he pulled her out of the water, another guard who was conducting crowd control grabbed her from his arms and carried her to the first-aid kit next to the large chair, precisely where the damn light was waiting.

"Excuse me, people, please, step aside and make some room!" one of the guards shouted. "Can we please back it up, folks? This woman needs some air."

I held one of the pontoon ropes taut to trip him up with the hope that he might lay her down a safe distance from the light, but he just stood his ground and placed her down right in the center of the fucking light.

I fell to my knees and begged for freedom. "Please, I can't take it anymore! I quit! I am not protecting one more person. I can't withstand this terrible feeling of loss another time." I could not help the tears from trickling down my face. I had had enough. "Why do I have the power to protect life if I can't save everyone who is in harm's way?" I looked around as if I would receive a reply to my question, but as always, the voices I heard were mortal and not the ones intended for my ears.

The conversation of the crowd overlapped. "Is she dead?"…"What happened here?"…"Did she get bit by a shark?"…"Dude, did you see that guy almost trip?"…"Someone call an ambulance."

I watched as the men worked on her, attempting to force air back into her lungs and get her to breathe on her own, but their efforts were to no avail. She would never get the chance again to see the sun set. Time for her had expired, and with all of my attempts, I was unable to protect her from the deadly light. The hellish glow heckled me when it won the battle between life and death. The ambulance pulled up, and the crowd dispersed as they loaded the woman into the back of the rig.

Looking up at the sun and then out over the cool green water of the Atlantic, I was all alone and realized I always would be. Just then, I remembered Kitten, my goddess of the Atlantic. I booked down the beach so I could gaze at her beauty for a little while longer, possibly the rest of the afternoon, but she was gone. All that remained of her was the slight impression of her chair in the sand and a small castle she had made of dripping sand.

I had to find her. I looked everywhere, but she was nowhere in sight. "Damn it!" I wondered if I would ever see her again. I truly hoped she was a local. If she was local, why was it that I had never seen her before? I darted up to the boardwalk and roamed for hours in search of the woman who had captivated my mind. I wandered from Webster Avenue down to Hiering and back down all the way to Fourteenth, but things were quiet for most of the day. I had covered over five square miles but could not pinpoint Kitten's location.

Night had come, and because it was Friday night, I would have my work cut out for me. I was sitting on the tiny roof of the Grant Avenue beach badge booth, watching the sights of the summer night. It was a display of music, lights, and voices. Bodies were in motion all about the wooden planks of the boardwalk, people laughing and shouting. All of these noises consumed the salty air around me. I loved just taking it all in. I decided to take a walk being that there was nothing going on, and no sooner did I think about it, I turned the corner, and there it was: that dreadful light.

The heavy stench of alcohol filled the air, and this kid did not look good. I could smell the whisky as clear as if I had the shot right under my nose. He turned and stumbled to look at the little sexy chick that had strolled on by, and then he tripped over the parking meter and fell face first down toward the sidewalk. I knew that it was my turn to step in when the light showed its ugly self. Using my quick reflexes, I zoomed down to the street smacked a large stuffed animal from a tourist's hands, and it flew in front of the bumbling drunk softening the blow as he fell to the ground. The instant the stuffed toy hit the center of the light, it had gone dim, and I knew it would not be returning for now.

Releasing a large sigh of relief, I realized that I could continue my search for the little Kitten that I discovered on the beach earlier. I was anxious to see her again, and she was all I could think about, her long flowing hair and beautiful lips. I walked around for a few hours but could not find her anywhere. I figured a beauty such as she would be hanging out in a classier place. Nothing this close to the boardwalk would do. I went down to the Top-of-the-Mast restaurant that overlooked the beach down on Twenty-Third in Seaside Park.

It seemed to me that if she would be anywhere, it would be here; besides, a better class of people dined here, and the atmosphere was breathtaking. A tall, dark, blue-carpeted stairway curved up toward the restaurant. The upstairs was serene with tall, glittery popcorn ceilings. The entire back wall of the restaurant was glass, and the view of the beach was spectacular. The moon rising over the Atlantic Ocean was the first image you saw as the gentle summer night wind caused the dune grass to sway from side to side. Music played by a DJ filled the background air, and one could view evening anglers surf fishing on the stretch of beach just outside long into the night.

Dining onlookers watched from the balcony as they ordered lobster tails and danced the night fantastic. The bar at this particular restaurant was always jumping with action, and the girls were always trying to outdo one another at looking pretty. This was where all the large paycheck men spent their money, and it was every woman for herself when it came to hunting down and landing themselves a man. Women would literally body-check each other when a new man appeared.

It was funny watching them try to pose and primp their bodies without being noticed for trying too hard. I had to laugh about it. I can't begin to tell you how many women I have saved from the light by catching them with a chair as they were falling because they couldn't walk due to their six-inch-high heels. You would be surprised how many women almost die, because they are trying to look sexy, sucking a cherry off the stem. What a joke! These women would have choked to death if it had not been for my intervention. I spent over four hours hanging around the restaurant, and Kitten was nowhere in sight. I could see the sand in the distance begin to light with a green glow. I would have to put my search on hold for the moment and see what was going on out on the beach.

I glided across the sand, and as I approached the waterline, I could hear a gurgling scream muffled by the sounds of water pounding. Three men scrambled frantically to free a towline from the mechanical wench mounted to their jeep bumper. One man grabbed the end of the cable, ran down the beach, and dove into the water, swimming with all the strength he had to reach the drowning victim. The yelling came to a halt as the wench began to reel in the two men. *They caught a big one!* I thought to myself, but that wasn't funny. Really, it was not; the person was seriously injured, and it did not look like he had much of a chance to survive.

They pulled the bloody swimmer from the water and placed him on the sand just two feet from the brilliant light. Blood gushing from the stump of his severed leg spilled out, mixing with the ocean surf and turning the foam a brilliant red. I wondered why the light shone brightly only a few feet away. I could see the ambulance lights coming up the ramp of the pavilion when it hit me. Quickly, I dove into the water and searched the ocean floor for the severed limb that was missing from the individual who lay in agony on the cool wet sand.

As I emerged from out of the ocean, I could see the paramedics placing the gurney directly into the light. I knew for sure if they had placed him in that spot, he would have had no chance at survival, and his life would perish. Therefore, I pushed the water as hard as I could to force a wave that took the limb from my grasp and hurled it straight at them. Before they knew what was happening, this partially eaten leg came from out of nowhere and landed in the light. They jumped, and the gurney moved over just enough to be free from its deadly grasp.

"Holy shit! Did you see that?" one paramedic grimaced and yelled to the other.

"Yeah, man, that was sick. Where did that leg come from anyway?" the second man screeched as he rubbed his head in disbelief, shaking it from side to side.

"Who knows, dude? Let's just get this guy in the rig. Maybe the doc can reattach this thing. Try not to touch the end and get some ice packed on that fast."

They scooped up the mangled shell of a man, placed his leg wrapped in ice on his chest, and raced him off to the hospital. I wondered if he would survive this terrible ordeal, and if so, how long he would be amongst the living after what had happened. I was not supposed to spend time with my interventions longer than the initial distraction. Whatever happened to them later was none of my concern.

I could see the light glowing just under the surface of the ocean. It was strange, but at night, the light was very beautiful when it would illuminate the sparkling water of the dark sea. I guess that shark was still hungry. After all, he did have his dinner interrupted tonight. I did not mind looking at the light when it had come for the fish. It was like watching fireworks exploding in the water. The cool water was so inviting. I could see how that last victim could have been overwhelmed with the beauty of the ocean, forcing him to expose himself to the harsh reality of nature and swimming at night when there were no lifeguards to keep watch.

The ocean was one of the most beautiful and refreshing places on the earth. Besides the fact that I hated the mainland, the ocean was the only place that I could spend eternity without running out of beautiful sunrises and sunsets to keep my heart occupied. I dreaded the thought of going back to the mainland, which had been where I spent my last days as a mortal, and I did not look forward to ever crossing that God-awful Tunney Bridge that connected me to it.

The best action took place directly on the coast in this town anyhow. The boardwalk, which was filled with cretins who possessed such scandalous aptitudes for taking tourists' money in the peak season, demanded my presence here. Yet I could not resist looking for her. As I walked down the boardwalk, I managed to fight the crowd through the packed section between Porter and Sherman. It was madness, and the people were rushing around like ants under attack on an anthill.

Chapter Two

*T*he blinking lights and the music from the dance club were calling me, and I could not imagine why. As I headed down Hamilton, I found myself drawn to Dark Crystal. I hated the dance music, but I just could not keep myself from entering the doors from which it blared. There was a line of people waiting for acceptance into the club that spanned around the corner. I entered, and it was loud and hot. I have been up on roofs in August that were not as hot. The club was body-to-body people dancing, drinking, and talking loudly. There was a heavy cloud of cigarette smoke in the air, and I still could not figure out why I was in this place to begin with.

My eyes panned the room in search of whatever it was that had drawn me in. When I saw her, she was even more radiant then I had remembered. Her dress was long and flowing in the back, short and tight in the front, hugging her curves like a glove. It was pink, and she looked gorgeous. I could hear my heart thumping over the music, pounding out the beat of desire in my ears. She wore her hair down. I was still unable to see her eyes. I worked my way through the crowd to where she was standing and looked to see if she was alone or with someone. Just as I reached the spot, a woman motioned for her to follow to the women's restroom. In an instant, she was on her way, following closely behind. Her dress flowed like a handkerchief in the wind and so did her hair.

She was the most beautiful vision I had ever laid my eyes upon, but should I follow her into the women's restroom and invade her privacy? I just had to; I longed to see her eyes, and I wanted to find out what her name was. I slipped in the restroom behind her, but again, that damn light distracted me. It shone from under the bathroom stall, and I was panic-stricken just thinking it could be the one she was about to enter. Relieved to see her stop at the sink to wash her hands, I took a deep breath, but I still had not seen her eyes. I was too busy trying to figure out how I was going to stop the light from glowing in the stall beside her. I quickly made the toilet back up, and as the water began to flow up and out over the rim, another stall lit up instead. I created the same mess in the second stall as well, and the third stall went all aglow.

I continued to overflow the toilets in the women's restroom until all of them had caused running water to cascade all over the tile floor. I could hear the women rushing out the door. Even Kitten had gone, too. I had to get to her, but the glow of light was right there on the floor in front of the dressing mirror, but for whom had it shone? Suddenly, in barged a woman who could just about walk due to her over-consumption of alcohol. The water did not seem to distract her whatsoever and neither did the backup of paper and muck. I knocked over the garbage can to distract the woman, but she still headed straight for the light. Tripping over her own two feet, she fell smack dab straight into the center of the hellish green glow. Her life ended right there on the floor of the women's restroom.

I exited the restroom, and my eyes panned the club for Kitten. She was standing right next to the bar, summoning the bartender to get help for the faulty plumbing in the women's room where I found her. She motioned with a wave as she called out to her friend, notifying her that she wanted to leave. Her eyes, they were dark and mysterious, beautiful, almost catlike. I had not yet seen her smile, but I was sure it would only add to her beauty.

Now her smile was my quest. I needed just a little more of her then. Every time I would see her, my heart yearned for just a bit more. I followed her out the door that had originally led me to her and down the block that I had just walked alone in my search for her only moments ago. She seemed to be in a hurry and began talking to herself.

"Why did I even go there with her? She is such a bitch. Why do I always do what everybody else wants me to do? What about me? When do I have some fun?" she mumbled under her breath as she stormed up Hamilton towards the boardwalk.

I guess she did not like that club either. What a nice girl! It seemed so sweet that she was just there for her friend. I wondered where she was running. I followed close behind her, looking on as the men she passed watched her go by with their mouths hanging wide open. I could not blame them; she was gorgeous.

On the way, I had come across a couple of distractions, and a few people were in need of my attention. I worked quickly to fulfill my duties, knowing that if I had ignored just one of them, I would be in breach of contract. I saved a baby carriage from utter annihilation and prevented the death of a man almost mowed down by a tourist out driving drunk, not too shabby, considering I was more interested in Kitten than anything else. I could not let myself lose sight of her, so I acted in haste with each intervention and continued on my way.

I needed to know her name. My mind was trying to imagine what it would be, but there was not a name in history that coincided with her beautiful face. To me, she could only be Kitten, but I am sure whatever her name turned out to be, it would complement her beauty. This was all just too exciting for words; the anticipation of knowing her name was making me anxious, but I was not sure where she was leading me. I followed her as she walked along Ocean Terrace breezing through the buzzing and ringing coming from the arcades that lined the strip until she turned down Sheridan Avenue and advanced up the ramp leading to a dingy biker bar.

My angel was going into a dirty, swanky biker bar. I could not believe it. Why would she want to hang out in a place like this? I could not even begin to imagine. The floor was gray cement, and the stools were mismatched. The bar spanned from the boardwalk entrance clear down to the very back of the building. There were strange people scattered about the room, some shooting pool, and the jukebox was wailing hard rock and roll. She walked straight up to the bar and motioned to the bartender, smiling as she caught his attention. He was rather large with muscles that covered his entire body; they seemed to stack up, one on top of the other. I thought to myself, *This must be her boyfriend; why else would she be in a place like this?*

She spoke briefly to him. I could not hear what she said, but he pointed to the side deck just outside the sliding glass doors, and again, she was off, headed just in that direction. That was when I saw her beautiful smile. Her lips curled up on one side, and her eyes seemed to smile along with them. She was gorgeous, even more beautiful than before. *What more could I discover about her?* I thought to myself. Her name, I needed to know her name, and then I could get back to my work. The moment I discovered her name, I was sure to lose interest. On the other hand, should I say I hoped that I could lose interest in this woman who had me chasing after her like an alley cat in heat? As she approached the outside deck, I could tell she was on a mission, pushing past the crowd of people and heading straight toward a man dressed in the typical biker attire, leather vest and black jeans with his arms and chest covered in tattoos.

Oh no, this couldn't be her boyfriend. What could this sort of man possibly have to offer this magnificent beauty? I watched as she wrapped her arms around this clown and gave him a big hug.

"Hello, sexy, almost didn't think I would see your ass tonight. I was beginning to lose hope," the tattooed freak said with a sinister-looking grin.

Leaning in, she whispered something in his ear, and he nodded yes to her. Reaching down into the front of her dress then into her bra, she withdrew some money. They exchanged something for the money; she smiled happily and walked away, making sure to swing her hips so everyone watching would notice her. As she made her way to the women's restroom, again, the light summoned me. It was at the base of one of the pool tables down in the middle of the bar. I ran over and before I could react, SLAM! A pool stick came crashing down on top of the head of an unsuspecting patron. Your typical, full-blown bar brawl had broken out, and my work had begun.

I swung the overhead lights to separate the crowd. Three murderous green lights had gone dim. Another light grew bright, but it was too late, the person that had received the blow to the head had fallen directly into the light, and there was not a thing I could do about it. When she came out of the restroom, I could hear the police sirens in the distance, and apparently, so did Kitten, because she rubbed her nose and like a flash of lightning, she was out the door and headed for the parking lot.

I could hear her fumbling with keys in the darkness. She popped the trunk of her car, reached in, and pulled something out, but I could not see what it was. She stepped into the front seat and pulled something from out of the console. I could not gain access to the passenger side but longed to sit beside her. I watched through the window as she cracked open a beer and tossed the bottle cap into the back seat. Grabbing a piece of paper from a notebook, she folded it in half and began to dump out what seemed to be marijuana directly into the crease of the folded paper. Was she rolling a joint? Could my angel be a pothead? How could that be? She did not seem like the type of girl that rolled her own.

I watched her every move, and as each second passed, I found myself even more captivated by her beauty. When she was finished rolling the marijuana into a cigarette, her tongue gently parted her lips, preparing to seal the deal. She chugged down the rest of the beer, slipped the number into a cigarette pack, and headed back to the trunk of the car. I had concluded that the big biker at the bar just happened to be her dealer. That was a relief; I only hoped Kitten was unattached.

She grabbed a beach bag out of the trunk and pulled a small lunchbox from out of it. Opening a large cooler, she scooped a few fistfuls of ice and dropped them into the lunchbox, plunging about four beers in right behind, and packed them into her beach bag. She cantered up the boardwalk ramp and headed down to the beach. I stared at her face, studying every curve. She appeared to be extremely sad, and just as I thought about it, she began to cry. What could be wrong? Why was she crying?

"Why do I have to be alone? What's wrong with me?" she said to herself as she got closer to the water.

The tears were streaming down her face as she reached into her bag and pulled out a blanket.

"I don't need a man to have a good time. I don't even need a friend. I'm fine all by myself. I don't need anyone."

Still crying, she placed the blanket softly on the cool sand and had a seat. I could feel my heart sink a bit as each tear fell from her eyes, and I felt sorry for the girl. How could such a beautiful woman be spending this time in solitude? Just then, the dreaded light was back, beckoning me to come forth and make with an intervention.

There were three kids setting off fireworks on the beach at the end of Fremont. I could see it glowing ever so bright, how it taunted me, two lights shining brightly just waiting for them to step within. I rushed over to see what I could do to dismiss their present fate and save their lives.

"Check it out, Tanya; I'm the Statue of Liberty!" one of the kids shouted as he held a bottle rocket above his head.

"Check out Jonathan shooting fire out of his hand," a voice came from behind the resting lifeguard chair.

The dumb shit was lighting bottle rockets and holding them in his bare hand. He should know that he could get a nasty splinter, or worse. I tell you, kids today live in an alternate reality. I heard an ear-piercing scream over a loud whistle just before an explosion.

"Ahhh, my fucking hand, my fucking hand!" The boy stood there staring at his mangled hand.

The bottle rocket gave him a nasty splinter all right, sticking directly into the palm of his hand. The rocket lodged itself into his skin and blew up. I looked over at the boy; he was shaking from shock and looking down at the ground. I looked down, too, and there lying on the sand at his feet was one of his fingers.

"Oh shit! What the fuck? That was crazy dude," the kid behind the chair said with disbelief.

The injured child fell hard to the ground unconscious. The damn light had not gone away. The Zinno lighter he had used to light the rockets stayed lit when he dropped it, and it fell right into the bag of fireworks. Knowing that if I did not act fast, his girlfriend was going to die right there on the beach in front of everyone, I gave the lifeguard chair a hard shove and pushed it over directly between the bag of explosives and the girl. Landing on her butt, she kicked her legs frantically until she had traveled over to her injured friend.

"I'll go and get help!" the girl shouted and darted to the boardwalk screaming for help.

Then in a colorful, yet life-threatening array of explosions, the bag went up. Roman candles spit fireballs up and down the beach, some exploding off toward the boardwalk. The people began to scream and run in all directions to protect themselves from the dangerous balls of fire.

"Mommy, I see the pretty colors!" a child shouted as he jumped up and down with glee clapping his hands.

I could hear police whistles coming from the boardwalk, a crowd began to gather as the fireworks died down. The light was gone, and the four-wheelers were tearing up the sand toward what was left of the glowing pyrotechnics. The cavalry had arrived, and it seemed that they were safe for now. I suppose you could live with a few missing fingers. It was better then the alternative. I watched as they collected the boy's digits and turned back to see if Kitten was okay, but she was gone.

I headed back up the beach to search for her and found her on the other side of Casino Pier sitting on her blanket, looking out aimlessly over the water with her chin up, finishing another beer and still crying her eyes out. I sat down beside her on the sand, looking into her swollen eyes. I wiped a tear from her cheek. She shook, startled at the touch of my disembodied hand, and looked around as if she were looking for the person who had just touched her face. I could see the goose bumps popping out from her arms and up the back of her neck as if she had seen a ghost. I could feel her pain as the salty tear ran down my finger and wondered how such a beauty could be feeling this much pain. Reaching into her cigarette pack, she pulled out a joint, lit it, took in a rather long pull and held it in for a very long time. She exhaled and fell back onto the blanket.

"Oh yeah, that's the stuff!" she said, with a sigh of relief. "That's what I'm talking about, baby!" she shouted and put the joint between her lips for another hit.

Grabbing another beer from her lunchbox, she popped it open, flicking the bottle cap between her fingers and sending it flying through the night air into the sand. She even began to show the hint of a smile. This made me extremely happy. I hated seeing her cry, but I loved sitting in her presence, such a vision of beauty. I was glad to see that she was feeling better. If only it had been I and not the marijuana that made her sweet face smile. Well, I suppose I could settle for being the creator of goosebumps.

I watched her every move, memorized her every feature, and could not help but wonder why she captivated me so. Maybe it was the absence of love, or was it the way she seemed so alone that drew me to her? No matter what the reason, I felt so content basking in her beauty. She continued drinking and began to sing in a low, soft voice.

"Once I dreamed, love would come, and sweep me up away, but now it seems life's passed me by, I'm still alone today." She ran her fingers through the sand making the outline of a heart. She continued her song of sorrow. "Won't somebody love me?" The tears again began to swell up in her eyes, and her words began to break up. She stood up and cried out, "Why, God? Why?" She fell to her knees and grabbed her head. "Not tonight, I'm not going to get like this."

I felt the need to do something nice for her and make her smile again. I dove into the dark sea in search of something special. Well, there was a horseshoe crab and a rather large fish, but they would not do. I needed something special, something beautiful. Then I found it; it was perfect; I just knew she would love it. I forced a large wave onto the shore at her feet and released my perfect gift to her. When she heard the crashing wave, she lifted her head. The surf broke, and the foam carried the large conch shell up and placed it directly in front of her. Looking in disbelief, she rubbed her eyes and reached out to pick it up. Grabbing it with the utmost delicacy, she held it up to the moonlight and smiled.

"Oh, thank you. It's beautiful. It's the most wonderful thing that I have ever seen." Smiling like a small child, she brought it up to her lips and kissed it, then she put it up to her nose and smelled it, then to her ear.

I had done it. I was the reason she was smiling, and no one could take that away from me. She was so beautiful, and I thought that maybe I could be falling in love with her. I wanted to stay on that small patch of beach for the rest of eternity, but I knew that if I did not get to work soon, the morgue could be overflowing with the dead. I memorized every detail of Kitten's features, so in her absence, I could still bask in her unreserved beauty.

Now, I knew where I could find her. I knew that she would be coming back to the beach. Just like me, she seemed drawn to it. The sea seemed to give her the heartfelt sanctity she so desired. The wind whispered for me into her ear, "Goodnight," as the breeze gently raised the hair from her cheek. Seeing her lips curl into a smile as she caressed the shell was very stimulating. I yearned for her touch and longed to taste the sweetness of her lips. I turned around for one last look at the woman who mesmerized me. I anticipated when she would again grace me with her presence and was sad that I had no choice but to leave her and continue on my quest to intercept death.

I wondered around the boardwalk for a while keeping a close eye open for the light, and before I knew it, the dreaded light was beckoning me. I rushed up to a small crowd of people gathering, and when I got to the center of them, there she was, a frail shell of a woman gasping to take air into her lungs. The light was only about two feet from where she lay and began creeping slowly toward her. She seemed to have something lodged in her throat. I needed to find someone to give her a simple pat on the back. Looking at the people around me, it was obvious that none of these mindless tourists retained the capability to do anything for her.

Tourists, becoming vegetable brains before my very eyes from sniffing too much suntan oil, surrounded the gasping old woman. God, I hated them, but this little Jersey town would be nothing without them. It was hard to imagine that local businesses depended on three months out of twelve to account for a whole year of income. I looked down at the poor woman and came to realize that she was going to die if something was not done right away. I ran down to the corner, to the first-aid station.

"You need to go up the street now!" I hollered into the ear of a lifeguard.

She jumped to her feet and hurried out the door. I was relieved to find that she was one of those people that had a very suggestive mind. There were a lot of them, but running into one that did not fall prey to the power of suggestion in this kind of an emergency was not really what you would call good luck. When she reached the choking woman, instead of sitting beside her on the left side to protect her from the light, she knelt on her right and rolled her onto her back smack dab in the middle of the light. There was nothing that could be done to change the old woman's fate. What is the point of possessing the power of suggestion if it was not going to help in any way? I was really beginning to get sick of my work.

Chapter Three

*F*rustrated, I walked down to the beach and stood looking out over the water. I wondered when the woman who got me into this mess would come to me again and inform me of the length of my sentence for what I did all those years ago. Would I ever pay for my actions back then? When was enough going to be enough? I thought back on that day. That day, everything went wrong. I did not know what I was doing, not until it was too late.

I had just got to the livery, and my day was going very well considering the farm was in trouble, and I was on my way home from a big city bank that had just okayed my loan. You see, I needed money for my crop; I only needed enough money to plant a nice cash crop of corn. Jersey corn was the best tasting corn in the world. I had enough land to grow over sixty acres of Jersey corn, and that would bring in some nice cash.

I pitched an idea that I had about a new kind of device that would pick the corn faster than three men could, and they bought it; they also told a private investor about my idea, and he liked it, too. I received acceptance for a loan for the seed and received a nice big bonus for the idea. The man that was investing in my idea was loaded. He invited Sue Ellen and me to attend a lawn party in my honor that next evening. He claimed that we were destined to make a lot of money and that something like this called for celebration. I was so excited I could hardly wait to get home and tell my precious wife the good news.

She was beautiful, probably the most beautiful woman that I had ever seen before or since. Well, there was Kitten. Anyway, Sue Ellen was beautiful, her hair as golden as a wheat field and her eyes as dark as the sky during a thunderstorm. She had this way about her that was like no other. She sang to herself as she did the dishes, and while she washed our clothes down at the creek, she would sing to the frogs. She spoke and laughed with the horses as women of today chat at the beauty parlor, and she even kissed the pigs. I loved everything about her. She was my whole world, and I knew that I would be able to provide her with all the wonderful things that she deserved. I stopped in the mercantile on my way home that day to buy her a present for when I told her of our good fortune.

I looked around at all the beautiful things that they had behind the large plate-glass window: musical boxes, porcelain dolls, silver serving trays, and so much more. I entered the shop and saw incased in a glass cabinet were gorgeous gold and stone broaches. Sue Ellen's favorite color was green, and right smack dab in the middle of the case sat a rather large emerald stone with tiny little gold butterflies surrounding it. This was it; this was the perfect gift for my wife. I knew that she would love it. I knew that she and I would be together forever. I called to the shopkeeper to open the glass case and asked him if he could gift-wrap the symbol of my love for my wife.

"I'll wrap it, but it will cost you a penny extra," he smiled and said.

I laughed and gave him an extra dollar. He looked at me as if I had gone mad. I picked up a bottle of French perfume and told him to wrap that as well. Maybe I was mad, but she deserved it, and there would be plenty of money from now on, so why not spend some of it now? I looked around the store some more, and the yard goods caught my eye, but Sue Ellen could not possibly sew a dress for the party in just one night so I decided to spend a little more. I picked out the most expensive and most attractive dress in the store and purchased a bonnet to match. I had the shopkeeper wrap that as well and then picked out a new suit for myself. I figured that the class of people who would be attending the party would be dressed well, and I did not want to look like a typical dirt farmer when we arrived there the next day.

When I was through paying for my goods, I headed back to the livery and requested that the blacksmith have the harnesses cleaned up for the horses and shoe them up right for the trip back to the city. They were well fed, and I even paid the stablehand to give the horses a bath and a good brushing. I was ecstatic and smiled the whole way home. I took the long way home so I could pick some wildflowers for Sue Ellen. The flowers covered the meadow this time of year, and you could smell their fragrance in the air for miles around if the wind was right. There were yellow ones and pink ones popping up covering every inch of the meadow. She loved the color pink, and I would always bring her the pink ones. She loved how they made the house smell, and sometimes, she would put the pink petals in her bath when she was feeling blue. Everything I did, I did for her; I loved her with all of my heart. I knew she would be so excited to hear the good news, and I could not wait to tell her.

I approached the small dirt road that led to my farm. It wouldn't be long now, soon I would be telling her the good news, and she would be smiling and kissing me. All of our troubles would be fading fast, and life as we knew it would never be the same. It was going to be magic. I could hear the sheep in the distance, and the dogs had already picked up my scent. I could see the dust from their feet as they ran down the road to greet me. Butch was the first to come; he jumped up and licked my face. I could smell the fish on his breath. This was the only dog that could catch his own dinner. It was amazing; he would sit on top of an old log that hovered over the creek and would watch and wait until a fish would swim directly underneath him. Then, with no hesitation, he would plunge his head directly into the water and pull out a fish. He was self-sufficient and well fed. I looked up the road for Sparky; he had not come to greet me. This dog was a mangy cuss. He was ornery, the type of dog that would not let anyone on the property that didn't belong. I wondered why he hadn't come. He would always greet me with a loving nudge but always was there to protect his territory. Yet he had not come. I wondered where he was. I began to get worried, and I feared the worst. It was not like him at all; I'm talking about a dog that would chase a bear.

This dog saved my life while I was hunting for deer in the woods. I had been gone for about three days, and the game was scarce. I finally stopped to get some rest when all of a sudden, a huge bear came into camp. It had taken me by surprise and would have killed me if it weren't for that mangy dog. He was fearless and attacked that bear without hesitation, barking and snarling with such fierce enthusiasm that I could not run away. I just lay there in amazement; my companion had put his life before mine, protecting me.

I hurried up the road. The air was still, and there was a strange feeling in my bones. I could hear barking coming from the barn. I thought I locked him in the barn when I left for the city early that morning. Sue Ellen would have gone in to get the feed for the animals. Maybe she locked him in when she closed the barn door.

That had to be it. I opened the barn door, and Sparky lunged at me looking very happy to see me, but where was Sue? Hadn't she heard Sparky barking? When she did not come outside to see what the all the commotion was about, that too made me worried. What if someone else locked Sparky in the barn? What if it was not a mistake? I needed to find out. I was concerned that something terrible had happened. I dropped all the parcels and ran to the house.

I grabbed the doorknob, and it would not turn. I gave it a hard kick and broke it open. There was only one key, and I had left it with Sue Ellen. The house was quiet, and I proceeded in through the hall with caution. I searched every room on the first floor and made my way up the stairs. The house was empty. I could not find her anywhere. Nothing was out of place. I laughed to myself as the dogs followed me in my search, their tails wagging frantically back and forth.

I headed back downstairs, thinking of how crazy I had acted and assured myself that she was probably at the pond reading one of her poetry books or down the road talking with the Widow Stein. I went to the kitchen to find something to eat. I had been on the road all day, and with all the excitement, I had not stopped to fill my stomach.

There was a basket on the table filled with delicious fried chicken. I loved Sue's fried chicken. She had a flair for cooking. When the town hosted its annual county fair, people would come from miles around trying to beat Sue Ellen out of first-place blue ribbons. She had won almost every competition for the past five years. She had so many ribbons they covered one whole cubby of our kitchen.

There was some potato salad, so I grabbed a spoon and dug in. I figured she would be home anytime soon, and if she had not come home by the time I was done eating, then I'd just go down to the pond and see if I could find her there. I savored every bite of the delicious chicken, and as I bent down to pick up a bone that I had dropped, I noticed the cellar door. My heart sank, because it was the only place that had slipped my mind. She could be down there, hurt, or worse. How could I sit right above her enjoying a meal while she lay down there all alone? I jumped to my feet, pulled at the ring, and lifted the floorboards. As I raised the wooden planks, I could not see anything. It was just too dark down there. I quickly grabbed the lantern and struck a match to light it. I hurried down the shaky stairs and looked around. I found nothing out of place. I breathed a sigh of relief and rubbed my head.

I climbed my way back up to the kitchen and cleared the remains of my meal. I wanted everything to be perfect. I let the dogs eat what I couldn't finish, and I went out to the water pump to wash my plate. When I was through, I gathered up all the gifts that I had purchased for her and brought them into the sitting room. I hid the dress and my new suit under the loveseat and slipped the perfume bottle and the broach into my pocket. I wanted to surprise her in the morning with the dress, just to keep the good times coming. I loved to see the expression of surprise on her face. She had the most beautiful smile.

I walked out of the house and attempted to shut the front door, but because I had kicked it in, it would not close all the way. I pulled on it with all my might to force it closed figuring I would fix it later. I looked into the water barrel to get a glimpse of my reflection. I did not want to look mangy as the dog when she saw me. I wet my hands, slicked back my hair, and washed my face. Then I checked my pocket to make sure I had the gifts and began to head for the pond. I was sure that she would be there; she didn't expect me home until the next day, and I knew that I would surprise her. Things had gone so well and so fast in the city that I was back home a day early.

I headed out to find her, and on the way, I imagined what she would be wearing and how her hair would look. I pictured her sitting on a soft patch of grass talking to the animals. She loved to feed the rodents, and they seemed to know her. She treated the squirrels as if they were her own kin, and the birds would sit in her hand and eat the special seed that she ordered for them from the mercantile. She was my world, and I could not wait to see her and tell her the good news. I walked over the rickety footbridge that crossed the creek leading down to the pond when a terrible memory flashed inside my head: the sound of a runaway team of horses that had thundered down the road years before. It all happened so fast nothing could have stopped them, not even myself. Even with the powers that I have now, I would not have been able to stop them.

The stagecoach had been intercepted by a band of would-be robbers. They killed the driver while trying to hijack the bank notes on their way to the city, and in the fallout, all the terror had spooked the team, and the stage was set off barreling down the road like a menacing bolt of lightning. The coach had broken into a thousand pieces. The wreckage lay strewn about, and we were finding remains three years following the aftermath.

Moments before the accident, Sue Ellen had just placed a blanket down in the front of the yard, setting up a picnic for my son and myself. Junior was just a little man. I can remember the day he was born. My wife was so strong; she never made a sound. She just did what she needed to do, and that was that. There was no midwife, no doctor, just her and I alone. She carried our son around in a bassinet that she had woven by hand. He had not had his first birthday when the horses came that day.

As I turned to see where the thundering sound was coming from, a big cloud of dust covered the entire yard making it difficult to see. I rubbed my eyes and cleared my throat running to where Sue Ellen and my son were, but they had vanished.

I heard Sue Ellen calling out, "Junior, junior, where are you?"

My head was all in a turnaround. I could not think straight to figure out what was happening and why it was happening to me. I ran over to Sue Ellen and looked her over to see if she was badly hurt. Besides a few scratches and bumps all over, she was fine.

"Where's the baby? I can't find the baby!" she cried.

We searched and searched, but he was nowhere in the yard, but when the dust cleared and the last bit of the road drifted back to its place on the ground, we saw the trampled remains of his basket torn to pieces.

Sue Ellen fell to her knees. Without having the strength to raise her head, she cried, "Why has this happened to us?"

I slowly walked toward the shattered remains of the bassinet. There was no sound or movement. I knew he was gone. As I rolled the tattered remains of the once beautiful bassinet over, I was relieved to see that my son was not there.

"Honey, he's not here!" I shouted.

She looked up at me. "Oh Lord, we have to find him."

We frantically ran around the yard looking everywhere for him but could not find him. I could hear Sue Ellen screaming. When I turned to see at what, I saw her fall to the ground and reach into the creek. I ran to her as fast as I could, and as she pulled my son's tiny lifeless body up the bank of that creek, I knew our lives would never be the same. She cradled him in her arms with the love and affection only his mother could give.

"Yes, he is going to be just fine. I was really scared there for a minute." She looked up with a lost look as she rocked back and forth.

I knelt down next to my poor wife and put my arms around the both of them for comfort. I explained to her in a low, soft voice that my son had not survived and that he was gone.

I had been distracted from my mournful thinking, and I spiraled back to my present reality at the shore. That dreaded light had come back. I could see it smack dab in the middle of the pier. There was a man riding a bicycle headed straight for its menacing glow. I rushed past him and grabbed a fishing line from one of the unmanned polls that was resting on the handrail of the pier.

Moving quickly, I attached the line to the back of a passerby who was walking in the opposite direction. I hooked the line taut to his trousers, and as he strolled past the cyclist, they became tangled together, falling to the pier with a crash and taking down a few other people who were minding their own business. I was able to save the man, and there were only a few minor scrapes and bruises to show for it.

I looked around, satisfied at the job that I had done when suddenly, before I knew it, I could hear a woman scream. Apparently, her boyfriend was surfing and was having some trouble. He wiped out, and I found him caught up in a massive wave as it curled. It had thrown him from his board, and he ended up motionless drifting toward the jetty. He had not come up for air since he wiped out, and the glow of the light was just a few wave crashes away from where he was. I quickly latched myself onto a line casting myself and soaring off the pier heading directly toward the distressed surfer.

The ocean was lit up like a Christmas tree, and I had a hard time finding him in all that light. There was a flock of seagulls preying upon a small school of fish; they were diving into the water headfirst to feed on them. The bubbles were like a screen that enabled me to locate the surfer. I searched until I saw the bright colors of his bathing suit. I grabbed one of his legs, but I was not positive of which way to pull him. The ocean was still lit up rather brightly for the fish that were being eaten, and I was not sure which light was for them and which light was for my surfer friend. I jumped straight out of the water, so I could get a bird's-eye view of the water surface with the hope that I could somehow determine which light was intended for him. I spotted it right away, pulled the surfer away from the rocks, and back in towards the shore, just close enough for the woman to spot him and pull him out.

Chapter Four

I watched the people on the boardwalk for a long time. It was amazing to me how fast the years had gone by and how the people of this earth had changed. There were young adults dressed as the dead, and the music was nothing like when I was a boy. Nowadays, every part of the human body was altered. There were darts and studs pierced through every part imaginable with scars of brands and tattoos etched into the flesh of just about everyone.

The most common color of the night was basic black, and the beautiful blond teens were dying their hair black to rebel against their yuppie parents. It seemed the more dramatic the wardrobe, the more negative the energy that followed these people. They would carry weapons of violence, drink, and use drugs as if they needed to consume them just to live. The women looked like men, and the men looked like women. The music was loud, full of rage and hate. It was no wonder the world was in such a terrible state.

There was one person in particular whom I found myself drawn to. She was a young girl; she couldn't have been more then about fourteen years old. Her hair was painted in purple and black; her eyes darkened with heavy liner, lips as red as blood. The pale white of her skin shone bright, and she headed to the pier. I decided to follow her and see what she was doing.

She ducked into the bait store just on the edge of the pier. I followed her down a long hallway; she opened the door, and as I looked, I noticed that there were all sorts of strange humanity in this place. It wasn't a bait shop at all, for behind the storefront, hidden from the unsuspecting people of this small summer town was a gothic night club.

I exited the back of the club through a door that lead to the far end of the pier overlooking the water. It was a clear and beautiful night. As I looked down into the hypnotic waves of the surf, I could see a faint glow coming from under the boardwalk. As I moved in to get a closer look, I could hear the sound of a person choking. I turned to my left, and there she was, the girl that I had been following earlier. She was smoking some drugs, and it didn't seem that she had it under control. I pushed the wind, forced the small rolled article from her hand, forcing it to fall to the floor. She dropped to her knees and reached for it, but the wind made it roll and fall between the cracks of the pier and disappear into the cool water below.

One job was completed successfully and another about to begin. Even though she was clear from the dreadful light, I knew in my heart that it would only be a matter of time before her habits would become fatal, and her mortal life would end. Even still, my job would never be complete. I was damned to never rest from this wretched line of work. The increasing light coming from under the amusement pier directly below drew my attention. I had a strange feeling about this and was a bit uneasy. I had to investigate the situation, and besides, what else could I do? This was all that I knew.

I darted between the pillions and up to the dry sand. The light was very bright and a bit off color. Not like the usual eerie glow, this was more of a greenish-blue getting darker blue as you reached the center. I was sure that this was why my stomach felt a little uneasy. I was feeling almost nauseous, but more toward being scared. That was when it hit me. It was going to be a murder. I could feel my heart begin to ascend into my throat. I knew I had to get to them, but I just couldn't get my feet to move. Maybe it was because I was panicky, or maybe it was because I didn't want to be the only one that was destined to be the protector of life. I knew that I should be grateful for preserving life, but if you could walk one mile in my shoes, you would understand where I was coming from.

I got to the grimly lit spot, and I could not believe my eyes: there were two people feeding on one another's blood. Yes, their blood. He was sucking her neck, and she was nibbling on his shoulder. They were dressed completely in black, and I could smell marijuana in the still air. They seemed to be having a good time together. I could hear them panting and sucking. It was beginning to stimulate me. It had been so long since I felt the touch of a woman.

I imagined how my life was when Sue Ellen and I were together. Things were grand. She was so sexy, so beautiful. I loved to watch her work in the fields. She would pull the back of her skirt up between and through her legs to the front of her waistband and tuck it in as if she were wearing trousers. This would expose her luscious legs, muscles flexing and beading with her sweet thirst-quenching sweat. Her strength was extreme for a woman, and she was gorgeous.

I was there when she broke in our horse, Dante, a massive mound of animal flesh. This was the most handsome saddle horse, and big, he was over sixteen hands high. He was red chestnut in color and beautiful. She just jumped on his back and took hold of his mane as if she had done it a thousand times. This horse, never before ridden, did not like the idea of having Sue Ellen on his back. He bucked wildly and almost threw her a dozen times. She just hung on strong, showing him who was boss. The distressed animai didn't know what had hit him. She hung on until that horse trotted around the corral like a little pony. She rode with a huge smile on her face and laughed like a schoolchild. She was so beautiful, with her hair lively from the bouncing of the horse's massive strength forcing her off the saddle. When she dismounted, I grabbed her up into my arms and flung her into a pile of straw. She straddled my waist with her legs, and while in her scissor-like grip, we made love until nightfall. She was my every fantasy. I longed to feel the touch that drove me wild with desire.

Watching the two of them lick and suck each other's blood was getting me heated up. She was going to die from this torturing, ritualistic sex game, so I went to the pier above them and spilled about fifty gallons of water from the kiddy rides directly above their heads on the amusement pier. I knew that it would work, because it was the only way to get the animals on the farm off one another, like the way you would throw a bucket of water on a couple of dogs to get them apart. This action broke up the two lovers long enough for the person to realize that he was taking the kinky sexual act a bit too far. The hellish blue-green light had dissipated as he carried her out from under the pier screaming for assistance. I was confidant that the girl was going to be all right. I let out a large sigh of relief and took a seat down by the waterline.

I was wallowing in my own misery, the dreaded light, Sue Ellen, and my son, not to mention the pain I felt longing for Kitten. I just did not understand why all these torturous circumstances filled my life. Before that dreaded day, I had tried to live my life on the straight and narrow. I went to church every Sunday. I worked the land for the food we ate, and I helped those less fortunate than myself. I didn't lie, cheat, or steal. I did everything in my power to make life special for all those around me. Where did I go wrong? Why did this have to happen to me? When would it all end? These questions I would never have the answers to; I looked out over the beautiful ocean view and smiled to myself for a brief moment, thinking how beautiful the world was, and for just a moment, I had a feeling that I wasn't alone. Where was that coming from? I had the strangest feeling. I took a walk to the stinky biker bar that my precious Kitten had gone. I figured that if I hung out in the bar, I would not see any of the lights outside, and being it was a biker bar, I assumed that there were probably people there that would eventually need my help. What were the odds of Kitten being there? I wasn't sure, but I needed to be close to her and didn't know where else to look. I was hungry to see her, even if I had to go to a dank pit to do it.

The place had the stench of a cesspool. I couldn't imagine how a person would intentionally come to this place and spend their money. You would have to pay me to drink in this place. I've drunk and gambled in saloons that had pigs living in them, and they never smelt this bad. I cringed at the thought of the public restrooms. Looking around the room, I searched for an interesting conversation to listen to. There were some hard-looking people here, but as I looked around, I noticed that it was a crowd of all kinds. There were so many tourists that they had overrun the locals six to one. It was funny how the locals got the better of them. They called them Bennies, Shoebees, and Cockroaches. The locals had the corner on kickbacks, and drunken tourists were always leaving money on the bar. The bartenders had a way of skimming the patron money off the bar when they weren't looking. I enjoyed watching everything that was going on. It was amazing how people even left their minds at home when they went on vacation. I could understand the feeling of losing your mind. I had lost mine and wasn't aware of what I was doing. Maybe it was because I couldn't believe it, or was it that if I didn't admit it in my mind, it never happened? Whatever the reason was, I was ashamed, and I have paid for my actions every day since then.

I could hear a few voices getting louder. There seemed to be an elevated conversation, a disagreement over a pool game. I thought, *Surprise, surprise, two men fighting over their balls. What a joke!* I went over to check it out to see if they needed my services. One of the men was an older local man, you could tell; he was wearing clothes that he obviously used for work. His pants were covered in speckles of paint and filth. He looked drunk. The other man was younger, wasted, and obviously on a mission to do some damage.

"Leave the guy alone! He is a regular in this place, guy! Why don't you just leave?" the bartender shouted.

The man pulled back his fist and swung, hitting the older man in the jaw, knocking him into the jukebox. Before he fell, he got in a shot of his own, and the crowd began to part, giving way to the two men. They wrestled around for a minute, and from out of nowhere, this little mangy dog ran in barking and started biting the hotheaded vacationer. The man turned to kick the snarling little dog, and the local man hit him upside the head with a billiard ball. Blood trickled down the side of his face. As he wiped it with the back of his hand, you could see the hatred in his eyes as he looked back at the staggering local. The bartender jumped over the bar and broke up the fight.

"All right, take it outside!" he said as he pushed them both toward the door.

The little dog, still barking and nipping at the man, followed them out onto the boardwalk. A small crowd followed the two men outside, and some of the people that were out on the balcony were hollering out to them. The aggressive vacationer began to kick the little dog, and you could hear the hollow sound of the dog's body, echoing as he was struck between the parked cars that lined the street.

A woman's voice fell over the crowd. "Don't kick the dog, you jerk; if you do it again, I'll come out and kick your ass."

The local man called to his dog, ordering him to get back in the flatbed of the pickup truck. When the police whistles began to blow, the vacationer melted into the crowd and was long gone before the cops had a chance to pick him up. It was all very exciting. I felt bad for the old man and his dog. It was a terrible thing, getting beat up in your own hangout. All he wanted to do was stop for a couple of beers after a hard day at work. You could see how the man who made up that bumper sticker that said, "Shit Happens," made all his money. It is true, and if some only knew how much of that shit almost happens to them, I am sure most would live a better life.

I began to get bored of waiting for my Kitten, and this bar was getting to me. I needed to get outside into the salty ocean breeze and collect myself. I wandered off, looking around at the people wandering alongside of me, staring blindly at the lights and spending money. They wore blank looks on their faces with eyes like the finely polished glass of a prize plush toy, not one of whom would know the true fate if had not been for my presence among them.

One zombie almost stepped on a nail, which would have caused a chain reaction of deadly light to come, but as the multiple lights became present, I knew just what to do to stop it. It was amazing how good at this I had become after all these years. To get the job done, there was not anything I could not do. I watched as the teens and preteens flirted with one another and saw how many of them were apparently drunk on alcohol and God knows what else as they stumbled around town.

I diverted an elderly man from walking directly off the edge of the boardwalk. There was no warning of the high drop. If it was not for the darkness of the night, I would have never been able to see the light. If he had fallen, he surely would have died. I roamed around for hours, searching for my goddess, but could not find her anywhere.

I planted myself on one of the benches, which overlooked the ocean and did not move at all. People kept passing, never to know that I was there, never to feel my presence or know my name. I longed for someone to talk to, and I was torturing myself as I thought about Kitten, and how I longed to be with her.

I craved for some eye candy. If I could not have Kitten's beauty to admire, the sun setting over the bay would have to do. I waved goodbye to the East and made my way across town to the bay. It was only a few blocks walk; this town was only two miles long and not more than one mile wide. While passing the bakery, my nose filled with the sweet aroma of fresh-baked goods. I remembered how delicious Sue Ellen's cooking was, and the scent of pie made my mouth water. My thoughts returned to my mortal past.

I had built her a large pie rack, and she would fill it up with tasty pies for the church social every Sunday. Everyone loved her; in the town, she was highly respected. She was always doing things for our neighbors, and if she had not been a woman, she could have been mayor. The noise from the bay brought me back to reality.

The coast was loaded with action. The wave runners ran as far as the eye could see, and the docks were filled with crab traps and fishing poles. Boats were all about, and the sound of laughter was in the air. The moon had less than an hour before it would rise and the birds were fighting over discarded bait. What a beautiful sight, it was like going to a different part of the world; the beach seemed to be empty, but the bay was still very much alive with activity.

I wandered up and down the fishing pier, looking for something, but I did not know what. I was not sure what I was doing there, but I knew that if I had left, I would have missed something. I watched a kid bait his crab trap, and then I saw it. The light shining off into the bay, but there was not a boat or wave runner in sight. I wondered and watched, but there was no sign of trouble. That was when from out of nowhere, a boat came speeding a bit fast for the area of the bay it was in. There were four small children sitting on the bow of the small craft. It hit a wave, and as the boat went airborne, one of the children was thrown overboard from the bouncing. I jumped with all my might off the pier and into the water where the child began to sink. The man who was driving the boat was not paying attention and did not even notice that the child was no longer part of the boat's crew.

I swam down to the bottom of the bay and scooped up the young child who was lying on the sea floor. I pushed her up slowly and prayed that someone would be there to pluck her out from her watery grave. As I approached the surface, the light was blinding. I moved to the left and then the right, but no matter where I went, the light seemed to get brighter. I figured that if I did not bring her body up to the surface at the time, maybe this child would not survive. I kicked my legs as hard as I could and pushed the child up onto the beach. The light was nowhere in sight; I was relieved to see that someone had spotted her. As the tiny waves of the bay washed the lifeless body up onto the shore, a man rushed to her side.

I hope I was not too slow in getting her to shore, I thought as I crawled out of the water. I could not help but feel frightened as I stood by and watched the man who was tending to the little girl try to get her to start breathing on her own. Soon after, an ambulance pulled into the parking lot. As it backed up, I held my breath as a saw the approaching light. "No!" I yelled, but as the paramedics swung the rear doors open to the ambulance, it was clear to me the small girl would not survive the ride to the hospital. The light shone bright in the sanctuary of the rig, and there was nothing that I could do about it. There was only one ambulance and the chances of another one coming were slim to none.

I speared the rear tire with a broken piece of wood that was lying on the pavement of the parking lot. As the paramedics wheeled the gurney toward the vehicle, one of them noticed that the tire had gone flat. They continued to work on the girl, and a bystander called emergency services on his cell phone. Fire and rescue pulled in behind them, and I knew then that she would survive this day, and there was a good chance that she would be sleeping in her bed tonight. I felt relieved and hung around until the child was off in the other emergency vehicle.

The paramedic that was driving looked at the tire and said, "I checked to see if there was anything in the way when I backed up, but it was clear. Where did that spike come from?"

"You could have never seen that in your mirror. Don't worry about it, man. Just be glad that rescue showed up and the girl is okay," the other man said.

As I sat there, I was feeling awful proud of myself. I had helped save the life of a small female child, a child that might live just long enough to graduate college and maybe have a family of her own. I thought about my son, Junior, and how I was lost in this lonely world without him. He was a rather large boy at birth. He weighed over eleven pounds and had an appetite that could surpass all. He bulked up nicely and before the first year he began to crawl.

The doctor joked and said, "If the boy continues to grow at this rate, we'll have a Paul Bunyan on our hands."

He was right; my boy was an amazing little man. I would sit by the creek with him in my arms looking out at the water as it flowed through the yard. I would imagine him at an older age out in the woods hunting with me. I dreamt about his first horse and the first time he would swoon over a girl he liked. I hated that he had to die that day. We were going to have a picnic; everything was supposed to be wonderful.

My mind stopped wandering, and my emotions became selfish. I hated the parents of that small girl. I was jealous that my son was not saved that day and their daughter had been today, and I was the one who assisted in saving her. My head dropped down, and I asked for forgiveness. I didn't know whose forgiveness I was seeking, but I knew that there was someone out there that knew what I was doing, someone who knew what I was going through. I just wanted an answer, any answer, to any one of my questions. This day would be a hard day to get through. All I could think about was the sorrow I felt for the loss of my son. When would this all end? When could I walk t hrough the pearly gates and see him again? Where was my Magic Garden? Would I ever be with Sue Ellen and my son again? I couldn't fight it any longer; I had to go to the church. I needed to see if I could make sense of all this. My heart was breaking all over again.

The red doors to the church were huge. I felt so small next to them. I entered the building, and as I walked down the short aisle to the front of the church, the beautiful glass windows blew me away. There weren't pictures of saints or the Son of God. The images on the panes of glass were of nature, beautiful, crashing waves on one window and a long vine surrounding colorful flowers. There was a sun rising behind the pulpit while dainty butterflies danced in the yellow rays. This had to be the most compelling house of God that I had ever entered in all my time on this earth. I was in awe; I sat on the pew and prayed. I prayed for my son, asking John, my son, to be all right and asking the same for Sue Ellen.

In my heart, I had forgiven her, the love of my life, the woman who bore the son whom I would never know, the boy who would never know the love that we had and felt for him. I couldn't forgive myself for driving her into his arms, the man that I called my friend. The power to return the man whose life I stole, I did not have it. I took it for my own, and now look where I was, stuck between two separate planes of existence for all of eternity, never to see my beloved family again.

I hoped that they would wait for me, no matter how long it took me to get to them. Looking at the beautiful glass, I could almost hear the gentle sounds of the ocean, which brought me back to reality, and I couldn't take my eyes off the beautiful sparkles of light across the water that had been enhanced from the rising sun. It was a sight to behold. I couldn't get myself to leave this wonderful place. I wanted sanctuary from my fate, and the light here was so beautiful, it made me dread that light of doom even more. In my mind, I thought if I could stay here all day, I could admire the light shining through the beautiful glass so I would forget about all my torment. That was exactly what I did. I stayed in the church until the sun was ready to set.

With my heart feeling full, I jumped to my feet and started back to the boardwalk and thought about what I was going to do next. The town was jumping with action this time of year, and the cops were on full force. Teenagers drinking in the streets and young girls looking for adventure were the perfect mixture to keep the cops on their toes. I approached a gas station filled with waiting motorcycles and trucks with anxious teens trying to figure out where they should go to get away from the cops. There were cops waiting just up the street for anyone to slip up and break the law. Most of the police were part-timers, and the majority of them were on some kind of power trip. They would pick on kids that were just trying to have a little fun. Because the Jersey Shore was covered in Pine Barrens, it was prime real estate for all off-road thrill-seekers. There were many dirt roads that led to nowhere, and the destination was perfect for teenage mischief. The cops weren't equipped to follow them into the woods, and that seemed to be the place to go for underage drinking. My services would be needed there tonight, I had a feeling, and I, too, needed to have a little fun, so I hopped into one of the pickup trucks and tagged along for the ride.

It definitely wasn't a wasted trip. The crews of kids that totaled four trucks, two of which were pulling quads, and a half a dozen or so motorcycles had been packed up and ready to go. With coolers full of alcohol and pockets full of drugs, they convoyed to the small dirt road that would lead them to party sanctuary. The motorcycles headed up the trail, as the quads were unloaded from the trailers. Everyone was excited to get a move on, and the girls were laughing and flirting with the boys. The quads were off to catch up with the bikes, and the trucks tailed close behind. You couldn't see anything except the beaming headlights and taillights of the vehicles as they popped in and out through the rough terrain of the dirt road. I myself was excited about the trip. The last time I had been on an adventure like this was with my brother. I didn't notice the bumpy road as my memories flooded my head.

We had run away from home because my father would get drunk and beat us. We saddled up the horses and took enough food and water to last us well over a week. Our pa had come after us, and he was madder than ever. He chased us through the woods for three hours, and watching the motorcycles dart in between the trees reminded me of that. My brother ran his horse off a small cliff and into the river; he made it out to safety, but his horse didn't. Pa stopped long enough to beat the life out of him, but when he was finished, he came after me. I ran my horse faster than he had ever run before, and Pa seemed to be right behind me. No matter where I went or how fast I would go, he was always on my tail. My horse ran out of life after a few hours, and I cried aloud as I lay by his side, trying to get up the nerve to unload my shotgun into his head. The poor thing was suffering, and I loved him so much that I couldn't take his life. When I saw my pa coming up over the hill, I tried to hide, but he heard me. We both knew what I had to do.

I thought to myself, *He is going to kill me*, but when he reached the distressed horse, he just looked at me and said, "Boy, you go on now, go back and see to your brother."

He patted me on the back, and much to my surprise, he did not freak out on me. I walked back to the camp where my brother was waiting and that was when I heard it, the shot fired that killed my best friend. He pulled me up on his horse, and we didn't speak during the long ride home. Pa knew what that horse meant to me, and we never spoke of it again. Even though my pa was a drinker, he did love us, and every day that passed after that day, he showed us just how much, never once raising a hand in anger again. I just wish that my best friend didn't have to die in trade.

Returning back to the excitement, the gang had reached the small pond, an oasis in the middle of the Pine Barrens. It was beautiful, like being in a different part of the world. The first to arrive had started a small bonfire. The surface of the water was reflecting the flames, and it looked like a scene from one of those beach party movies; you know the type, teenagers and beer, dancing and sex. Everyone was passing around marijuana; they turned up the music and went with it. One of the girls pulled a bag of marshmallows and a skewer from her bag.

She jumped to her feet and said, "Hey, Don! Why don't you tell us the story about the crazy guy that lives in these woods?" as she held the white, sticky treat over the open fire.

"Okay, I'll tell it, but I'm warning you, he doesn't like people to talk about him. In fact, I heard that one night, there was a party out here, and the kids that were drinking and having fun started to tell this same story, and that was when it happened."

The girls began to huddle close to the fire. "What happened?" one of them asked with concern.

"I'll tell you what happened, they heard a noise in the dark, and one of them went missing. The others thought that they were just trying to scare the rest of them and much to their surprise…"

"What? What happened?" they asked anxiously.

"A mind-curling scream sounded out over the woods, a scream so loud and so horrifying that the kids dropped their beers and scattered. The girls were hiding under the bed of a pickup truck frightened and crying when all of a sudden, they noticed that something was crawling around above them in the truck."

One of the girls asked, "What was it? Was it the crazy man?"

"No!" said Don. "It was the shattered, bloody remains of the missing person, dragging himself to the end of the tailgate."

"Then what happened?" asked the girl.

"Then, one by one, they all started to disappear until there was only one of them left. Only one left to tell the tale."

Another cut in and said, "Yeah, and the next day, when the cops went there to see what happened, they didn't find a thing. They sent the shocked survivor to the nuthouse. No one ever believed him, and they never found the rest of the other kids. They say that the lunatic is still in these woods watching and waiting for some kids to come back so he can feed on them like an animal."

"Did he really eat them?" one of the girls asked.

"Well, they never found any part of them. Where else could they have gone? They never made it home."

Another said, "That's bullshit, that guy is dead!"

"Dead?" the frightened girl asked.

"Yeah, dead, they found his body over a year ago. He was just some homeless man that lived out here. Vince said he seen him taking a bath in the pond when he was walking to the arcade one day."

"Vince, is it true? Did you really see him?" asked the scared girl.

"Yeah, I saw him; he was just some homeless guy."

From out of nowhere came the horrifying scream. "Aha! Help me! Someone please help me! Oh God, no."

The kids all began to scream and run around looking for the place the hollering was coming from, but they could not find it.

One of the girls said, "Don, where is Don?"

"I don't know!" another boy said. Then, with a thud, out jumped Don covered in blood. Everyone screamed, and Don started laughing.

"It's only a joke! It's just ketchup!"

The boys began to laugh along, and the girls were pissed off. I had to laugh, too. It was funny to see how one homeless person could cause such chaos.

The party continued into the night, and everyone was getting very wasted. One of the girls stripped down to her underwear and jumped into the pond. She was taunting one of the boys to join her, but he was too drunk to do so.

She called to him, "Chicken! Bock, bock!"

"I'm no chicken!" he yelled and jumped into the cold, dark water.

They began to swim toward one another when Don jumped up to grab the girl. With a heavy shove, she pushed him off of her, and he fell back onto a large rock and bumped his head. It must have been very hard, because in that instant, I could see the light begin to build up at the bottom of the cold, dark pool.

"Oh, shit!" I shouted and shook one of the kids who was getting busy with his girlfriend on a blanket close by.

The girl screamed, "Don, stop kidding around!" But he wasn't kidding, he was in trouble. Everyone was so drunk and stoned that they were pretty much non-responsive. I grabbed one of the beer coolers and pushed it into the water.

"Maybe one of you will get up and save the beer!" I screamed, and they did. As they heard the splash, they all lifted their heads up to see what the noise was.

The young woman screamed, "Somebody help me; Don is hurt!"

They scooped him up out of the water, and the light faded away, another job well done, I looked on as the wonderful high that they were all feeling drifted away and hitched a ride back to Main Street being that it was midnight and I needed to search for Kitten. It had been a long while since her beauty graced me. I needed to see her.

As we approached the main drag in town, the cops noticed the truck swerving a bit out of its traffic lane. They put their lights on, instructing the kids to pull the truck over. I felt bad for the kids and figured whatever will be will be, being it was something I could not fix. I watched as the police officer administered a sobriety test. As he discovered the driver was intoxicated, he motioned to his partner to assist him with the arrest. They smiled to each other and pushed the boy into the back of the patrol car. I looked on as the other kids packed up their stuff and trudged on foot with the remainder of their night.

I walked across the street, and a group of people caught my eye. They were laughing very loud, and I was not the only one who noticed them as they came out of the pub. One of the women was pulling the buttons off her shirt, exposing her blue lace bra. Her breasts were full and popping out of her undergarments. One of the men who was there tugged at her shirt, revealing more of her voluptuous body. She laughed louder and began to peel the remainder of her top off. She grabbed the man and started to kiss him, darting her tongue in and out of his mouth.

The other two women looked at each other and one said, "She's at it again. Let's get the hell out of here."

"Yeah, she is such a slut; let her walk home," she replied.

The two continued to make out, touching, feeling, and slowly made their way down into the adjacent parking garage.

Suddenly, the woman said, "We have to stop. I can't do this."

The man pushed her hard onto one of the cars and said, "Listen, you don't have to leave. Let's just talk."

"Yes, I'm sorry, but I have to get back to my friends. If they leave without me, I'll have to walk home," she replied.

"Listen, just for a little while. We could just talk," the persistent man said.

The girl started to walk away, and she mumbled something under her breath, but I couldn't hear what she said. Instantly, the man took a few long strides after her and tackled her down to the ground. The light was nowhere in sight, but I had a really bad feeling about this whole situation, so I hung around just in case I could be of some help.

The man dragged the crying woman deeper into the parking garage until they were in a dark corner away from prying eyes. He balled up his fist and with one shot, sent her into unconsciousness. He pulled up her skirt and ripped her panties off completely. She began to wake up, and when she did, she began to cry again. I tried to intervene, but I could not do anything. I felt helpless; all I could do was look on as rape continued for the unfortunate woman. She was bleeding badly; the man did not seem to care at all. He pulled down his shorts and spit in his hand as he readied himself for penetration. He plunged his semi deep into his victim, and you could hear her silent screams as his hand cupped tightly over her mouth. He proceeded to bite her breasts and a small trickle of blood became visible. I was shaking; that's when it happened, the light, and the blue-green light that was so frightening to me appeared. He was going to kill her. What could I do? I ran quickly out of the garage and over to some people who were walking past, making the wind blow the money from their hands forcing it down into the garage, but the stupid asses didn't see it happen, and they just kept on going.

"Damn tourists!" I shouted. I heard the sound of a shot. I couldn't believe my ears, and I was petrified at the sound I had just heard. He shot her, and she was dead? I rushed over to see the carnage I had missed. There in the dark, a figure stood wobbling from side to side. The scent of gunpowder was in the air, and the smoke cloud was still hovering in the darkness. I walked over and looked down, to get a glimpse of the dead girl's body, but the horrible blue-green light was still burning bright.

Why had the light not gone out? The murder was complete. That was when it became apparent that the body on the garage floor was not that of a beaten woman. It was the body of the sexually aggressive man, who only moments ago had originally caused the woman harm in the first place. She had shot him. Yahoo, he is the one who is dead, but what about the light, why was it still burning for death? That was when the girl, still holding a smoking gun, fell to her knees and pointed the gun at herself. Oh Lord, what was she doing? Why was she doing it? Just then, the shot went off, and the girl went down. The blue-green light changed to bright orange, and there, in the eerie glow of orange, came forth a figure. Who was it? Oh no, was it her?

I had waited for this moment for so long, to see the woman who came for me all those years ago. Would she be coming for the girl now, and could I stop her? I had so many things I wanted to say, so many questions that I wanted to ask. It seemed like a lifetime as I waited for the figure in that bright orange light to show herself.

The girl's lifeless body lifted off the bloody concrete of that parking garage. It hovered silently for a few seconds, and in the distance, I could hear the sound of bells ringing, just as they did when the church bells rang before mass at that beautiful church on Sunday morning. That was when the figure revealed itself. The face of a man became clear. He was easy to look at, tall with light hair and eyes. I could see the girl's spirit lifted from her mortal body. She smiled at the ghostly figure that had come for her, just like I did all those years ago. He stretched his hand toward her and motioned for her to take it. That was when I intervened. I could not let this poor woman reach for the hand of doom. She would never rest in peace if she took this tyrant's hand. I blocked the beautiful soul from harm and shouted.

"No, no, you can't have her! Not so she can be damned for all of eternity."

"Don't scare off my angel. I want to go with God!" she cried.

"He isn't taking you to be with God. He has other plans for you, my dear."

"Go ahead. Tell her why you are here!" I shouted as the scoundrel sneered at me and said, "She did it to herself, and she took a life. With that comes a price."

"But she was raped, and she did what she had to do. Why does she have to pay? What about that pig that deserved to die? What price does he pay?" I exclaimed.

"He didn't kill anyone. He was murdered, not her. And besides, what do you care anyway?"

"Why do I care? Why do I care? I'll tell you why I care; I care because she shouldn't have to suffer an eternity of hell just because she defended herself."

His reply was, "I don't have a say in the matter, and I just bring them in. I do not pick or choose who it is, that is not my job. I just lead the way, and that's it."

The girl could not understand what was going on. She just looked at me as if I had ruined everything for her. I was sorry. I tried my best to make things right but failed. The pirate grabbed her hand, led her up into the horrible light, and in a flash, they were gone. Because of the pandemonium, I did not get to ask the questions I longed to have the answers to.

"When will I have paid off my debt? When will my job be complete?" I needed to know, but I supposed I would have to wait a bit longer.

Chapter Five

I was determined to find Kitten. I trudged my heavy heart up the ramp to the street and continued on my quest. I needed to look upon the beauty that she possessed. I knew that Kitten was the only one on this big blue planet who could turn my frown upside down. I hungered for a glimpse of her beauty. I needed a fix. I figured she just might be at that rank pub, so I booked to the stinky scene. The bar was quiet, which was unusual for a place like this. I spotted the biker dealer, back in the dark corner of the bar. If she was coming, I was sure that he would be the first person she would talk to. I listened to the crummy conversations that this scab dealer was having and just laughed at all of the addicts who begged to be fronted their night's festivities.

It was funny to me how drugs made people grovel. This went on for hours; I began to give up hope. I did not think I would ever see my girl tonight. I dragged my butt off the stool and began to walk toward the exit. That was when I saw her; she was breathtaking. She smiled at the bartender as she glided in the entrance. He motioned to her that the stinky biker was in the back of the bar, and her stride became swift. She skipped over to him and flung her arms around his neck. She hugged him and whispered something into his ear. He patted his hand on her butt as the money passed along with the drugs. I wondered why she did this to herself. Why did she need to use drugs? Why was she always alone, and how could I possibly have her? All of these questions raced through my head as I stood in awe, gazing at her, watching her every move.

She ordered a beer and walked toward the restroom. I followed close behind, determined to find out what sort of drugs she was purchasing. She washed her hands and gathered her gorgeous long hair, twisting it into a pretzel before she entered a private stall. I slipped in behind her and waited to see what she was going to do next. She pulled off a few strips of toilet paper and placed them over the toilet seat, hiked up her skirt, and gently pulled her panties down around her knees as she squatted, hovering a few inches over the nasty urine-soaked toilet bowl. I turned my head to give her some privacy. Knowing all along that she could not see me, I did it anyway.

She finished up, reached into her purse, which was resting on the toilet tissue holder, and came out with a baggie filled with cocaine; she rolled up a twenty-dollar bill and shoved it into the baggie. She looked up to the ceiling, took a deep breath, and let it out slowly, put the bill to her nose, and inhaling deeply, she sniffed more then half of the content of the baggie up into her nose. Her head swayed a bit, and her body leaned into the corner of the stall. She exhaled and snorted again, letting out a great sigh of relief.

"Oh yeah, baby, that's what I'm talking about," she moaned quietly.

She gathered up her things and walked over to the sink, washed her hands again, and wiped the remaining residue from her nose. She fluffed her hair and walked back out to the bar, where her beer was waiting for her.

She pulled out some money, but the bartender said, "No, it's taken care of."

She smiled and said, "Thank you."

"Don't thank me, thank him," he said as he pointed to the balcony.

I looked over, and there was a dude holding a mug up in the air and smiling at her. She smiled back and started to walk over to him. This person was clearly drunk, and about ten minutes before she walked in the bar, he was begging some old woman to take him home.

Why was Kitten accepting drinks from this bum? She looked down at him and said, "Where the hell have you been?"

"I've been here waiting for you, baby," the person replied.

"Yeah, sure you have," she mumbled.

He put his arm around her waist and pushed his face into her breasts saying, "Oh, baby, please don't be mad at me. You know I love you."

I could see her fighting tears that were welling up in her eyes as she said, "Yeah, right. Sure you do. That's why you don't come home for days at a time, and when you do come home, you just sleep and fight with me. Oh yeah, but you love me, right? Whatever!"

"Oh, baby, don't be like that," he said.

She pushed him off her and started to walk out of the bar.

He yelled, "I'm sorry, baby! I'll try harder, I promise. You know you are the only one for me. Besides, who knows you better than I do?" He jumped up onto a stool and shouted, "Attention, may I have your attention please? I wanted to inform all that are present of my unconditional love for this beautiful woman. She is smart, beautiful, and a great kisser. She's my girl; she belongs to me."

She stopped dead in her tracks, her chin drooped down to her chest, and she turned an ear toward him.

"I'm sorry. I love you, baby," he said with self-loathing in his voice.

I could tell he was just telling her what she really wanted to hear. She could not buy this line, not from this clown. This guy was a bum, but she turned toward him and smiled.

"I'll have a shot!" she shouted to the bartender.

The creep laughed and put his arm on her shoulder.

"That's more like it. You want to shoot some pool?" he laughed and reached into his pocket.

She nodded and pulled some money from her pocket. "I guess you need some of this too, huh?"

"Oh, baby, you're the best." He leaned over and kissed her.

His shave was over a day old, and I am sure his breath was the same if not worse. I could not understand why she wanted to be with a guy like this. What could he have that she wanted? What could he be holding over her? I wondered.

I watched as she took her first sip of beer. She drank almost half of the bottle before putting it down and had a strange painted smile on her face; she did not look the same. I moved in closer. I could not help but want to intervene in this mess. She was perfect, and this Devin was a nasty flea, a blood-sucking parasite lurking behind one of my angel's two thousand parts. I did a mental inventory of her parts and wondered if I could possibly burn him off?

I need to find out what it was going to take to get her away from him. I watched as he pawed at her ass, and the way he constantly mashed his face into her chest made me want to kill him myself. I listened as he spoke in a rude tongue about her to any passerby that would stop to listen. I desperately wanted to be alone with her and wondered where the hellish light was when I needed it. I remembered what she looked like only moments ago, she looked just like an angel, and now, well now, she just stared with blank eyes. How could this happen? Where had she gone? Her body was here, but her heart was somewhere else.

After about an hour of beer drinking and shooting pool, she began to get agitated at the way this Devin guy was acting. I could tell that she knew the truth about him when her head dropped, and she ordered a double shot of black licorice.

The bartender said, "Why do you put up with this asshole?"

"I don't know, Tiger," she replied.

"You know he was hitting on Lady Remington before."

"Lady Remington? That old bitch that drinks Bloody Marys all the time, the hairy bitch that has never heard of a razor in her life?"

"Yeah, that's her. I heard him tell her that he would take her home if she paid his bar bill," the bartender said.

"What? He said what?" she shouted.

She steam-rolled over to him and jabbed her fist into his kidneys, pushing him about three feet back. I smiled with pride and followed her as she bounded for the door.

"Yes!" I cheered. "See you later, Devin."

She ducked around the nearest corner, shaking her head saying, "How could I be so stupid? What kind of a stupid chump am I?"

She ran her hands along the chrome handlebars of an unmanned mountain bike lying against the side of the building. She had that look in her eye that she was about to be up to something. No sooner did I think it, and off she was, peddling her legs as fast as they could go. I started after her, following her down Central Avenue past the police station and up the ramp to the pavilion. She shoved the stolen bike behind some tall grass in the sand dune to hide what she had just done. Giggling to herself, she shuffled her feet through the sand down to the waterline and plopped her butt down in the moist sand.

She wiped tears from her eyes and let her body fall limp. Her hair looked so stunning lying there on the sand; I wanted so badly to kiss her. She pulled the drugs from her pocket as she rolled over and twisted up a bill, snorting what was left of her cocaine. I could see the pain in her face as she looked out over the ocean. Her bottom lip began to twitch, and her eyes filled up with tears yet again.

I looked out over the water with her; the deadly light was shining everywhere from a pod of dolphin feeding far off in the distance. If only she could see them, I knew it would make her smile. I pushed the tide in fast to bring them in closer, and I coaxed one of them into jumping high up, out of the water. It worked; she had seen them and was smiling. Kitten had the most striking smile; I wish she never had a reason not to smile.

I could not take being this close to her any longer. I had to do it. I got right next to her, so close that if I could have I would have used the same air to breathe. She smelled so wonderful, like the way the earth did after a storm, clean and fresh. Her lips were full and inviting, pink from the habit she had of nibbling on them. Her eyes smiled at the sight of the mammals frolicking in the sea. I could see how content her soul was at that moment, and she looked like an angel. I was falling deeper in love with her. I pressed my lips against hers and stole a kiss. She seemed to have kissed me back. She pulled away and fell to her knees.

"Oh thank you, thank you. I knew you were watching. Thank you for the kiss and the beautiful dolphins," she said as she wrapped her arms around herself, holding on tightly.

Whom was she talking to? Was it me? Was she talking to me?

She stretched her arms up over her head, smiled, and said, "I can't believe it! Mother Nature kissed me!"

Wow, she thought I was Mother Nature. I could live with that. She went back to the bike and began her journey. Where would we be going now? I had to follow her. I needed to be with her to make sure she did not go back to that bum, Devin. She rode for about thirty minutes and rolled the bike up a long driveway, dismounting as she approached a garage. She ditched the bike in the bushes and traipsed up the steps that led to a small apartment. It was nice, considering it was over top of an old garage. She had a small fire escape that looked over a quaint little garden. She grabbed a beer from the fridge and leaned over the railing flicking her bottle cap into the flowerbed. The sun was almost down, and the tiny accent lighting in the garden grabbed the attention of some moths, which danced in the dim light. Kitten spotted them and lifted her beer high in the air.

"Here's to you, little friends. Have fun tonight, and be careful; watch out for frogs now," she said smiling as she sipped her drink.

I loved how she would talk to the animals. She seemed so kind. The more time I spent with her, the more I longed to have her by my side forever. If only things could be different, I would love her like no man has ever loved her or ever could love her, but what was her name? I snooped around the apartment to see what kind of life she lived. There were pictures of animals on every wall, from snakes to skunks. She had a glass tank full of fish and one with frogs. There were two bowls on the kitchen floor but no trace of what kind of animal they belonged to. I heard a dog bark outside and wondered if it was hers.

Then she jumped to her feet and yelled, "Kitty! Here kitty, come on, baby." She jumped to her feet and reached for the empty bowls, filled one with water and sprinkled some dry food in the other. No sooner did she place the bowls back down on the floor, then Kitty had come home for dinner. He was a big gray cat that looked as though he had been in a fight.

As he rubbed his cheek on her leg, she said, "Are you okay? Guess what, Azreal? Mother Nature kissed me today." She knelt down and patted his head. "Have a nice supper, baby."

I sat there for hours watching her drink one beer after another while she talked to the crickets singing outside.

"You guys are really out of tune tonight, aren't you?" she giggled.

The large gray cat jumped onto her lap purring louder with every stroke of her hand.

She whispered, "Azreal, I think my luck is changing. Maybe I'm supposed to be alone! Just you and me, buddy."

I looked at her precious face. She seemed lost, like she was looking out over the frozen tundra of a wasteland. Continuing to drink into the night, she listened to the radio and played with Azreal. The night air was cool and comfortable. I could see her breasts becoming tight from the cold. Her nipples began to show through her blouse, so I forced the wind to blow a little harder in their direction so I could get a better look. I suppose I blew too hard, because she got a chill and went in the house.

She kicked off her sandals and made a beeline for the bathroom, dropped her shorts, and pulled her shirt up over her head. I could feel myself blush as she pushed the door closed. Azreal was right behind her, and he pushed the door open again. Oh yes, the cat came through for me. It was good of the kitty cat to open the door for me, helping me to keep her in view. I missed her getting into the shower, but I could see the silhouette of her body projected onto the glass shower-stall door. She looked astounding. I could see the water cascading off her breasts, the soap foam from her hair dripping down the center of her back to the crease of her luscious backside. Her form was supreme; she was a goddess.

As she caressed her body with the bar of soap, I could feel myself becoming aroused. I could not help myself. Not many men would have been able to. She was a vision, the sexiest woman I had ever laid eyes on. Just the way she washed her body led me to believe that the show was not over yet. She seemed so compelled to rub and fondle herself. I was lucky to be a witness to the intense appreciation she had for herself. Letting the water remove the final traces of soap and bubbles from her body, she shut off the water, and my heart skipped a beat as she opened the shower door. Never had I seen such magnificent breasts in all of my existence. They only compared to her smile. She wrapped a small towel around her waist, held it with one hand, and wiped the foggy mirror off with the other. She shook her hair and turned on the blow dryer. I began to feel a bit uncomfortable. It made me think, how could I invade her privacy like this? What gave me the right? I left her to herself and went out on the fire escape. Not long after, she followed.

The fragrance of her perfume engulfed my lungs. She sat down, cracked open another beer using the end of the silk shirt she had on to protect her hand. I watched as she leaned back on her chair and slipped her hand between the buttons on her blouse. I could not leave her side. I was excited and about to steal a kiss when the phone rang.

Kitten staggered to the phone and answered with a slurred voice. "Hell-O." There was silence. "What do you want?" Her eyes were beginning to roll around in her head. *Who could this be?* I wondered. Then she screamed, "No!" and hung up the phone. Reaching her hand to her head, she pushed her hair back. "He better not come here tonight."

She sucked down the remainder of her beer and flopped onto the couch. In no time, she was sleeping like an angel. Keeping a close visual, I looked through her purse. I needed to know her name. I flipped open her wallet, and when it was about to reveal her identity, I heard stumbling footsteps outside her door. A knock came soon after.

"Baby, let me in!" exclaimed the voice.

She rubbed her eyes and stumbled to her feet. "Go away!" she yelled to the door.

"Oh, honey, please let me in. I need to talk to you," the voice replied.

"No! Go away!" she yelled even louder.

"Why did you steal my bike? You knew that I would come and get it." It was Devin.

"Oh shit, sorry." She sighed.

She opened the door, and there he was, Devin, that rat. I hated the guy. He was slime. He smiled like the cat that ate the canary and strolled into the apartment as if he owned the place.

"Take your bike and go," she said.

"You know you don't want me to go," he replied laughing.

He grabbed her and pushed himself onto her. They fell on the couch, and he began kissing her neck. She frantically tried to push him off, but he persisted.

"You know I love you, baby. Why do you fight it? I know you want to," he muttered.

He continued to run his nasty tongue along the side of her throat, and I could tell it was getting harder for Kitten to resist. She pushed her chin up higher so he could gain full access to her neck, and as he did, he slid his hand between her legs.

I heard her say, "This is the last time."

I could not watch. I hated this man, and I could not see this happen. *You had better believe this is the last time,* I thought. I turned away and headed back for the wallet. I needed to know more about her. I could hear Kitten's gentle moan. The hair began to rise on the back of my neck. It was such a sweet sound.

I flipped the soft leather over my thumb, and there she was. I had seen many photo identification cards, and every time, it was the same thing, a photo in which the bearer resembled a criminal in a police mug shot. Not one, not two, but every photo looked this way. My lips would never mutter those words on this night. On this night, I was at a loss for words. The photo was breathtaking, a vision, with the brightest smile my eyes had ever seen. I tried to imagine watching her, standing on that long line at the motor vehicle office. How could anyone smile so big on such a long, putrid line? Many people have almost died on that musty line, but not Kitten, she was as happy as happy could be.

The decisive moment was upon me. Now, I would know her name. I could feel the lump rise in my throat as my eyes slowly turned to the perfectly typed print. Kitty Morris, my Kitten's name was Kitty. Oh, my gosh, how could I have known? I turned my head in the direction of the couch. That filthy Devin was all over her. I needed to put an end to this and fast. This slime didn't deserve my Kitty; she was way too special for a creep like him. Not being able to take the torture any longer, I scurried down the stairs of her apartment and sat down. I looked over at the bike leaning against the bush. My head fell in such sorrow. I wanted so badly to be with her. She was becoming everything to me. I needed to get away, just knowing that a loser like Devin was upstairs having his way with Kitty made me sick. I headed back to the beach. My hate grew stronger for that Devin, and I wished that the light would come for him.

Chapter Six

*T*he streets were very quiet. I needed to think, so I went to the Beach Park Sanctuary. There were barricades to keep the tourists out and warning signs posted for those who journeyed past them. I figured, no people, no problem. Here, I could think.

The sun was about to come up over the dark ocean. I could see just a hint of orange in the distance. It was amazing to look at. I could not believe my eyes as the gold and yellow sparkles on the waves grew longer and reached their radiant glow to the sand at my feet. Birds scouting for food and a few land crabs scurried in the dunes behind me. A bright blue butterfly fluttered past, and all I could think about was Kitten and how she would have loved to see this beautiful sight. How I longed to see her! Just as I longed for the answers, I was sure I would never get. I fell back onto the sand and closed my eyes, listening to the morning sun whisper in the wind. I needed to be in my mind, pretending everything would be all right.

I could hear a faint voice in the distance calling out to me. "Who's there?" I called. "What do you want?" I jumped to my feet and followed the gentle, soothing voice. It was coming from an old observation tower once used by Fish and Game to scout for new wildlife activity. As I got closer, the voice had stopped. I called out repeatedly, but there was no answer. Who was calling out to me? It was just one more question I would not have the answer to anytime soon. I waited for hours to see if the voice would call out to me again, but it never did.

The sun rose high in the sky so I worked my way up the beach to the boardwalk. I had work to attend to, and I needed to get to it. The sand was wall-to-wall tourists, and the lifeguards were on full staff. Action filled the air, and the sweet smell of suntan oil surrounded me. I could not see any green lights, and after the night I had, I was not looking forward to saving anyone anytime soon. I could not keep myself from her any longer. I needed to see her. I hurried to her house, and when I came up the driveway, there it was, that bike, Devin's bike to be exact. How I hated him and wished him bodily harm. At that moment, I could hear Kitty and Devin yelling back and forth at one another. The apartment door flung open, and all his clothes floated down the stairs.

Kitten was screaming, "I told you not to go into my purse! What were you doing with my wallet? Taking money again? Get out of my house, and don't come back. I knew I was making a big mistake giving in to you again."

I smiled and laughed as he fumbled down the steps. Dodging high and low, he avoided the beer bottles that Kitty was throwing at him as he gathered up his things on his way down. My kitten was a tiger. I loved it. This was the best day of my life. The loser got dressed, hopped on his bike, and rode off down the driveway. I wished for a truck to mow him down as he entered the street, but no such luck.

I ran up the stairs and peered into the apartment. Kitten was weeping on the couch. She reached for her cigarettes and walked over to the fridge to grab a Coke.

"What the fuck was I thinking letting him in here? He isn't going to change." She popped open the cold soda and took a seat on the balcony. "I wish he was out of my life for good. Oh, Azreal, what do we do now?"

I felt so sorry for the girl. Why did she deserve this abuse? She deserved better than she had, and I made it my quest, she would be the one I saved this summer. I would devote all of my time to Kitty. She needed me, and I was the only one who could help her. From this day forward, I would never leave her side, no matter what the consequences may be. I watched as she pulled a joint from her pack and lit it up. The tears were just running down her cheeks. A dove landed on the railing next to her, and she smiled a happy grin.

"Good morning, Mr. Dove! How are you today?" The dove just stared at her for a minute, and just as it was going to fly off, she reached her hand out, and that bird sat there and let her stroke his feathers. She thanked him by blowing him a kiss.

I watched as she headed to the shower. Once again, I would bask in her beauty as the soap bubbles cascaded down the small of her back. This woman was a rare beauty. When she was finished drying off, she put on her bathing suit and packed up a duffel bag with a towel and some lotion. She called up a friend and waited for her arrival at the edge of the driveway. A few minutes later, a small convertible pulled up to the house. It was a younger girl who did not look old enough to drive an automobile. She hopped into the car without opening the door.

"What's up, Girl? How's it going?" Kitty asked.

"Nothing much. It's a good thing you called when you did. I was just about to cross the bridge. If I had, you would have had to walk," the young girl replied.

They sped off down the road with the wind blowing in their hair. The sun was shining, and they smiled at each other when the boys on the street whistled at them. They pulled up to the bay, and Kitty thanked her for the ride and offered to give her some money for gas.

The young girl laughed. "After what my brother puts you through, you don't owe me a dime!"

"You're not working; I know you don't have any money. Please take it. Your brother tried to steal it; you might as well have it. Please, just take the money," Kitty insisted.

"I don't know why you put up with his junk anyway. You should just break it off with him for good. I know he is my brother and all, but, Kitty, why do you stay with him?"

"Just shut up, and take this money, will you? I can handle him." Kitty shoved the money into her hand and held it tight. "You know you are like my sister, don't you, Gwen?"

"Yeah, you are the only sister that I have. My brother is useless, and my mom is never around. She is more interested in finding a man than worrying about picking up groceries for her kids." She slowed down and pulled slowly into the parking lot. "I just wish my brother was normal. If he would just do the right thing, you could really be my sister."

"Listen and listen good. You are my sister, and you will always be my sister. Don't let your brother bring you down. Go out and have a good time; you are young and in your prime. Go shopping and buy some shoes or a new beach bag," Kitten instructed.

She pulled out another twenty and shoved it into her hand. "Thank you for the ride. I'll talk to you later. Come by the bay if you aren't doing anything later. I'll be here." She gave Gwen a hug and reached for the door.

"I love you, Kitty," Gwen said smiling.

"Just stay out of trouble."

"I will."

Kitten got out of the car and waved goodbye to her friend. I liked this girl even if she was Devin's sister. It was great that she hated him as much as I did and did not want Kitten to see him anymore. Now, I just might have an ally.

I followed her down to the edge of the bay where she placed all of her things. She was not happy at all. I could see the confusion in her face. This just was not my girl. Why did she do this to herself? She deserved so many wonderful things in her life. I just wished I could be the one to hand them to her. As she flopped onto her beach towel, I could tell she was beginning to relax a bit. Letting out a heavy sigh, she closed her eyes, and her lips curled up a bit, exposing just the hint of a smile. I thought to myself that this could be a great day. I looked on as her feet wiggled gently into the sand, pushing away the warm, dry sand from the surface, exposing the cool damp sand just underneath. She watched children running up toward her.

"What ya reading?" the little girl asked.

"Nothing yet, I just got here." Kitten looked up at the child peering over her sunglasses. "What's in the bucket?" she asked.

"I'm Cindy, and this is my sister, Sarah. We're looking for sea monsters. Have you seen any around here?"

"No, but I'll keep my eyes peeled for them," she replied, giggling as she said it. "Hey, can you girls do me a favor? Would you fill this up with water for me?" Kitten reached into her bag and pulled out a small inflatable pool.

"Cool! What is that?" Sarah could not keep her feet still. She began jumping up and down with excitement.

"This is my wading pool. I use it to keep cool." She put the tube to her lips and blew it up. She placed it where she had cleared the sand and pushed more away to make room for the pool.

"Why don't you just go in the water? You can get wet all over that way, you know," the little girl explained.

"I don't want to get all wet. I like to put my feet in." She reached down and made the hole a little deeper.

"Why don't you just put your blanket down by the water? You can put your feet in if you get really close." Cindy stood there with her hand on her hips quite annoyed.

"Because if the tide comes in, I just have to move, and I don't want to move. I want to read my book. Do you always ask so many questions?" Kitten pulled her glasses off and lifted herself up to her feet. "May I please borrow your bucket to fill up my pool?"

"Cindy, give her the bucket."

"I don't want to. Let her get her own bucket." Cindy pushed the bucket behind her back.

"How about if I give you some money for ice cream? Then can I borrow the bucket? Look, I'll only be a minute, two minutes tops."

"I want ice cream! Here you can use the bucket. Wait, I'll help you. I'm a good helper." She ran down to the water and pushed the bucket in filling it with the bay water. "I got it, I got it." She ran to the pool and splashed the water in.

"Thank you, but next time, please don't splash. Put it in gently so it doesn't spill out all over the place." Kitten reached for a small towel and brushed it over her legs where the water had splashed. The little girls laughed and took turns filling up the bucket and pouring it into the tiny pool.

"This pool is nice. I wish I had one for my dolls. They would love to swim around in here, and I don't have to worry about them getting lost because there aren't any waves in a pool. Where did you get it?"

"I got it at the dollar store up on the boardwalk. Here you take this five dollars, and be sure to split it with your sister." She squinted her eyes at the child. "Make sure you each get a pool and an ice cream."

Kitten handed over the money, took the bucket from the young girl's hand, and finished filling up her pool.

"Thanks for the bucket, girls. Have a great day."

"Oh we will, we will." The little girl ran off. "Mommy, can we go to the boardwalk and get a pool like the lady has. She rented our bucket for five dollars, and she said that's where she got it."

Kitten looked on as the kids ran down the beach to their mom. I wondered what she was thinking. Was she remembering her childhood or something else? I would never know. The look she was wearing seemed somber. She settled in her seat and placed her feet in their cool pool of water.

"Ah, that feels so good, just what I needed today." She reached down, picked up her book, and began to read. I watched her running her fingers through her hair and nibbling on her lip as she continued to read. There was a dog barking.

"Now what?" she muttered. A big black dog came bouncing off the pier and ran straight for her. He was all wet and carrying a big broken board in his mouth. "Killem, what are you doing here? Where is Jack?" She got to her feet and looked around to see where Jack was. "Oh hello, Marge. How are you feeling lately?" Walking toward her was a hard-looking woman.

"Oh, it's you. What are you doing here?" the woman snarled at Kitten and gave her a once over. "Are you alone?"

"Nice to see you, too, Marge. I thought Killem was with Jack."

"No, Jack got a job in the city, and he left the dog with me until he gets back. You look um, good." The woman rolled her eyes and called to the dog.

"Let's go, boy, time to go home." Marge latched a leash to Killem and began to pull him away.

"Well, it was nice to see you again, Marge. Tell Jack that I said hi." The woman never turned to say a word; she just kept pulling on the poor dog's leash.

"Witch!" Kitten sighed. "Poor Killem."

She headed back to her seat, grabbed her purse, and headed toward the pavilion eatery just down the beach. I loved watching her walk, especially in the sand. I did not know what it was, but when my Kitten was in the sand, she was radiant. Could it be the salt in the air or the cool and gentle waves on the shore? I was sure that I would never know. To tell you the truth, I did not even care; all I knew was I was falling in love more and more with each passing minute, and there was nothing I could do. I was trapped, hopelessly trapped in everything my Kitten was and determined to turn her life around for good.

As we approached the pavilion, there was not an eye on the entire beach or pier that was not looking at her. Men parted from her path as if they were honoring royalty. She walked through, owning all that was around her with every step she took. As she stood in line to place her order, the person in front of her offered her his place in line. She smiled politely and declined his offer, thanking him for the opportunity.

Calling out, "I'll have some carnival fries please, oh and a Coke if it's no trouble," Kitten placed her order.

As she handed the burly cashier money for her order, he said with a sly grin, "What is that a tattoo of?"

She replied with a huge smile, "You'll have to surve me more than some fries to find out." She took her change and her snack and strutted off, back to her little blanket on the bay.

The bay was very quiet; it was usually only senior citizens who sat on this side of the island. It was not a far walk from the parking area to the waterline and at the far end was a boat ramp. Most people who came here only came here to place their boats in the water; they never hung around much after that. I could see why Kitten came here. It was peaceful and beautiful. I could smell the vinegar coming off the fries she was eating, and I thought I might lose my mind as I watched her lick the salt from her fingertips.

I could not get that thought from my mind. I wanted so badly to kiss her and tell her how much in love with her I truly was. I hated this job, and I hated my so-called life. There were some children playing in the water just in front of where Kitten was sitting, and the splashing from their play was getting her fries all soggy. She carried them off to the garbage can, on the way, changed her mind, and decided to feed them to the seagulls instead. She threw one up in the air, and in a downward swoop, the first bird arrived. Before you could blink your eyes, two more gulls were calling out in a loud squawk for her to throw more food up to them. She laughed and tossed up another French fry. Now the three birds had turned into about twenty, and the noise of their calls was extremely loud.

She shouted, "Okay, okay, you can have them," and threw them all up in the air for the birds to take. She laughed aloud and did a little dance. "Okay, now, be nice to each other. There is enough to go around."

As I followed her back down to her place in the sand, there it was, that dreadful light haunting me to make it disappear. Why did it always come? Where were all the other souls destined to the light? Why was I the only one of my kind here on the island? I would never understand the length of my sentence. Would I ever be free to do what I wanted? Probably not, but the light was not going away anytime soon.

I could see a bike rider approaching; the light was just in his path. There did not seem to be anything that could cause harm to him, but I went over to check it out. Before I could get there, the bike stopped short, hurling the rider up over the handlebars and into a pile of discarded chunks of blacktop. There was nothing I could do. The rider was knocked out cold, and the thick, deep red liquid was running from his nose, mouth, and ears. He was a goner; it was just a matter of time before he would take his last breath. Just then, a small child, who could not have been more then five years old, looked directly at me.

"Is there anything that you can do to help him?"

I turned around to see to whom the child was speaking, but there was not anyone there. Was this child talking to me? No, that wasn't possible. I didn't acknowledge the boy; I just stood there.

The child persisted, "Hey! Isn't there anything you can do for the man? Don't you hear me?"

I was blown away, but I mustered up what courage I could and said, "No, what is done cannot be changed."

"That's too bad!" he said.

"You can see me?" I asked.

"Yes, I see you perfectly clear. If you are an angel, why don't you make him better? Are you here to take him to heaven?" the boy asked in a quiet voice.

I did not know what to say. How did I explain to this small child why I was there? Did I dare speak of my agenda? I was petrified, and to top it all off, I was confused. This was the first time in years I was able to have a conversation with a live mortal. Why now, and why this young boy? He continued to look at me with those innocent eyes taunting me to answer his questions.

I was at a loss for words. I just looked into his eyes and said, "When you're dead, you're dead. There isn't anything that anyone can do for the bike rider, not even me."

"Why are you here then?" he asked again, but this time, he spoke with anger in his voice. I just stared at the boy. I could feel a lump become lodged in my throat, and my speech was nowhere to be found.

"What good is it to be an angel if you can't help people? Were you too late?" he asked.

I wasn't sure what the rules were, but I knew that if I didn't try to explain myself to the boy, this incident would surely scar him for life. I knelt down beside the young man. I could hear the sirens coming up the road. I knew that the biker was dead, and I think the boy did, too. He reached out to touch me, and his hand passed right through my shoulder. I explained to him that it was my job to help people avoid being hurt, and that I could not always be there in time to save everyone.

"I bet you feel bad when that happens?" he asked.

I replied, "More than you know, kid."

The boy's head hung low, and his mother came running toward him, as she began yelling for him to come to her.

He looked at me and said, "Bye, bye!" I watched his mother take him away, and I could not help but wonder how that boy could see me, how he could talk to me and hear my words. I had lost all of my bearing and did not remember what I was doing before that moment.

That was when it happened. Time seemed to stand still. All movement around me came to a dead stop. The people that were on the pier and all that were on the beach were suddenly on pause. Not even the waves of the ocean had movement. What was happening? I could see a bright orange light in the distance and directly in the middle of it came a figure. Who could this be? Why was this happening? I was petrified, could not move an inch, as the figure grew closer to me. I could not see a face, but the voice was familiar to me. It called out, "You should know better than to converse with the mortals. Your place on this earth is to intervene with the tragedies you come upon, not to respond to those who have the power of sight."

I called out to the figure, "Who are you? Why don't you reveal yourself?"

The figure just laughed. "You have been here all this time and you don't know?"

They just laughed and faded into the orange glow of the light. I scrambled toward the figure desperately trying to catch up, but it was too late, they were gone. As I looked around, time began to go on as if nothing had happened. The waves began to flow, and the people continued their activities. I was confused. What was that all about? Why couldn't I talk to mortals who had the ability to see and speak to me? Again, I had more questions that needed to be answered and no one to answer them. I had a hollow feeling inside me. Now what was I supposed to do? I just did not know.

I walked slowly back down to the beach where Kitten was sunbathing. She was rubbing lotion on her body and getting ready to read a book that she had pulled out of her bag. I sat next to her and couldn't help but wonder what it would take to get her to hear me. Why was that small child able to converse with me and not my Kitten? I longed to have her touch my face in a loving way and tell me that everything was going to be all right, but I knew in my heart that could never be. I would never feel the touch of the woman whom I loved more than anything in this world. I spent the rest of the day watching her every move, enjoying every moment of my time with her.

As the sun set over the bay, Kitten smiled wider than I had ever seen her smile before. She said, "Thank you, God, for making the world that we live in so beautiful. I will never get tired of your beautiful sunsets."

With that, she began to pack up her things. She walked down the coastline with her feet in the water, letting the gentle waves caress her ankles as they rolled onto the shore. She giggled all the way to the pier and flopped down on a bench for a rest. Reaching into her bag, she pulled out a cell phone and called someone to pick her up. I waited for her travel arrangements to arrive, and to my surprise, it was a man. I thought all along the convertible would be coming for her, but it was not. I did not recognize this old muscle car. As it grew closer, it was clear to me who was driving: that sleazy biker, the drug dealer. Why would she go out of her way to call this loser? Deep down, I knew why she had called him, but I wished that she had called someone else to pick her up. He pulled up with great speed, and as he slammed on his brakes, dust flew up from the dirt parking lot, leaving everyone behind choking from it.

She ran toward the car and motioned for the passenger to get out and sit in the back. Out popped a sleazy-looking woman. She had no teeth and rags for clothes. I thought to myself, *Why would she want to hang out with this element of people?* Drugs were the answer. Drugs made people do the strangest things sometimes. I went along for the ride.

"Thanks for the ride, Ed," Kitten said. "Who's the chick in the back? Where did you find her?"

Ed replied, "Oh her, she's just here to suck my dick. I'll give her a gram and kick her out of the car." Kitten laughed and looked at the pathetic slut in the back seat.

"Why don't you just give me her gram, and after you get your head, throw her out of the car anyway."

Ed smiled and said, "Only if you do it instead, baby." Kitten shook her head no and laughed.

"Okay, why don't you just give me some because you are a nice guy? I do spend a lot of money here, you know."

"Okay, okay, I'll give you some, but you have to buy some, too."

"Cool, no problem. I have money at the house. You can come up, but your friend has to stay in the car. I don't want her in my house."

"Sure, baby, whatever you say!"

We pulled up to the house, and Ed ordered the whore to stay in the car. She agreed, and Kitten made her way up the driveway. Ed was close behind, staring at her ass as she climbed the steps to her apartment. I could hear him breathing heavily and could swear he was extremely angry as he watched her make her way one flight up. She fumbled for her keys and swung open the door. To her surprise, there he was, Devin. That jerk was in her house!

She shouted, "What the fuck are you doing here?! How did you get in?"

"You left the window open, baby. I thought you would be happy to see me."

Ed said loudly, "Is this jerk bothering you, Kitty?"

"Yes, as a matter of fact, he is." No sooner did she say that than Ed had picked Devin up off the couch and pushed him toward the door.

"Okay, I can take a hint. I'll leave, but I'll see you later, Kitty."

"Don't count on it," she replied and slammed the door behind him. "What an asshole! I told him yesterday that I didn't want him around here anymore. Why doesn't he get it? Now I have to change the lock and be sure to lock my windows before I leave the house from now on. This really sucks!"

"I'll take care of it, Kitty. I'll be back in the morning to change the locks, and I'll make sure that he doesn't bother you again."

"Thanks, Ed, you are a lifesaver. But please don't hurt him. He is just a drunk, and most of the time, he doesn't realize what he is doing."

I was surprised at this man. I thought he was just a dirty drug dealer, but it turned out that he had some good qualities as well. Kitten reached into the kitchen cabinet and pulled out a coffee can filled with money. She handed him some of it, and in turn, he passed her the drugs.

Ed smiled and said, "Here are a few extra for your troubles. I know how it is, a girl like you. Men must do crazy things to be close to you."

Boy, was he right! If only he knew about me. I wondered what he would think about that. She gave him a big hug and thanked him with a kiss. He told her that he would see her in the morning and headed back to his whore in the car.

Kitty ran to the porch and hollered, "Make it around one o'clock; I'm probably not going to get much sleep tonight, if you know what I mean."

Ed laughed and said, "Sure one o'clock, I got ya!"

She closed the door and sat on the couch. She opened a baggie of cocaine and just like before, rolled up a bill and snorted up almost half of the drug inside. She held her breath for a while and exhaled. The sound of relief filled the air, and she fell back onto a big pillow. Closing her eyes, she said, "You are my only friend. You make me feel good, and you don't cause me any trouble."

I hated to see her do such terrible things to her body. I could not watch her any longer, so I left the house and wandered through the busy streets.

I could not get that child out of my mind. I needed to know how and why. I ended up wandering around the marshlands. There were many animals about, and the light was flashing all around me; spring peepers catching insects, and snakes eating frogs, life's cycle never changing. The sounds of the crickets brought me back to my home. It reminded me of the quiet nights I spent with my family staring up at the stars dreaming of the future, never knowing that my whole life was going to change into this hell on earth.

I was remembering when I went searching for Sue Ellen, the empty house, the dog locked up, and my journey across the creek bridge. I could see myself crossing over the creaking wooden planks. I made my way down the path to the pond. I could hear laughing, but it was not Sue Ellen. The laughter was deep and hardy; it was the laughter of a man's voice. I slowed my pace down to a slink and peered through the branches of the trees. As I grew closer, I could see a large figure holding a woman in a long, flowing dress. Could this be? I had to know for sure.

I got closer still, and as I focused on the two I was spying on, it became clear to me. In a fit of rage, I picked up the largest rock that I could find and hurled it at the man. As he turned to see where the projectile was coming from, my heart stopped. It was Jacob, my best friend, holding my beautiful wife in a way that only I should be. She jumped to her feet and tried to explain to me that it was not what it appeared to be. I could not hear a thing. All I could do was stand there in dread as she began to fasten the buttons on her dress.

I picked up a large stick and jumped onto Jacob's back, beating him as hard as I could. Sue Ellen begged me to stop, pleading with me to put down the stick. She tried to get in the middle of my rage, and I tossed her away like a small rag doll. I could feel the hot liquid splashing about my head and arms. It was blood. I was covered in his blood. I continued to beat him until he stopped moving.

Sue Ellen fell to her knees. "What have you done? What have you done?"

Her body shook, and she turned her head away from me. I threw the stick and pulled her arm, lifting her off the ground. She began to scream and begged me to spare her life. Pleading with me, she pledged her love for me and said that we would never speak of this again. I looked her straight in the eye and said, "No! It's over now. I thought you loved me. First my son was taken away, and now this? I loved you so much." I pulled the gifts and the business contract from out of my pockets and tossed them at her feet.

"This is why I came back early!"

She picked them up and looked at me with such regret. "I'm sorry!" she said as the tears rolled down her cheeks. "What do we do now?" she asked. I shook my head and thought to myself for a moment.

"What else can I do? I have nothing to live for, and I took a man's life. I am going to turn myself in."

"They will hang you for sure! No one has to know about it. We could go on just like any other day."

I hated her and Jacob for what they had driven me to. I knew that I could not live knowing what had transpired between them, even if he was gone. That just was not who I was.

I made my way back to the barn. As I looked around, all I could think about was my son, how I would never know what kind of man he would have been. Then I thought even harder and realized what this incident would have done to his innocence and how he would have had to live without a father. I petted the dogs and walked into town. As I got down to the road, I heard a shot. The sound of my revolver echoed through the air. I knew that she was gone.

When I got to town, I was greeted with smiling faces and "how do you do's." Not a soul knew what had happened, and boy were they going to be surprised when I let out the news about what I had done.

I stopped in the saloon for a last belt of whisky. As I walked up to the bar, all eyes were upon me.

"Hey, John, did you just make a kill?" one man asked.

The bartender stated that I looked as if I had just come from an Indian slaughter. I ordered my drink and then another. It went down hard, but I ordered another to soothe my suffering. As I stood there drowning my sorrows in that glass of gold liquid, I felt a tap on my shoulder. It was the sheriff. I told him that I had done something terrible and I needed to talk to him in private. He agreed and we walked the wooden sidewalk to his office.

I explained what had happened and assured him that I had not killed Sue Ellen, only Jacob was my victim. I asked for the judgment against me to be quick. I did not want to spend more than a day in the jailhouse.

He patted me on the back and said, "John Davis, I have known you all of your life. Why? How could you do such a thing?"

I just looked at him. I did not know what to say. I begged him to get the men together and have me hanged the following morning. I did not want to live another day without Sue Ellen. My life was over, and I was ready for the end.

I refused to eat a last meal, but I did have my share of whisky and beer. Murry left my cell door open, and we played chess all night. The beer was cold, and the whisky, warm and steady, kept my mind from wandering.

"John, you really should think about this. Sue Ellen is gone, and you are waving your rights to a trial. The worst that could happen is you'll be hanged anyway, but there is a chance you could go off scot-free. It was a crime of passion for goodness sake! You could get off."

"Murry, I can't live with this! I have to do it. It's the right thing to do."

The door of the cell was locked tight. I had remembered that conversation word for word; it would be the last one that I would have.

As the sun came up over the hills, it pierced through the bars of my cell. This would be the last sunrise I would ever see. I never expected my life to turn out this way. What would be the final price when this all came to an end? I would have never expected it, not in a million years. I could hear the crowd begin to assemble. The voices were all familiar to me; people whom I grew up with, people who looked up to me, shouting and gossiping about the slaughter on my farm. Anxiously awaiting my demise, the rabble was getting larger and louder with each passing minute.

I could hear the footsteps on the plank sidewalk getting closer to the jailhouse. The time had come for me to make peace in my heart. The time had come for my life to end. The door swung open; the sheriff and his deputy approached my cell.

"I did just what you asked," the sheriff said. "Are you sure you don't want a trial? I can have the court judge here in about a week."

"No, thank you," I replied. "No sense in dragging this whole thing out. Let's just get it over with." My voice cracked as the words came out. This was it, my final hour.

The large key inserted into the lock on my cell door and made my heart stop. The sound echoed in my head. My ears began to ring as they led me out of the jail to the waiting mob, thirsty for my blood. I was placed into a wagon and driven to the hanging tree on the hill beside the meadow, the very same meadow in which I would pick flowers for Sue Ellen. I could see the crowd's lips moving, but I could not hear a voice among them. Not one person's voice reached me. The clapping of the horse's hooves and my heartbeat would be the only sounds my ears would hear. The hill drew near, and my throat began to close. I could feel the panic kicking in, and I could not breathe.

When we reached the tree, I looked up at it. Never had it looked so large to me. I had been to my fair share of hangings, and the tree never looked this big. The men strung up the rope and asked me to stand in the wagon to measure the proper length. I did not hear any words, but I stood up just the same. The sheriff asked if I had any last requests or statements to make. I stared blankly out at the crowd for several minutes. I do not remember blinking. The last thing I heard as a living mortal was the sound of the horse being slapped on the rump to get it to gallop away from the tree and the snapping of the rope as the weight of my body fell like a stone.

I have to tell you, I did not feel a thing. All I remember is stumbling to my feet in the beam of a truly bright light, not like the sun's reflection off the water which is somewhat bright or even when the snowy hills blind you. This was not hard to look at. In fact, it was almost hypnotic and euphoric to me. As I began to focus, I fixed my eyes on her for the first time. She was spectacular! A goddess, I would say. She definitely was not of the earth.

Her only words were, "Please come with me." She had the most magnificent smile I had ever seen. The smell of wildflowers was in the air, and my heart felt at peace.

I asked her where she was taking me, but she just sighed and turned away from me. I wanted so much to know where I was headed. I began to suddenly see what was to be. In my mind, it was all explained to me. The light and my destiny were the two things that would bind me to the earth forever. I wondered to myself, *was this hell*? If it was not, it sure began to feel as if it was.

The input into my brain flashed faster and faster still. I saw it all before I got to my destination, how my life would be from then on, diverting death from people I did not even know. I never asked how long my sentence would be. If I could go back, I would have asked that question first.

When everything was said and done, she grasped my hand and kissed my cheek. I never knew such a gentle touch. She was almost angelic. I dreamed that this would all be over soon, and I would be waking shortly from a strange yet wonderful dream. We reached what looked like a mirror in the splendid light. I could see bright green grass and trees in the reflection. Turning around to see what was behind me, I saw that the wonderful brilliant light was gone, and I was in the meadow just along the outskirts of town.

Everything looked more splendid than I had ever remembered the world to be. The bird's songs were in harmony with the whispering winds through the tall reeds in the marsh. Even the dragonflies seemed to be chiming in. Large white clouds graced the brilliantly blue sky. This was more beautiful than I had ever seen. I wondered what was going on. Was I dead or still just dreaming? I made my way to the mercantile and got a glimpse of the weekly newspaper. When I did, that was when I knew that I was dead. Right in plain view was the date. More than five years had passed since I fell from that tree.

I wondered how that short journey could have lasted so long. What was really going on, and how would I know what to do?

The tears falling down my cheek brought me back into reality. I was back at the shore, standing in front of the little church. The place that made my heart full of life was before me, and I had to go inside. I reached for the door, and before I could open it myself, it swung open. No one was there. The door just opened up for me all by itself. I was a bit hesitant to continue in. Looking around for a minute, I mustered the courage to enter. As I approached the pulpit, the smell of flowers was overwhelming. I sat in the first pew and asked God why he had forsaken me. When would my journey be over, and why I had been here for so long? There was no reply. I looked up at the beautiful colors of the glass, and the splendor of nature suddenly began to become animated.

I watched with my mouth open wide. The colors swirled, and the animals suddenly came to life. I was not sure what was happening, but I looked on as the brilliant colors meshed into dark and dismal shades of black and gray. I could hear the sound of thunder and the flash of lightning shone through the glass. A voice cried out to me, "What are you looking for? Why are you here?"

I replied, "I need to know. When will this all be over?"

The voice got louder. "Get out of this place, and do not return!"

"Why? Why can't I be here? Who are you?"

The voice just laughed and said, "You have no place being here. You have to go now."

The doors to the church opened, and the rain started to come down hard. I left the church and wondered what had just happened. I moved across town slowly in a trance-like state. I could not figure out what was going on. Who was contacting me, and why were they so nasty? *Just a few questions, why did they not ever answer any of my questions?* I asked myself repeatedly in my mind.

Chapter Seven

*T*he rain was coming down hard, and the thunder boomed loudly. People were rushing to duck for cover from the harsh weather, and there were kids splashing in the puddles across the street. I walked around for hours with the hope that I might be contacted again. Cars were driving past, splashing me with every puddle on the road, and the children laughed as they drove by.

I wished that I could have some fun. I remembered how when I was a kid, we would go down to the creek and wade all day long, rain or shine. Catching frogs was the only challenge I had and how I was going to explain to my mother how I got my school clothes all saturated when she told me to come straight home from school and to stay away from the creek.

One of the children playing jumped off an overturned garbage can to create a big splash when he slipped into the street directly in front of an oncoming car. The light began to shine brightly.

"Peter look out!" the other child screamed. I dashed out into the street and gave Peter a hard shove, forcing him to the curb.

"That was close!" he said confused. "Who pushed me out of the way?" the child asked with fear in his eyes.

"No one pushed you, Peter. You almost got creamed by that car."

Reaching out, the child helped his friend to his feet. "We better get home before Mom starts looking for us." The boys took off running up the street at full speed.

I continued to walk until it stopped raining, continuing to keep a close watch for the light. The sun was beginning to come up high in the sky, and I wondered how Kitten was and if she was okay. I made my way to her place and just as I was coming around the corner to her driveway, I heard tires screeching behind me. It was Ed. He was turning into her driveway. I looked on as he grabbed a bag out of his trunk and slowly ascended the steps to her door. Rat a tat, he knocked loudly.

"Just a minute. Who is it?" Kitten yelled.

"It's me, Gorgeous, your knight in shining armor! Don't you want your locks changed?"

"I thought I told you to come at one o'clock?"

"Darling, it's three o'clock. Now, are you going to let me in?"

I could hear her fumbling around the apartment, bumping into things as she made her way to the door.

"Oh shit, I never locked it, come on in."

Smiling the whole time, Ed said, "What do you need the locks changed for if you aren't going to use them?" He laughed and bumped her with his hip as he headed toward the table.

"I'll get started on the locks just as soon as we have breakfast." He pulled a couple of bagels out of the bag and handed her some orange juice. "You are going to need this, baby."

She flopped down in the chair and made a growling sound.

"Boy, are you a cranky kid in the morning. This is why you shouldn't party so much."

She grimaced and said, "You wouldn't be able to pay your rent if I quit."

Ed laughed and said, "I know you would have put my first kid through college if he hadn't dropped out." Kitten just gave him a look and drank down some of her juice directly out of the carton...

"Hey, easy there, girl; save some for me. Don't you have a glass or something?"

She pulled the carton from her lips and tilted her chair back, reaching for a dirty glass from the sink.

"Gross me out, Kitty. I'll get them myself." Ed walked over to the sink and began washing the dishes. "Kitty, you need a maid."

She smiled and said, "Well now, I seem to already have one."

He placed the glasses on the table and poured the juice for her. "Now isn't that better? Why would you want to drink out of a dirty glass?"

"It's too early in the day to be worrying about washing dishes. Besides, why are you so Hazel all of a sudden?"

"Hey, I'm your friend, Kitty. Now do you want this bagel or not?"

"I hope it's an everything."

"It is. I know what you like."

"Thanks Ed. You are the best." I could hear Kitten making yummy sounds as she gobbled down her breakfast.

"Man, that was good. Thanks, babe."

Ed assured her that it was no problem and began working on the locks. She went into the bathroom to take a shower. Ed's cell phone rang, and he talked to the person on the other line briefly. He hurried with the lock and knocked on the bathroom door.

"Kitty, you're all set; I'm going to leave you a little something on the table, and I'm splitting. Make sure you come to the bar tonight. I have a little job for you."

"Thanks, Eddie. I'll see you tonight. You're the best."

"I know. I'll see you later. Make sure you lock this door when you come out. I can't lock it from the outside without a key. I'll leave the keys on the table, too."

"Okay, I'll see you later, buddy."

Ed closed the door and got into his car. I went over to the table to see what he left her. Alongside the keys was a sandwich bag filled with marijuana. *It figures. Just what she needs, more drugs.* I was tempted to remove the pot from the table, but just as I was thinking about it, out she came, soaking wet and wrapped in the smallest towel I had ever seen. What a vision. She was a spectacular example of woman, even more beautiful than Sue Ellen. She walked over to the table and smiled when she saw what Ed had left for her.

"Kitty! Where are you?" Drying herself off, she skipped toward the door to bolt it shut. I looked on as the droplets of water flittered about the room with every swish of her hair. Crying out again, "Azreal, here kitty!" she opened the window, reached down, and filled up the bowls with food and water. The cat jumped through the window. As it jumped on the counter, I got a sudden chill deep in my bones.

"Damn? What was that?" I could feel the cat's eyes looking deeply at me. I moved my head in for a closer look, and it hissed at me.

"Damn!" The little cuss just saw me.

"What's wrong, baby? Are you mad that I didn't wash out the bowls, too?"

I backed up, and the darn thing just stared me down. I did not want to upset my girl so I thought it best to leave, and quickly. I hopped out the window figuring that it was time to get to work. I was beginning to slack in my chores. Destiny was a cruel and torturous girl, mocking me throughout the endless days. It was about time for supper, and the streets were covered in the filth that trickled down from the northern part of the state. The air was heavy and filled with the hustle and commotion of the shore.

Hearing a wholehearted laugh coming from the nearby liquor store, I could not help but head for the sound. I needed a good laugh. In addition, maybe, just maybe, trouble would follow that laugh. When you hear a laugh like that, you just know that someone is on the other end of the joke. I just had to know what and whom it was about.

There was a burly dude blocking the way. I could not see what was beyond this mountainous pile of flesh. I climbed on top of the pyramid of twelve packs to get a better look. As I glided over the cardboard cutout of a beer model, I could see his face. Smiling and as goofy as they come, he was cross-eyed and slack-jawed, not right in the head, if you know what I mean. The young men who worked there were getting the best of him. Sad, how the purest hearts are meant to endeavor the worst, most impossible tasks throughout their lives.

The man was named Michael, and his eyes shone brighter than a child on Christmas morning.

The shopkeeper came out from the back of the store. "You boys leave Michael alone, and hey, there is plenty of stock to put away."

"Have a good night, Mr. Dunkin. See you tomorrow."

"Take it easy, Michael, tomorrow it is." The mountainous child smiled and waddled out the door, pulling his pants up with every twist of his gluttonous gut.

I figured I should follow him just in case he was walking into trouble. Usually, I do not just come across people for no reason. There is always a reason. My very existence revolved around some stupid reason that was beginning to become very unreasonable to me. The people around him were staring and looking with hateful, prejudiced judgment on their faces. I was disgusted by the awful feeling Michael must have had as he tried to walk down the street unnoticed. What kind of a life did this poor man have? Did he live through this battle as I did, alone?

Ducking into a driveway with bags in hand, Michael knocked on the first door he came to.

"Anthony, it me, Michael."

"Come on; it's open." I could hear the words "dumb ass" foilow as Michael pushed his way through the door. Who was this person and why was he coming here to visit him?

"Did you get what I asked you for?" he asked in a snide voice.

"Yes, I did just what you asked me to. It's all in the bag, Anthony, all in the bag." Anthony reached into the bag and pulled out a bottle.

"Why didn't you get cold beer, you idiot?" A bottle hit Michael on the side of his face, throwing his head to the side.

"I'm sorry, Anthony, I'll go back. I'll get it right this time, I promise."

The poor lad bent down to pick up the bottle that just removed another tiny piece of his dignity and walked over to the table. His head was hung low, and he shuffled off with the rest of the beer and put it in the refrigerator. Anthony came up with a backhand, right upside his head.

"Put them in the freezer, dickwad."

"Right, the freezer. That's where I meant to put them." Rubbing the back of his head, he walked down the hall to the bathroom.

"Make sure you don't back up the toilet again, you fat bastard." The door shut quietly. I stood outside the door and looked in the hallway. There were rows of photographs and shelves lined with crusty yellow doilies while tiny glass figurines covered in cobwebs stared blankly back at me. I looked around the rest of the house. It was an old woman's home; she had most likely died from the stress of taking care of the special child and his pathetic brother.

I watched as Anthony began to gulp down his warm beer, wiping his chin on the front of his dirty tee shirt.

"Michael, you better not be touching my stuff again. I'll kill you this time, jerkoff."

I couldn't hear a sound coming from that bathroom. I got close to the door and was about to sneak a peek when I saw the light creeping up the hallway out of the corner of my eye.

"Damn, I knew it. Get the fuck out of the bathroom, moron. I told you not to fuck with my stuff."

Anthony kicked the door open, and Michael looked up in shock with fear in his eyes as he crammed a bundle of something into the hamper.

"I told you I was going to kill you this time, didn't I?" He slammed his fist down hard on Michael's chest and continued to hit him, blow after blow in a fit of rage. Michael stood up with his back to his angry brother, and while his head hung low in the sink, he said, "No, no more, Anthony!" As he swung around, I could see the straight razor in his hand. Anthony backed up, and the light began to creep slowly towards him.

I could not believe that I was going to have to save the slime I thought would kill Michael, the gentle giant. I forced the door closed in Michael's face and broke off the doorknob to assure the heartless beast would be safe. Anthony stumbled down the hall, out the door, and into the driveway. All I could hear was the sound of gravel being kicked about, the clicking sounds on the glass as it flew up at the windows. He was out of there. I felt bad for the giant behind the door. What could I do for him? My purpose was served, and my services were expired.

I took one last look at the photos on the wall, small children in a wading pool with genuine smiles on their faces. There was a portrait of a once proud mother with her two sons at her side. They seemed to look normal. I could not imagine what could have gone wrong. Years of heartache and pain the three of them must have endured. It was a pity it ended up the way it did. Was Michael always special, or did he turn out that way from neglect? Did Mommy go out every night looking for a papa for the boys and end up on the wrong side of the tracks? Or did Anthony get his manners from the abusive father who left after the damage was done? I was sure that I would never know.

I left the sad home, and my head began to flood with hate, hate for my job. I was getting sick of helping the people who were not worthy. Why were they allowed to walk this beautiful earth day after day, wreaking havoc on good-hearted people? Why did they get away with it? Why did I have to save them? I was getting mad because I had no answers, and there did not seem to be any comfort as I made my way toward the beach.

The sun was beginning to go down, and the humid air conformed around everything, making the world seem fuzzy to my eyes. This was strange; people seemed to be walking in slow motion, and I couldn't put my finger on it, but I was sure something besides moisture was in the air, but what? I had a strange buzzing in my head and began to feel nauseous, but why? Why was I feeling this way? I darted toward the boards. As I passed the tall waterslide, I could hear the faint sound of a distressed woman's voice.

"I'm falling off! Oh Lord, please help me!"

I zoomed up the rickety platform to where the sound was coming from, and when I arrived at the top, I could see a rather large woman hanging onto the bright yellow flotation device as her body dragged behind. She began to pick up speed when I saw the light.

It was straight in front of her just at the bend in the slide. I had to do something and do something fast. I pushed the raft as hard as I could but the speed and the force was almost too much for me to handle. *What happened to the slow motion?* I wondered. As the raft bumped the woman, she somehow was set adrift on the soft plastic and glided down to the pool creating a large wall of water that crashed up onto the foam padding that lined the edges of the pool. I kicked up my feet and gently rolled into the pool behind her, another deed complete. Several whistles blew, signaling the patrons to gather their things and head to the gates; the water park was closing, and the guards demanded their prompt removal from the water.

I finally made it to the beach. The smell of snacks and greasy sausage filled the air, and the lights flashing on the midway signaled me to head for the bar. Kitten would be meeting Ed soon, and I did not want to miss her arrival.

As I ascended the wooden ramp leading to the crowd of people shouting and spending, I thought about Michael and what would become of him. I wondered if he would make it through another beating from his brother, or if brother dear would come back with police and have poor Michael committed, placed in a hospital, locked away from the beauty of the world. Maybe that was the best thing for him. Maybe he would be better off in a place like that, a safe environment away from judging eyes and hateful hearts. Poor Michael, what would become of his pure heart?

As I approached the bar, I could smell the foul stench of drunkenness. It was a God-awful smell; even a skunk would run from it. It was crowded and dark. The lights were still not turned on. It was dusk, and the bar seemed even more stagnant than ever. I listened in on the conversations as I worked my way to the balcony where Ed preferred to do his business. There he was, like a fixture, in the same place he always was, surrounded by dirty dos and perverts. Why does Kitten hang around in a place like this? I could not stop thinking how soon my precious girl would be consorting with such loathsome characters.

I took a seat on the railing beside Ed, awaiting the arrival of the goddess. I was beginning to get bored with the chatter of mindless dribble coming from the mouths of these creatures when she appeared, strutting through the door. She was wearing a short orange mini-dress, backless with silver hoops at the waist. I could see the small of her back peeking out as if it were saying, "Look at me." She smiled the widest smile at the bartender and pushed through the crowd as if she was cutting through the jungle with a machete. Pulling some money from her dress, she tossed it at the bartender and ordered.

"Hey, baby, give me a shot of Black and a beer back."

"Anything for you, beautiful? Are you going to stay a while?" the bartender asked with a sparkle in his eye.

"I'm not sure. Is the jerk around?"

"No, he hasn't been here all day. Why? Is his bike outside? Jimmy kicked him out last night and told him not to come back."

"Cool, maybe he'll mean it this time."

"You know how Jimmy is, when he drinks, he forgets. It's only a matter of time before that happens, and he'll be back." He handed Kitten her drinks, and she refused to take the change.

"Thanks, I'll get the next one."

"Cool, I'll be back; don't worry." She pushed the barstool over with her foot and kicked back the shot with her eyes closed. I could almost feel the heat in my stomach as she licked her lips and took a swig of her beer.

Ed saw her coming and told the people who were sitting with him to take a powder and make room for the lady. Kitten smiled and brushed off the bench before she sat down. Throwing her arms around him, she whispered in his ear.

"Tell me more about this job. How much do I get?"

Ed laughed and shook his head. "Is it always money with you?"

"Well, it is with you, silly. It's always about money, and you should know that." She laughed and took another drink of her beer.

"Okay, it's like this. I got a truck, and I need you to get me a few cars. You know how you do it. There's four hundred bucks in it for you."

"What's the catch?"

"There is no catch; just do what you do best."

"I want half the money now. You can pay me the rest when you recover the finder's fee, okay?"

"You got it, darling. Now drink up, we have some work to do."

I stared in amazement and could not believe my ears. Was my Kitten a car thief? Was that how she made her living? Up until now, I had never seen her work or even heard her complain about it to the animals. Could this be? Was she a criminal for real?

"Okay, Eddie, but you have to take me home first. I have to pick up a few things."

"Whatever you need, Kitty, whatever you need."

I became angry with her. Was she the person I thought she was? She could not be, not after hearing that. I could not get myself to leave. I had to follow them; I had to see what she was about to do.

Ed summoned the bartender. "Bring us a few more shots and a pitcher of beer!" he shouted over the noise. I noticed that all eyes in the bar were focused on my Kitten. The men were bragging about how they could have some of that ass, and the women were fighting about what the men were saying. It was trouble just waiting to happen. I kept my guard up just in case.

As they drank down the shots, Ed said, "We'll leave at about eleven o'clock; it should be a good time to do it."

"Remember, I have to stop home first."

"I know, love; we will."

I wondered what was so important at the house that she needed to get. I hoped in my heart that it was not a gun. The bar was beginning to get crowded. All eyes were on Kitten as she shook the points out of the pinball machine in the corner. The bartender brought a couple of shots over to her.

"Give me just a second. This is my game; I can feel it."

"Take as much time as you like, sweetheart. I'm not in any hurry."

The bells and whistles were ringing loudly, and Kitten began to jump up and down with excitement.

"I did it! I got the high score and a free game. Take that, Arnold. You won't be back this time!" she shouted with glee. "The Terminator has been terminated," she sang out. "Who is the best? I am the best!"

"Nice moves, Kit; I knew this machine would go down for you sooner or later. Do you want to have this shot with me now, or are you going for another record?"

He lifted the shot glasses from the tray and passed one to her. She reached out to grab it, and she spilled it all over herself.

"Now look at what you've done." He reached for her hand and licked the whisky from her palm.

"Oh my gosh, are you hitting on me, Tiger?" she said in a sexy voice.

"Kitty, I'm your bartender. If I can't hit on you, then who can?"

"Okay, then, we drink our shots to you, my personal palm-licking bartender, for without you, I couldn't catch a buzz tonight."

"No, we should drink to you, because if it weren't for you, I couldn't have this much fun being a bartender."

"Okay, to us it is!" Kitten shouted with a smile on her face.

They laughed and drank down their shots. I could see Ed getting a little jealous as he stood up to get a better look at the two of them laughing and carrying on in the corner.

"Tiger, you are a great guy, but I'm afraid that if we mix sex in our relationship, it could ruin my kickbacks for life." She moved in close. "Besides, if you and I were to get together, I just know that it would ruin you for all women. After me, you wouldn't want another woman." She leaned in and gave him a hug.

"Oh, Kitty, you know how I feel about you. You have already ruined me for other women. Can I just have one kiss? Just a peck?"

"Okay, Tiger baby, you got it."

She leaned in again, but this time, she smashed her body against his, wrapped her fingers around the sides of his face, and pressed her lips tight against his. She opened her mouth slightly and wisped her tongue gently over his upper lip. She graced him with one of the greatest gifts of all. As she pulled away from him, his eyebrows raised and his body wobbled.

"That was everything that I imagined it would be. Come here, baby." He grabbed her and kissed her again. "Was it as good for you as it was for me, doll?" he said smiling.

"Oh yeah, it was great. Is it hot in here or is it just me?" She began to fan her face with her hand and turned bright red.

"Oh, it's you all right."

Ed came rushing over to them. "Okay, if this game of spin the bottle is over, we have some work to do," he said sternly.

The two of them were locked in an embrace, neither one of them willing to release one another. Kitten smiled and said, "Okay, okay, I'm ready to go. Sorry, Tiger, we'll have to pick this up some other time. Duty calls."

"Okay, but I'm going to hold you to the picking-back-up part."

They released from the embrace, and Ed pulled at her arm to guide her out of the bar.

"Okay, Ed, what's the big idea pulling me away from a perfectly good kiss like that?"

"You need to stay focused on the job, baby. I can't have you kissing my bartender."

"Oh come on now, you are acting like a jealous boyfriend. It was just a kiss."

"Okay, this time, it was just a kiss, but the next time, it won't be. Then you'll be in real trouble. You know how much he likes you. Now you are never going to get rid of him."

"Who said I want to get rid of him?" Kitten said with a sneer.

"Come on, Kitty, you and I both know that would never work. Not many men can have a relationship with you. You're a nut." He patted her head and gave her a slight tap on the butt. "Now, let's get to work."

I followed close and got into the car with them. I rode along, staring at Kitten and thinking about her beautiful lips and how I wished that I had been the one who had just kissed her.

We approached her apartment, and as we pulled into the driveway, Kitten yelled, "Get the hell away from my garage!" It was Devin; the little creep was trying to get into her house. Ed got out of the car after him.

"If I catch you, you are going to die, asshole," Ed yelled as he jumped from his car and darted up the driveway. Devin was long gone, and Ed was a bit out of breath as he reached her garage door. "See, I told you we had to change the locks."

Ed stood guard as Kitten opened the small doorway in the middle of the large garage door. I heard her fumble for something, and in no time, she was out, and shoving something into a duffel bag.

"Thanks, Ed, will you come over in the morning and help me board up the windows in the garage. I don't want him breaking in and taking any of my stuff."

"You got it, sister. Can we go now?"

"I just need one more thing."

Now what was she getting? I dreaded to think about it. She trotted up the steps and into the apartment and never turning on a light, she was out in a flash.

"Okay, I'm ready; let's get going."

Ed smiled. "Man, I love you!"

"That's what they all say. What if I can't pull it off?"

"You always pull it off; that's why you are my best girl."

"Best girl? Dude, you don't even have boys that work this hard for you. Just remember me when you get paid; share the wealth."

"Don't I always?"

Kitten just smiled a cracked grin and gave him a side glance.

"Yeah, right," she growled.

They got in the car and were off. Ed took her to a dark street and pulled over.

"Okay, what's the make?"

"It's a Honda."

"Color?"

"Blue."

"And the tag?"

"Something with a 'Z' in it."

"A 'Z,' that's it?"

"I think there's a two, or maybe it's a seven."

"You suck, Ed. Meet me at the truck. I'll only be twenty minutes. Have the tailgate ready to drop. If I pass you up, meet me behind the self-storage. I'll wait for you."

"Okay, be careful."

"Just go!"

Kitten crept into the shadows of the night, slinking around, checking out the area. How could she do such a thing?

"A 'Z' and a two or a seven; that's a lot to go by. I'm a chump. Hello, there you are. It's not even a seven, it's a damn three. What a ditz."

She walked up to the car and peered into the passenger-side window. She checked the door to see if it was locked; it was. Looking around before she made another move, she walked around the back of the car to the driver's side and tried the door, locked, too. She reached into the backpack and started to pull something out of it when I heard a man's voice holler.

"What are you doing to my car, bitch?"

Kitten turned slowly and smiled at the man.

"Oh, is this your car?"

"Yeah, it's my car. What the fuck are you doing to it?"

Kitten smiled and began to move her body closer to the man. Sticking her finger into her mouth and with a look of innocence on her face, she said, "It looks like the first car I ever had. My daddy bought it for me, and I was admiring it. I like the color of yours better."

The man smiled at her with a fiendish smile as his eyes slid up and down my Kitten from head to toe, soaking in the orange dress with its shining silver rings. Kitten acted drunk and stumbled into his arms.

"Do you want to go for a ride?" the man asked.

"Can I drive?"

"Okay, if you kiss me first, then I'll let you drive."

Kitty pulled on the door handle. "It won't open."

The man reached into his pocket, pulled out a set of keys, and opened the door.

"I said you have to kiss me first."

Kitten reached her hand out for the keys and kissed him, pressing her body into his. She sat down in the car and started it up. The man hung down, trying to steal another kiss, when she closed the door and told him to go around. As she reached over to unlock the door, she smiled at him and floored the gas pedal. The car sped off into the night, leaving the man in its dust falling in the street.

Kitty quickly drove up and down the side streets through town, keeping a watchful eye on what was around her. I hopped in the window and looked on in astonishment as my Kitten rifled through the man's tapes one by one, until she found one that was to her liking. She popped it into the tape player and cranked up the volume; heavy metal loud and strong was coming from the speakers. She pulled into a dark area behind a gas station, and there was Ed, with a big smile on his face.

"I knew you could do it, girl. You are the one," Ed said smiling.

"Drop the gate and get this thing out of sight."

Ed jumped out of the truck and pulled down the back gate. The truck was covered with a large white canvas. Kitten drove the car up the ramp and into the secret depths of the tarp-covered truck. When she got out, Ed quickly closed the hatch, and they took off.

"When do I get the rest of my money?" she asked, sounding a bit irate.

"Just as soon as I take it to the repo depot. Get the title out of the glove compartment, will you, babe?"

"Just get me my money please."

"You got it."

Ed pulled a beer out from behind the seat and handed it to her.

"You deserve this, and this."

He pulled out a joint and handed it to her as well. She smiled and put it between her lips as she giggled.

"How many more do we have to get tonight?"

Ed smiled back and said, "As many as you want."

She sat there smiling; her eyes had such a glow to them. Kitten loved it. My girl was an expert at her job. I wondered if this was all that she did.

"Okay, Kitty, are you ready for the next one?"

"How much will I get for the next one?"

"You said you would help me collect a couple cars, darling; that was only one car, and the night is still young."

"Okay, let's do it."

"Now, I must warn you, Kitty; this next job isn't going to be as easy as the last one."

"And why is that?"

"Because the person you are taking it from carries a gun."

"A gun! You never said anything about a gun, Ed."

"I know, but if you make this one and get out clean with the car still intact, I'll add on an extra hundred bucks to your cut."

"If the car is still intact? What about my head? I can't drive without a head, Ed."

"Just relax, girl; be cool, you'll do just fine. I have faith in you."

"Yeah, and who is going to feed my cat?"

They pulled up to Ed's car and parked the truck. Kitten jumped in the driver's seat and told Ed to get a move on. He told her to go to the gentleman's club on Route Nine.

"Ed, I don't feel like sitting around while you shove money down some coke whore's thong."

"No, Kitty, that is where the job is."

"Whose car are we swiping? Don't tell me it's Tony G's?"

"No, no it belongs to his sister."

"Not Carla?"

"Why? You know her?"

"Everyone knows her, Ed. She's the girl that drove through the parade last Easter. Remember?"

"No, when was this?"

"Dude, she killed two eggs and the Easter Bunny! Kids are still having nightmares."

Ed laughed, "Oh shit, that's funny!"

They parked the car around the corner. Kitten turned to him and said, "If this crazy bitch kills me, I'm going to come back and haunt you."

Oh no! That was exactly the situation with me. I was not her friend or her lover. I was a haunting spirit, stalking her.

"It's the red vet. Now be careful. That thing is made of fiberglass; don't damage the goods. There aren't any keys."

Kitten rolled her eyes and pulled on the door handle.

"Now you stay put. I'm going to scope out the vet, and I'll be right back. Don't split."

"Okay, babe, I'll be right here."

Kitten got out of the car and crept around the back to where the little red vet was parked. She crouched down low, eyelevel to the base of the tinted glass. She ran her fingers across the rubber weather stripping and attempted to slip a thin piece of metal between them, but to no avail. Her attempts proved unsuccessful. She needed the keys.

She headed back to the vehicle to where Ed was waiting for her, and she popped her head into the window.

"Listen, Ed, I have an idea. Do you have any coke on you?"

"Yeah, a little."

"Give it to me."

"Why?"

"Do you want the car to be in one piece?"

"Yeah."

"Well, I'm not thinking about the car, Ed. I'm thinking about myself, and if you don't give me the coke, I'm going to get my head shot off. Please!" Ed laughed as he hand her the drugs. "Oh and give me some money, too."

"What for?"

"Just give me twenty bucks." He handed her the money and made plans to meet her at the truck. "Just wait for me; I don't know how long this is going to take."

"Cool, I'll have time to get something to eat. I'm starved."

Kitten smiled as she reapplied her lipstick in the reflection from the side-view mirror of the car and said, "Be ready for anything."

"What is that supposed to mean, girl?"

Kitten just laughed and headed toward the bar.

I could hear the music before we got in the place. The building was plain and simple. It looked more like a storage unit than a club. Kitten swung open the doors, and much to my surprise, the place was ultra modern. Black lights hung from the ceilings, and neon lights illuminated the glass bar. There were cages in the corners and private rooms for frolicking. The dancers were of a higher quality than most of the ones that I had seen, and the crowd was as rowdy as any.

She walked up to the bar. When the bartender asked her what she wanted to drink, her voice changed, "Yeah, a…Hi, you're kind of cute. I'm here to see Carla. It's about a job, a job dancing or something. Do you think she'll think I'm pretty?"

She was acting like one of those mindless dancers with her high-pitched squeak and how she twirled her hair and shook her hips with every word. I had to laugh, and she was funny.

The bartender said, "I think we can find something for you to do. What would you like to drink?"

"I'll have one of those white wine things with the bubbles in it."

He smiled and fixed her the drink.

"So what brings you here tonight? Don't you have a boyfriend?"

"No, we just broke up."

"Can I help to cheer you up? Maybe later, after you show me your stuff?"

He looked at her body, moving his eyes slowly from her breasts to her luscious ass. I hated this. The girl drove me crazy, and I hated for anyone to look at her in that way.

"Sure, you seem like a lot of fun, and you're cute, too."

It sickened me to hear those words pass her lips.

"I'll talk to the boss. You have a seat. I'm sure I can get you an audition. I'll be right back."

"Gee thanks, you're really nice."

Kitten sipped her drink and had a seat while watching to see where her new friend had gone. Her eyes followed him up a flight of stairs and through a door to Carla's office. I followed close behind.

"What is it, Bill?" Carla asked.

"Sorry to bother you, Miss, but there is a girl outside that wants a job. Is it okay if I give her a demo?"

"Who is she?"

"Just some hottie, nobody. She looks good, tight ass, nice tits. I think she would bring in some customers if they could get a look at her. She's dressed for it. Take a look."

Carla walked to the glass door. "Where is she?"

"She's at the bar, the one in the orange dress."

"She doesn't look like anything special to me. Go ahead, Bill, and do what you want."

Bill raised his eyebrow and headed down the stairs.

"Okay, princess, it's up to you to whip this crowd into shape. You get them to spend some money, and you have yourself a job."

"Is there a dressing room or something where I can get ready? I have to look my best."

"Sure, doll, whatever you need. See that door over there?" He pointed to the door next to the bathroom.

"Sure, I see it."

"Straight through there. Now don't take too long. You have twenty minutes."

"Thanks!" Kitten said and strutted off to the dressing room.

I followed her closely as she opened the door to the dressing room. There were a few girls getting ready when she walked in.

One of them said, "Hey, who are you?"

"I'm Vicky; the bartender said this is where I get ready."

"Since when do you work here?" another woman shouted.

"Since now, do you have a problem with that?"

"And what if I do? What are you going to do about it, bitch?"

"Well, I'm not going to share my coke with you; that's what." The girl smiled and walked over to her.

"You can have my seat, sister. Come over here, and I'll help you fix your hair." Kitten smiled and poured the cocaine onto the counter.

"So, where are you from?"

Kitten just thought for a minute, rolled up a bill, and said, "Well, tonight, I'm from the motor lodge down the street." She snorted up the coke.

"Can we jerk guys off for some extra money around here?" She passed the bill over. The woman laughed as she snorted up the drugs.

"I can see it's going to get better now that you are here."

"Better? How so?"

"We don't have many gutsy chicks around here. You're like a breath of fresh air, kid. Okay, you look great; now go out there and have a good time. Remember smile and flash the guys, the tips are better. I'm Christy, what's your name?"

"I'm Vicky. Do I look okay?"

"I told you, you look great."

"Thanks again."

Kitten hoisted up her breasts and rubbed the lipstick from her teeth. She smiled at herself in the mirror and walked back to the bar.

"Okay, I'm ready."

"You look terrific. Do you see that little guy over in the corner playing the pinball machine?"

"Uh huh."

"Well, you go and dance, but not for him, if he stops playing, you won't get the job."

"That's it? All I have to do is dance but not for the little man?"

"That's all you have to do. Now go."

Billy smacked Kitten on the backside; she stumbled off to dance but headed straight for the little man. As she walked along the bar, there was Ed sitting there with a big smile on his face. With bills in hand, he turned and grabbed Kitty's arm.

"Hey, baby, will you dance for me?" I could hear the laughter in his voice.

"Ed! What are you doing here? I thought you were going to meet me at the truck," she said, grinding her teeth.

"What and miss this? Not for the world, baby, not for the world."

He continued to laugh as she walked away. I could tell she was mad because she was biting her lip more than usual. I could not wait to watch her dance. I just knew it would be a treat. She shook her hips and poked out her chest as she approached the tiny man. She got very close to him, and he ignored her, never taking his eye off the speeding ball beneath the glass.

"Hi, I'm Vicky. What's your name?" The man just kept playing.

"Would you like a drink, honey?" Kitten asked.

"No, thank you. I don't drink."

Kitten looked puzzled. "You don't drink? Everybody drinks. Tell me what you want, and I'll get it for you."

"Nothing."

Kitten walked away and headed toward the bar. Billy just looked at her and said, "Give up so soon?"

"No, the gentleman would like to have a wine thing with the bubbles in it. Can I have one, please?"

"Sure, doll, whatever you need."

She took the drink over and stood in front of the man and leaned on the machine. It made a strange sound, and the man got mad.

"You tilted it! What is wrong with you?"

"Oops, I'm sorry. Was that a bad thing?"

"Yes, it's a bad thing. Now please leave me alone. There are plenty of guys to give you money. Why don't you go and bother them?"

Kitten pressed her body tightly against his. Pressing her lips against his ear, she whispered, "Please, don't be mad," and flashed her boobs at him. He just looked at her.

"What are you trying to do, miss?" he said with disgust.

"I just want you to be happy. Don't you think that I could make you happy?" She grabbed his hand and put it to her breast. "Does this make you happy?"

The man took a step back and called to the bartender. "Get this slut away from me. She is ruining everything."

Carla had been listening from the top of the stairs and saw the whole thing.

"Billy bring her up here, now!"

Billy led Kitty up the stairs and into Carla's office.

"Here she is, Miss. Do you need anything else?"

"No, Billy, close the door."

The woman looked at Kitty and shouted, "What kind of a place do you think I'm running here? I have vice breathing down my neck as it is. I don't need you coming in here and getting me shut down."

"Gee, I'm sorry, I didn't know."

Carla walked around the room. As she continued to explain how things ran, Kitten's eyes scanned the desktop. She backed up and leaned against the desk and grabbed something. I couldn't see what it was. Carla called for Kitten to come over and take a look out the glass window.

"See those men down there?"

"Yes, there are a lot of them, aren't there?"

"Yes, and do you know why they are here?"

"To drink?"

"Yes, to drink and relax. They don't want to be bothered by women. They just want to look at them. That man you were harassing is a good customer. He pours over one hundred dollars a night, every night, into that stupid machine."

"But the bartender told me to do it."

She leaned on the desk and palmed something in her left hand.

"I'm the boss around here, and you do what I say. Now go and take some of those clothes off; get into your bikini and dance in the cage over by the phone."

"My suit is in the car."

"Then go and get it then."

"Okay."

Kitten walked down the stairs. As she passed Ed, he laughed at her.

"Just go to the truck, jerk," she said and rolled her eyes at him.

Ed got up and left. Kitten walked out into the parking lot and looked around to see if she was alone. There were two loud men getting out of their jeep. She tried not to draw attention to herself, but this was Kitten. How could she not?

The men began to hoot and holler across the parking lot at her.

"Hey, baby. How much?" one man yelled.

She flipped them the finger and continued on her way. The Vet was parked around back, and she was almost there. She pulled the keys from the back of her dress, which was funny because the dress was backless, and jammed the key in the door lock. She jumped in the car, and as she made her way to the end of the driveway, she buckled up her safety belt and sped off with the peddle to the floor. She turned on the radio and found half a joint in the ashtray. Smiling, she pushed it into the cigarette lighter and laughed.

"Oh, man, I love this job. I get to be whoever I want."

She pulled up to the truck, and Ed greeted her.

"Like I said, you are the best. Is it okay? You didn't break it, did you?"

"No, you idiot, it's fine. I got the keys."

"The keys? How did you get the keys?"

"I have my ways. If I told you, then you would know all of my secrets, and I can't have that, can I?"

"Good job, baby."

Ed reached into his pocket and tossed her four one-hundred-dollar bills.

"Hey, you said that you would throw me an extra hundred if I got the car to you in one piece."

"Here take this eight ball."

"No, no. I want the money. You said that you only had a little coke."

"Okay here, take this, too."

He tossed her a baggie filled with something that I had never seen before. She put it into her bra and squeezed his cheeks.

"Are these what I think they are?"

"Yep, take it easy, though; this is high quality stuff."

"Thanks, Dad!"

"Okay, babe, are we square?"

"Yes, but if you come across my car, let me know."

"You got it, baby. I'll come over in the afternoon to work on the windows in the garage. Take my car. I'll pick it up in the morning. Just leave the keys under the mat."

"Okay, I'll see you later. Thanks."

Kitty got into Ed's car and snorted some more of the cocaine. She pulled out the mystery baggie and opened it up.

"Haven't seen you guys in a while," she said into the bag as she dug her nose deep into it to get a better whiff. "I'll have you later; it will be magic."

She turned up the radio, grabbed a few mints, popped them into her mouth, and drove away.

I sat there in that smelly car and gazed at her face, feet, and hands. I got really close to her, close enough to smell the scent of the mint she was sucking on. Her lips were bright pink and her breasts jiggled from the run down suspension on Ed's car. She tapped her fingers to the music on the steering wheel as she drove along the boulevard. Pulling into the quick deli for some supplies, she came across a friend who was parked in the space beside her.

"Hey, Kitty, how the hell are you?"

"Holy shit, Kenny, what are you doing here?"

"I knew that you would be here, so I figured what the hell?"

"Shut up, you did not."

"Really, I had a feeling that I would see you, and here you are."

"Oh, Kenny, you tell me the same thing every time we run into each other. You're full of shit."

I had never seen this guy before; he was handsome and clean, nothing like the guys that she had been hanging around with. I wasn't happy about this, not at all.

"So what really brings you here, Bear?"

"Oh, I love it when you call me that. It reminds me of the days when you would make me breakfast just before you would throw me out."

"Let it go, Kenny; that was a long time ago."

"I know, but you never forget the important things that happen in your life, do you?"

"I guess not. Where are you staying?"

My heart sank. This was someone whom she had obviously had a thing with in the past, and now, she was asking him where he was going to stay. This wasn't good.

There was a construction site just across the street. There was always a construction site at the shore. Over the years, I had seen millions of homes and business being built and torn down one after another. I could remember when Jersey was nothing but farmland and pine trees, with wildlife as far as the eye could see. Not anymore, the only wildlife you could see now were the ones being scraped off the blacktop of the roadway.

I heard a screech coming from the direction of that site and hurried to see if I could be of some assistance. The light was shining bright and a man's life dangled, a shadow directly in the middle of it. Hanging two stories up, the light sat steady on the ground below him. I examined the situation but to no avail. There just was not anything that I could do without being noticed. Everyone in the area rushed over to see what all the commotion was about, and by this time, there was a whole crowd of people. I thought to myself, *How I can possibly save this man without being noticed?* This was my job, and there was not anything that I could do.

Wait a minute, I glanced over at the bucket truck, which was filled with dirt from the excavation. That's it; in a flash, I released the handbrake and rolled the enormous truck directly underneath the desperate man. The crowed dispersed as the truck parted them. I forced the truck to stop, and the man, still hanging with every last bit of energy, cried, "Someone, please help me!"

The police arrived and looked on as the man pleaded with them to help him.

I could see his fingers losing their grip as the crowd gasped. The fire trucks were beginning to arrive when the man lost his hold and fell straight into the earth-filled truck. Dust and debris flew up into the air, creating a large cloud that wafted over the crowd of people who watched on. The light was nowhere to be found, and once again, I had successfully intervened with death. I could hear one of the police officers remark about the moving truck in amazement.

"I don't know how the hell that happened, but whatever moved that truck just saved that man's life."

Another fellow exclaimed, "Do you think he is all right?"

The ambulance driver climbed up into the truck and gave the thumbs-up sign to his partner.

"He looks like he is going to be okay."

The crowed cheered, and I looked on with pride at what I had done. The construction worker stumbled to his feet with some assistance and shook the loose dirt from his hair.

"Am I dead?" he asked.

"You almost were, but the brake on this truck was never set, and it saved you from a fatal fall."

"I set that brake myself. There is no way that truck rolled alone."

A bystander hollered, "It was God; God is the one who saved you."

Then from beneath all of the voices, I heard just one. The voice was faint and to the point.

"It wasn't God who saved you, it was him."

When I focused on the person who was speaking, he was pointing directly at me.

"Who?" asked one of the police officers.

"Him, the guy over there. The one standing next to the truck; he didn't save the man on the bicycle, but he saved this man."

It was the boy, that child who spoke to me once before. He smiled at me and walked over.

"Great job, I saw everything. You are fast. I thought that man was in real trouble, but you saved him."

He smiled at me and reached out to touch my hand.

His mother grabbed him and said, "Who are you talking to?"

The boy replied, "The man standing right over there. Don't you see him, Mommy? He just saved that man over there from falling."

The boy's mother looked directly at me, but I knew she could not see me. The crowed looked as if he was joking.

One of them said, "Maybe it was an angel. I hear angels can save lives."

A police officer approached the young boy and said, "If you know who did this, son, I really need you to tell me. They won't get into any trouble."

"He is standing right there; don't you see him?"

The boy pointed to me again. The majority of the crowd began to laugh and the boy's mother tugged at his shirt.

"Come on, baby, it's time to go home."

She pushed her way through the crowd and made her way down the street away from the prying eyes of the crowd.

The boy looked back at me. He seemed sad that not one person in the crowd believed his story, not even his mother. As they turned the corner, I followed. I just had to speak to a child who had the ability to see me, and what I had done. When they got to their home, the boy's mother said, "Okay, Timmy, you can play in the yard, but don't go anywhere. Stay in the yard, okay?"

"Okay, Mommy, can I play in the sandbox?"

"Yes, baby, play in the yard."

His mother went into the house and closed the door.

I could see the boy playing in his sandbox. I watched him for a while and thought about talking to him. What would I say? I did not want to scare the youngster; after all, he was the only one who could see me. I moved in toward the fence. I could hear him talking to himself while he played with his action figures. He was copying the scene that had just transpired at the construction site.

"I'll save you," he said to the little green alien he held in one hand as he flew his Superman figure in and pushed a toy truck to break the alien's fall. I smiled to myself. Now I was Superman. I could live with that.

The boy noticed me sitting behind the tree and said, "Hey, will you play with me?"

I turned around to see if he was talking to someone else, but he was looking directly at me.

"If you want me to," I said.

"Why am I the only one who can see you?"

"I'm not sure; I was wondering the same thing."

"I liked the way you saved that man. That was the best. You are just like Superman. He's my favorite super hero, you know."

The boy was so young, and I was not sure how to go about talking to him. I had never had the chance to see my son grow up, let alone speak to him about anything. I was not even sure what questions I wanted to ask at this point. I just smiled at the boy and said, "Your name is Timmy, right?"

"Yep, what's your name?"

"My name is John, John Davis."

"Can I call you Superman?"

"Yes," I told him. "You can call me Superman."

"So Superman, do you save people every day?"

"Well, I try to, but sometimes, I don't get there in time."

The boy let out a sigh. "Like the man on the bike, you didn't get there in time then."

"No, I didn't, but I wanted to. Sometimes, there is nothing that I can do."

"Does it make you sad when that happens?"

"Yes, it does, but sometimes, I'm just not fast enough."

The boy just smiled at me. I looked into his eyes, and he had such innocence about him. I had not remembered how wonderful it felt to speak to another person. It had been so many years since I was able to do so. I felt myself getting all choked up. I began to think about my son and how I would never get to see him, let alone speak to him.

I asked Timmy if he spoke to his mother about me.

"Mommy doesn't think you're real. I know you are. You're Superman! Can you fly?"

I smiled. "Well, sort of, I need something to help me along."

"Like what?"

"Well, a breeze could help, or a wave. Sometimes, I use the Ferris wheel at the amusement park."

"That's cool! Can I fly with you?"

Now I was not sure what to think. I knew that I could manipulate people, but I was not sure that I could control the actions. I was told never to hang on to mortals for too long of a period. I never tried, for the fear of what might happen to them. My instructions were very clear on this subject. I could not get myself to experiment with the idea.

"No, I'm sorry, but it wouldn't be safe for you, but we can talk more later if you want."

The boy looked up at me with bright eyes. "You don't have many friends, do you?"

"How did you know that?" I asked.

"Your eyes look sad. Are you sad?"

"Everyone gets sad sometimes, but we're friends, right?"

He smiled and said, "I'm Superman's best friend!"

The boy's mother hollered from the kitchen window, "Timmy, who are you talking to?"

"Superman!" the boy replied as he flew the action figure about in the air.

I got to my feet and said, "Well, I have to go now."

"Do you have to go and save more people?"

"Yes, but would it be okay if I came back sometime, and we could talk again?"

"Sure, I would like that, Superman."

He waved goodbye and smiled the widest smile. I waved goodbye, and as I made my way up the street, I wiped a tear from my eye and headed over to Kitten's house.

Chapter Eight

The sun was high in the sky, and flocks of seagulls were overhead screeching at each other. Below, in the parking lot of a fast-food eatery, kids were throwing French fries, and the birds were catching them in midair. As I began to turn away, I caught a glimpse of the light. It was directly in the middle of the parking lot were the children were playing. Entering the driveway was a carload of teenagers. The music blasting and the amplified sound of laughter that was coming from the car combined with the waiting light told me that trouble was afoot. I hurried over to the children at play, looked around, and spotted a garbage can. There was a pimply-faced food worker pushing a hand truck loaded with buns, so I gave him a shove, and he toppled over the garbage can pushing it and the buns directly into the path of the loud and dangerous vehicle.

The driver slammed on his brakes, and the automobile fishtailed to the right, its rear fender crashing into a parked car. The children screamed and rushed to the sidewalk shaking with panic. Patrons ran to the windows and doors of the establishment. The manager ran out with a cell phone in his hand asking if everyone was all right. There were a few onlookers dialing the police on their cellular phones.

Everyone in the car was okay, but the vehicle took the worst of it all. The woman who owned the innocent car was screaming at the driver in Spanish. I did not understand what she was saying, but I knew it must have been a colorful array of adjectives that were not very nice. Back on the sidewalk, parents hugged their children in tears, thankful that they were safe.

I could hear the loud sirens of the police and emergency units that were responding to the scene. It did not take long for a response; Seaside Heights had a full-force staff. A bicycle response was the first to arrive, assessing the scene of the accident and getting the minors under control. As I reached the end of the block, the patrol car was coming around the corner.

As I approached Kitten's house, the music was loud enough for me to hear it before her driveway came into view. She listened to hard rock, that heavy metal that sounds so angry and violent it makes you want to tear something or someone apart. She loved it, and it showed.

I could see Bear talking on his telephone as he paced from one side of the driveway to the other. Kitten was making her way down the steps with a cooler when Bear hung up the phone. He walked over to her and gestured for her to hand over the cooler. Smiling, she dropped it into his hands.

"I'll get the sandwiches out of the car, and we can eat. The table is around the side; just follow the path of seashells."

She walked toward the car parked in the driveway. I could see by the way she was looking at it that she obviously had a love affair with vintage automobiles. My eyes could not focus on anything but her tight backside, which was a masterpiece in itself.

She trotted around the garage and flopped down onto the bench across from her friend who greeted her with a fiendish grin, eyeing her up and down. I could tell just by looking at him there were more than just reminiscent thoughts about old times on his mind. It appeared to me that Kitten seemed to feel the same way.

She leaned in toward him and said, "So, where have you been all this time? No phone call, not even a postcard. That hurts, you know."

"I'm sorry, Kitty, you know how it is. It's hard picking up good cars. It's your fault; you got me into this business. There isn't anything left in Jersey for me to pick up."

She smiled as she wiped the mayonnaise from the corner of her lip.

"Not anymore, there are lots of steel beauties down here. You've been away for a while."

Looking surprised, he said, "You back in the business? I never thought I would see the day. What are you working on?"

"Come with me." She led him to the garage door. "Now, I haven't had much time to work on him. I've had this one for about a year or so. I just don't have the time with jobs coming up here and there, and I'm not really a morning person, you know."

She turned the key, smiled, and lifted the door open. As the sun hit the interior of the garage, I could see it was one of the most organized and fully equipped mechanic's offices I had ever viewed in my life. Since automobiles were invented, I had always been fascinated about the way they worked, how one person could take them apart and put them back together again. Kitten was one of these people? I could not believe my eyes. What a woman!

Bear smiled at her with admiration in his eyes.

"You always had the best shop, everything neat and clean and everything in its place. So, what's under the tarp?"

Kitten grinned from ear to ear as she lifted the massive tarp revealing a vintage Barracuda. It was a thing of beauty. These were the cars that screamed to be driven. The only place that an automobile of this kind belonged was on the open road. Kitten had a tear in her eye as she ran her hand the length of the front fender to the driver's side door.

"Check out the inside, all original, chrome dash and bucket seats. Nice cockpit, huh?"

"Oh, baby, this is sweet. Where did you get her?"

"Him! He's a he, not a she. I found him on a job over in Whiting. You know how many old people live there. When they retire, they buy homes over in the senior citizen communities, and most of them can't drive anymore. I found it there. Got it for a steal, only cost me five hundred bucks. The lady I got it from said that her son died years earlier, and this was his car. She said he loved it, and she wanted it to go to a good home. It needed everything from brakes to headlight motors. The parts were hard to find, but what I couldn't find I improvised."

"When are you going to get him finished? Doesn't it call out to you in the night when you're lying right above it in your bed?"

"I try not to listen. I'm usually preoccupied with other stuff."

"Oh, I forgot about Devin. How is he anyway?"

"I don't see him anymore; Ed is seeing to that."

"Ed? You still hanging out with that dirtbag? Now I know what is keeping you from the project. It's the drugs, right? Are you still using? Are you still overdoing it?"

"Not overdoing, I only use what I need to keep going. My life hasn't been all that great, you know."

"I'm sorry, Kitty. I shouldn't judge. Who the hell am I anyhow? You have never listened to any advice I have ever given you. If anything, it only drove us apart. Or did you forget why I left the last time?"

"You left because I caught you in bed with that slut from the bar. I threw you out, if you don't remember! And, as I recall, you were dealing at that time. I got my shit from you remember?"

I was beginning to dislike this guy, too. He was probably the one that got her hooked on it in the first place. They looked at one another and smiled then reached out to embrace.

"Okay, Kitty, I'll tell you what, let's finish eating, and then we'll go to the parts store, and I'll spring for the battery. Let's get this bad boy started; I want to hear this mother run."

She smiled. "Okay, you win. Truce, no more old crap to get in the way."

They continued to reminisce, and I began to get annoyed very quickly, feeling it begin to burn in the pit of my stomach. I was angered to see her having a conversation with this guy, knowing I would never get the opportunity to tell her how I felt. She would never know the love that I felt for her in my heart, the burning truth that she was the one. She was the only spirit that kept me going on this long and lonely journey. From the first time I laid eyes on her at the beach, there was a connection to my heart.

I had a job to do and sitting around feeling sorry for myself wasn't getting it done. Maybe I hadn't changed at all. Was I claiming her for my own? Had I not learned my lesson after all these years? Could this be why? Had I finally answered my own question? I looked into

Kitten's eyes and realized that I could not possibly have loved anyone more, not even my wife.

I decided to head over to the Skateboard Park. There was always something to do there. Kids were always having close calls. I had been of some assistance there before, and it seemed like the thing to do. Hitching a ride on one of the board breezes was a hoot. I loved it. It helped me to feel free. That was actually one of the little perks of the job, probably the only one.

There were hundreds of elemental rides I could harness, but the feeling of flight was my favorite. Soaring through the air was exhilarating. It helped me to feel free, no boundaries, just me.

There were dozens of skaters, some young, some a bit older, zooming past, jumping the obstacles on the course. I enjoyed watching them and how they would defy gravity. It was fantastic. They each had their own style, and I have to tell you most of them were fearless. It was a rule of the park that all of the kids had to wear helmets, but not many did. I suppose there were not enough attendants to enforce the rules.

I could not help overhearing a group of kids who were a lot rowdier than the rest laughing and getting loud, so I diverted my full attention to them. I could hear the park security guard shouting to them to pack it up and get going.

The boys laughed and pushed their boards to the exit ramp. I hitched a ride as they made their way to the open parking garage of the hotel across the street. They darted in and out of the parked cars laughing and screaming back and forth to one another. One of the boys jumped onto a handrail and fell on his landing, tearing his pants at the knee. They laughed and dared him to try it again.

On his second attempt, there in the foreground shone the light of doom. Its glow was bright and defined in the distance. I raced behind him hoping to catch a breeze as he approached the light but to no avail. My attempts were a loss. As he hit the handrail and flew through the air, there was nothing that I could do. As his body flew high into the air, the daring young man slammed his head into the cement brace that hung down from the ceiling above. It was like he was hit by a Mac truck. There was little left of his face when his body went limp and fell to the ground in a lifeless lump.

The other boys looked on in horror, and two of them ran screaming in terror. Another of the boys fell on his back and with all of his might, pushed himself across the garage floor crashing into a parked car and crying uncontrollably. The injured boy's lifeless body lay quietly, not even a sound could be heard. I could smell the fear as the other boy sat shaking with anguish. I looked up at the bloodstain on the cement brace, still fresh and dripping with gray matter. It was a horrible sight, even for me to witness. The puddle beneath the boy's head was deep and dark crimson, thick and gooey. I hated the smell of blood; the sweet stench of death made my stomach churn. But there was an attraction to it as well; I had a hard time driving myself to look away from the carnage and death.

I had failed, and this boy was dead. Was I losing my touch? I could not understand. What was the point of having all of these special abilities if I could not save the innocent? Why did he have to die? Who got to decide who stayed and who went? Why was this boy chosen to expire? What was the point? I felt like I needed a break from all the pain and suffering. As I headed to the beach, I could hear the ambulance coming down the street. A bicycle patrol officer was coming up the ramp, and a small crowd had begun to gather.

It was my fault. The boy was dead, and I could not help him. The same question would always arise: Why was I here and for how long would I be damned to this line of work? Had I not learned my lesson? How many lifetimes would it take me to fulfill my destiny? I began to think about how I begged to die and to have a very short jail stay. I refused a trial and demanded to be hanged. Why did I do that? If I had only known then what I knew now, I would have taken the last few days to repent to a preacher, as if that would have done any good. I received my last rights and what good did it do me? I longed to know who was in charge, who ran this thing, and how I could get their attention.

I had a lot to think about, and I was beginning to be afraid of the terrible things that were beginning to cross my mind. So many years had gone by and all the good that I had done seemed to be for nothing. Why if all these good deeds were not getting me any results, did I continue to do them? What if I used my power to harness the elements to my advantage? It was something I had never done before.

Why not give it a try? Besides, I wouldn't hurt anyone, and I could still do my job. I needed more than one perk to this job, and it was high time I reached for the unreachable. It was high time I got closer to my Kitten, and I knew just how to do it.

The boy could see me, and he could talk for me. Now how did I get them at the same place and time? I walked around for days thinking up the plans of my path to happiness. The church seemed to be the place to go.

I stepped through the large doors. It didn't matter what day or time I entered this remarkable house of peace, I always found hope for myself within its wondrous walls. The bright green and yellow sparkles cascading across the air filled my heart with warmth and serenity. I had never felt so mortal in all of my existence.

I slid into the pew that called to me. When I knelt on the beautifully hand-forged brass legs which adorned the deep red velvet cushions for comfort, my existence on these vibrant articles almost made it feel like I belonged. It was perfect.

I began to think about the boy, how he was able to see and communicate with me, how I roamed the beach searching for Kitten and dreaming of the day she would be aware of the deep-hearted love that I had felt for her. Perhaps one day, she would be able to express the same feelings for me.

Praying for mercy and blubbering at the fact, I began to hear bells, no, not bells, chimes, but not the kind of chimes you hear on the Jersey Shore. This sound was eloquent and spiritual. My heart began to pump with enthusiasm, looking for a sign of true hope. That was when she appeared to me, a wondrous vision that glided through the light of the stained glass floating down and coming to rest beside me.

I was speechless as I looked into her eyes. They were filled with the hope that I desired, and without saying a word, she filled my empty heart with love. I asked her why she was here. She reached out and held my hand.

"I was sent here to answer some questions for you."

I smiled and could feel the tears falling down from my cheek.

"Don't cry, you have a purpose here. Haven't you figured it out yet?"

"I have been walking this earth for many years, helping strangers, but why?"

"You are the only one who can. You and others like you are the only thing keeping this world in balance."

"I have seen what this world is like, and it was a much better place years ago."

"Now you see why you are so desperately needed here. But I was told to remind you that speaking to the living isn't part of your job."

"Are you talking of the boy?"

"Yes, he is young and has sight. It is not good that you are communicating with him. They are getting angry with you. You really should keep away from the boy."

I became a bit angry. "Why? The boy is the only one who can see me, the only one I can communicate with, and I don't see others like me."

"You won't see others like you; that is not the way it works."

"Please tell me how it works. How long will I be here and will I ever get a chance at peace? Will this task ever be done?"

She looked at me with sadness in her eyes and said, "If you change your way of thinking and continue your work as it was intended, maybe someday you will have paid off your debt."

"My debt! Haven't I done that already?"

She began to rise from the pew.

"You will know when the time is right, for now, you must be patient and do what you do best, what you were meant to do. You're special, John. That is why you are still here. You are needed."

I looked up at her and pleaded for her to stay with me. It had been so long since I felt the touch of another, and I longed for it again.

"Please don't leave me. I don't know what to do."

"Don't worry, John. You will be fine. I'll be in touch, I promise."

"When? When will you be in touch? What is your name?"

Confused and sad, I looked up at the woman who floated into my life and just as quickly, floated out of it. "How do I contact you?"

She smiled and said, "I am called Tabitha. I will contact you. You are my new assignment. I'll be watching you."

"Why? Why are you going to watch me?"

She disappeared into the shimmering light of the multicolored glass and was gone.

I sat in the pew for some time and wondered why I was being watched. Was it the boy? Was he the reason for the surveillance? My mind was lost in the beauty of the glass around me. I pictured the woman who came to me and wondered if she was just a figment of my imagination. I was still angry, none of my questions were answered, and the longing for companionship hung heavy in my heart. All of my abilities and I was still unable to satisfy my desire.

I mustered up the last of my strength, dragged my sorry self off the bench, and slowly headed to the exit. I pushed the large doors with all of my might, and as I stepped onto the sidewalk, I realized that the day had been long gone and a new morning was about to begin. I was not sure what to make of the situation; it had just worried me more. What about the boy? What could the consequences possibly be for speaking with him? I really did not want to think about it. I could feel the hollow loneliness begin to kick in. I needed to see my girl; Kitten would be my only salvation.

On the way to the garage, I wondered what was on Kitten's agenda. Would she be home? Would she be alone? I hoped the answer to both of my questions was yes. As I turned the corner to approach her apartment, I could see the light appear in the middle of the street. I was not sure whom it was for, but I headed into the street to check it out. Just then, I heard a noise coming from a cluster of garbage cans, and the screeching of car tires turning the corner quickly. A squirrel darted out into the middle of the street, and before I could focus on the situation, the squirrel was no more. All that was left of this meek little fellow was the squashed remains of his frail little body imbedded into the blacktop of the street. I sighed and walked away.

Kitten was home; I could hear the music as I approached the steps to her apartment. How exciting, my heart began to beat faster with every step I took toward the door. She was talking to someone; I hoped it was a friendly conversation.

"What do you mean, Ed? How does she know who I am?" she shouted.

I could not hear Ed's half of the conversation; she must have been on the phone.

"If anyone starts getting close, you better call me...Now I'm going to have to keep a low profile...How do I keep getting myself into these situations?"

Who was looking for Kitten?

"Just let me know what you hear...I'll talk to you later." She slammed down the telephone and paced around the kitchen mumbling. "How the hell could she possibly know who I am? I never met her in my life."

Frantically, she reached into the cupboard and pulled out the mystery pack that she got from Ed. I was not sure what the substance was, and honestly, I was eager to find out. She poured a bottle of spring water into her teapot and used a match to fire up the burner. Azreal was purring and rubbing his body against her legs, and she spoke to him.

"What do you think, baby? Should Mommy save some or use the whole bag?" Azreal looked up at her and leaned in to nip her foot. Kitten jumped and smiled. "Okay, I'll just have a little bit."

She reached her hand out over the table and snapped her fingers together, beckoning for Azreal to jump up to her level. As he did, she leaned in to kiss his head. Then she gave him a hug.

The teapot was whistling for attention. She placed a mug on the table and began to fix herself a cup of tea. It was a pleasant change from her usual drink of choice: beer. She sat with her chin in the palm of her hand and dunked the teabag up and down to brew it in the water. There was a knock at the door. Kitten looked surprised.

"Who is it?" she shouted as she covered up the mystery pack with a placemat and headed for the door.

"It's Frank! I have a lot of stuff for you this week. Almost everything you ordered came in."

"I'm here," she said, as she opened the door.

"Do you want any of the boxes up here, or you want them all downstairs?" the deliveryman asked.

"How many do I have?"

"About eight or nine," he replied.

She slipped her flip-flops on and followed him down to his truck. The sign on the door read, "Callaghan Auto, Lakewood, NJ." She opened the entrance to the garage and turned on the light. With a loud pop, the garage door opener began to grind and slowly open the large double door. She smiled as he stepped out reaching for one of her boxes.

"You sure have a beautiful shop, Kitty. I never get tired of delivering here. You always have the hottest cars. Where do you find them all?"

"Now, Frank, if I told you that, then I wouldn't have them, you would. I'll sell it to you when it's done. Just like I always do."

"Are you really going to part with this one when you are finished?"

"Yes, unless you don't want it, but I can always find a buyer. This is a Cuda, baby. Lots of people are looking for one like this."

"No, no, I'll take it, but not until it's finished. You have the touch, kid. I'll see you next week."

"Okay, put this all on my account and tell Lenny not to screw with the pricing again this month, or you won't be getting any of my cars or my business in the future."

"You got it, girl. See you in about a week."

"Thanks," Kitten said smiling.

I watched as the truck pulled out of the driveway. Kitten began to unpack her delivery. Her feet were stepping to the beat of whatever music was playing in her mind, and she gently placed each item she unpacked neatly onto the workbench. There were filters, gaskets, and wires. There were things that I had no idea what they were. She seemed to be happy with her delivery. She turned away from the table and patted the hood of the car and said, "I'll see you later."

With that, she shut off the lights and closed all the doors before she went back up to her apartment.

I watched her run up the steps and quickly shut the door. She flopped down onto the kitchen chair and took a sip of her tea. Azreal was lying on the table looking at her when she said, "Well, this tea is too strong."

She dumped it into the sink and relit the burner to have another go at it. As she waited for the water to boil, she pulled the mystery bag from its hiding place and opened it up wide. I got closer to see what the substance was and was not really quite sure what to think. It looked like mold, or something like it. She pulled out a big chunk of the strange substance, smiled widely, and placed it on her tongue. The look on her face changed as she began to chew. Her eyes closed together tightly, and she began to swallow hard as she worked to get the nasty clump down into the pit of her stomach.

Why was she eating this stuff? For what reason would anyone eat this stuff? I thought to myself. She poured another cup of tea and drank some down quickly. Then she pulled out another chunk of this stuff, repeated the action, and finished her tea.

"Okay, Azreal, how long do you think it is going to take? Do you think Mommy has enough time to walk to the liquor store before it kicks in? We don't want to have another episode in the liquor store now do we?" Azreal just looked at her briefly and laid his head back down on the table. Kitten laughed out loud and patted him on the head. "I'll be back in a little while."

She scooped the keys up off the table, grabbed some money from its hiding place in the coffee can, and headed out for her beverages.

She walked, and as she did so, she avoided stepping on cracks in the sidewalk. If she failed to avoid them, she remarked with a sound of disappointment. Why was she so hard on herself? I could not understand or begin to imagine what was going through her mind. I wanted so desperately to take her in my arms, hold her tight, and assure her everything was going to be fine. She walked up to a mailbox and opened it up. There was a large pile of mail in the box, and it began to spill out when she opened up the door. She picked up what had fallen onto the ground and jammed the rest under her arm as she looked around. I followed her to the home of a much older woman. She was practically transparent when she came to the door. I could see every vein that made up her body structure, and her eyelids drooped like the satin lining in a coffin.

Kitten smiled at her. "Hi, Beatrice! I got the mail for you."

"Hello, Puss, come in and have some tea. Would you both like some tea?"

The woman gestured to me. I froze in my tracks. The hair on the back of my neck stood straight up.

115

"Bea, I'm alone, but Ed says hello. He wants to know when you are going to make more of that pecan pastry he loves so much."

"You tell him that I said he can come over anytime."

The woman was still trying to make it to the kitchen. Kitten was guiding her to a comfortable seat in the living room, but she pulled her elbow away and began to boil water for the tea.

"So where have you been keeping yourself these days, Puss? I don't get to see you. Is the new man in your life keeping you busy?"

I had still not recovered from the initial comment that she made, and here she was making another.

"What new man, Bea? I don't have a new man. I've been working a lot, and Devin is keeping me on my toes. Ed changed the locks to keep him out, but I'm still worried that he will be back."

"So there is no man?" She looked directly at me and raised an eyebrow.

"No, I wish there were, but I'm still too busy to even think about that. The Cuda has me pulling all-nighters, and you know I'm not an early riser," she lied, covering up the honest reason of narcotics and alcohol, revealing she knew the truth.

"You rise early enough to sort through my mail and throw away the junk that I don't need."

"I do that because most of the mail that you get is all garbage from dirtbags that prey on the elderly. It's always a deal for a small amount of money or a fake diamond pendant if you join some stupid club or make a donation to some foundation, all intended to steal your money right out from under you. Those creeps, someone has to protect you."

"Puss, you are the best person I know. Would you like to know something else?" She continued to look directly at me. I felt very uncomfortable. Did she really see me?

Kitten laughed. "What else do you know, Bea? Are you going to tell me the future again, like you did with Devin?"

Bea reached out her hand and placed it atop of Kitten's. She blinked her eyes quickly and hummed an old familiar tune. I did not know what it was, but I was sure that I had heard it before. She looked deep into Kitten's eyes and said, "There is a man in your life. He is tall and has caring eyes. He has been through a lot in this world, but nonetheless, he is your soul mate."

"My soul mate? I don't believe in that stuff, Bea."

Bea looked at her with disappointment and shook her head. "He is very close to you; it was love at first sight. There is something keeping him from you, but soon that will all be in the past. When he reveals himself to you, it will be as if you have known each other for a lifetime. Don't let this one get away. You were meant to be together." Bea smiled and patted Kitten's hand. "Now you go and find him."

She smiled and winked at me. I scratched my head and smiled back as Kitten ripped up the mail that was to be discarded.

"Okay, Bea, I'll see you. Next time I come by, I'll bring Ed. We'll make some pastry, and you can tell him what the future holds for him." They embraced, and Kitten kissed her on the cheek.

"Have fun, Puss, and keep an open mind."

"I will, don't worry." Kitten exited the house. "I'm on my way!" she said smiling.

I followed her to the end of the block, and on the way, I thought about what Bea had said. Did she really see me? She never really said that she did, at least not to Kitten, or to me, in fact. She had to be talking about me. She looked directly at me. Who else has been through more in this world than me? She was talking about me, but how am I going to reveal myself to Kitten? Could I? Would she really have the ability to see me? This information caused my mind to wander. I followed Kitten as she entered the liquor store, and I was shocked to see big Michael exiting; they brushed past one another... He was wearing the same clothes as before; the bruises about his face seemed to be larger and more defined. Kitten smiled at him as they passed one another.

Michael smiled back and followed her into the store with his eyes. I continued to observe his actions and waited outside while Kitten purchased her alcohol. I could not get what Beatrice said about Kitten and me being soul mates out of my head. I wondered when the day would come when Kitten would have the ability of sight and wondered how we could ever be together. Michael sat on the bench just outside the store, his eyes still focused on Kitten. Did they know each other? I wondered.

A very attractive woman walked into the store and shouted, "Kitty, how the hell are ya, honey?"

Kitten turned around, and a smile shot across her face. "Kelly! What are you doing here?" she said surprised.

"Same as you, getting some refreshments. I got fired today, and I thought I might use this valuable time to catch a buzz."

"What happened? Why did you get fired?"

"Jimmy didn't like the way I conducted myself at the convention in Vegas. He said this time it was for good, and he would never ask me to come back. You know what that means. Come Monday morning, he is going to call me pleading for me to come back. That place would shut down if it weren't for me. So, I'll take the next few days to relax and get caught up on my drinking."

"What did you do in Vegas to get fired? What happened?"

"I drank a bit too much, and before I knew it, I was over five thousand in the hole and escorted out of the convention hall. It wasn't a pretty sight."

"So you want to have a few beers with me? I got some mushrooms at the house."

"Mushrooms? Are you crazy, girl? I can't eat them. They make me freak out. You talked me into eating those nasty things once before. Don't you remember what happened?"

"Yeah, I remember, you took off all of your clothes at the bar and danced around begging everyone to throw fruit at you."

Kitten couldn't contain her laughter; she burst out into hysterics and covered her mouth to keep from being so loud. "How could I forget? You wouldn't come out from under the boardwalk. It took every bit of energy that Harry and Charlie had to get you out."

"I know, not one of my better moments, but it swore me off of mushrooms forever. You have fun, honey. I'm going to the beach. We'll catch up soon, I promise." She waved goodbye with her back turned, seeming not completely interested.

"Okay, call me." Kitten smiled with enthusiasm.

"You got it. Take care now," she mumbled.

"Bye."

Kitten paid for her order and grabbed a bag of ice on the way out. Michael stood up when she walked through the door and said hello.

Kitten smiled back and offered him some chewing gum. He accepted, and they stood there on the sidewalk looking at one another.

Kitten said, "Have a great day."

And she started to walk away. Michael followed behind her, and as she waited for the traffic light to change, he asked, "Do you like me to carry your bags for you?" She looked up at him and politely refused his assistance. "I could carry the ice for you. It goes in the freezer. I can put it in the freezer for you."

"No, that's okay, you don't have to. I can handle it on my own, thank you."

Michael stared at her with a confused look. "Okay, bye!"

"Bye!" Kitten smiled as she looked left and right at the corner of the street.

The light changed, and Kitten crossed the street, looking behind her to see if Michael was following. She walked at a slow pace and constantly checked to see if she was being followed. Michael just stood there on that corner and watched as Kitten walked out of sight.

Kitten reached her house, put the ice in the refrigerator, and the beer in the freezer and sat down in front of the television. She kicked up her feet and made a phone call.

"Ed, what are you doing?…I'm just relaxing with a few beers and some of those mushrooms that you gave me."

There was a pause in her statements. I could not hear what Ed was saying on the other end.

"Don't worry about me; I'll be just fine. You're a worrywart, Eddie."

There was a very long pause, and Kitten replied, "Okay, but I only ate a little bit, just enough to get me going. I'll be careful…Any word on Carla? Does she know who I am?…Who does she have out looking for me?…Is it someone we know?" There was a longer pause. "Well, keep me posted, I want to know whatever you find out. I'll talk to you soon…thanks…bye."

She hung up the phone and headed to the bathroom to take a shower. I watched her and fanaticized about touching her body, my hands gently caressing her soft, tan skin. I was getting excited about it. Her beauty was unsurpassed by any and made me lose myself.

As Kitten finished her shower; I watched as she dried her hair and made up her face. It was obvious that she was getting ready to go out. She sprayed perfume onto her neck and rubbed her wrists against the moist droplets. The fragrance was remarkable. I breathed her in. Her marvelous sent engulfed my lungs. I became anxious; I wanted to touch her body. To feel her close to me was what I truly needed.

She pulled on a tight black body suit and slipped a mini skirt over top of it. Reaching into the closet, she grabbed a pair of shoes and pushed her feet into them and looked into the mirror to check herself one last time. I enjoyed watching as she admired her own beauty, and the way she smiled when she did it made my heart sing. I could tell that my feelings at this time were beginning to become uncontrollable. I reached out and touched her face gently. She reached her hand to her cheek and tears began to swell up in her eyes.

Looking around frantically, she whispered, "Who is there? Is someone here?"

As she looked around the room, she was frightened and rushed to the fridge for a beer, but all she found was a dripping bag of melted ice. She lifted the bag and heaved it into the sink. She opened the freezer and pulled out the beer.

As she twisted the top to release her anxiety, the metal cap created a break in the skin. Blood began to trickle to her wrist, and the half-frozen beer erupted over the lip of the bottle trickling over her fingers.

"Oh crap! Oh great!"

As her tongue glided across the light pink of her flesh, I watched the crimson liquid absorb into her tiny taste buds. How sweet she must have tasted. I stood with her, face-to-face. I could smell her sweet breath and lost myself in her eyes. Kitten hadn't moved a muscle. It was as if time had been frozen for a moment. My heart grew hot so I leaned in for a kiss. Kitty's eyes closed, and without warning, she kissed me back. Her kiss was so sweet. I could feel our moisture meshing together, and it was bliss.

She stepped back and whispered, "It's just the drugs. This isn't happening. Man, I gotta get out of here."

I couldn't move. My feet wouldn't budge. Was I just fantasizing this entire experience? No, I was totally in control of the situation.

How is it that she could receive my kisses? She actually participated in the kiss that I attempted to steal from her. My head was floating, my heart was singing, and I was not sure how much time had passed. All I knew was that Kitten kissed me; this was the best day of my immortal life. When I finally regained consciousness, Kitten was long gone.

I mulled around the apartment for a while and opened the mystery pack. It was mushrooms. I knew that native people ate them to reach the spirit world, to contact their ancestors, but I never understood how it worked. I must say that if Kitten was able to experience me, then Beatrice might know what she's talking about. I had to go to her, and I knew just where to find her.

Chapter Nine

*T*he air was thick with humidity, and the tourists were loud and spending their money in the usual fashion. Children tugged on their parents' clothing asking for money to play games, and the bicycle patrol was peddling the boards keeping the peace. The women were dressed in tiny shorts and bikini tops, and the men conducted themselves as body-hungry wolves hooting and hollering at the flesh that passed before them.

I headed down to the bar where I knew my Kitten would be. It had been some time since she saw Ed, and after listening to her telephone conversations and discovering what the mystery pack consisted of, I knew that they would probably be meeting tonight. Kitten was taking mushrooms on purpose, but why? I entered a tiny novelty shop and headed to the back were they kept the unmentionables. Dope dealers and dope users frequented this area. They would purchase tools needed for their extracurricular activities. I entered hungry for information; there must be someone with knowledge of the mushroom drug in this place. I viewed the many items incased in the glass display units and read the sayings on the various tee shirts, which hung on the walls around me. One had a mushroom on it, and the caption read "Eat Me." I began to feel as though I might never get the education that I was seeking. Then I noticed the books that were on the back shelf.

I read the titles, and there was one in particular that caught my eye. It was the *Encyclopedia of Recreational Drugs.* I was never aware such a book existed. I knocked it over and flipped to the glossary. Mushrooms, I turned to page one hundred ninety-six, and there they were, photographs and articles explaining everything that I needed to know. It stated that people who used this particular drug were searching for something. The drug was intended to open your mind and spirit to the world that most people did not see with regular eyes. The drugs enhanced your ability to see things beyond the everyday, to put your mind and body in comfort to follow Alice down the rabbit hole.

Now I understood what it did, but why was Kitten using these things? I thought for a moment and realized if Kitten wanted to use such drugs, who was I to stop her? Besides, she kissed me back, and if it weren't for those wretched clumps of fungus, that would have never happened. Did Beatrice know that was the reason she would meet me? Could she have known? All this information only made me want to see Kitten even more. I left the small shop and continued on to the bar.

The music was loud, and the smoke was wafting out of the entrance door. There was no air-conditioning, and most of the patrons were dressed in the day's beachwear. The room smelled of suntan lotion, smoke, and alcohol with just the hint of urine. I noticed that the usual bartenders were working as I eagerly scanned my surroundings for Kitten. I headed for the balcony, and just like I expected, there he was, sitting in his usual seat surrounded by customers and kiss assess. There was a familiar voice coming from behind me. It was Devin.

"Hey, Ed, have you seen Kitty?"

Ed looked surprised. "Are you crazy, dude? You got a lot of balls showing your face around here. Kitty doesn't want anything to do with you, and she asked me personally to keep you away from her."

"Come on, Ed, you know that I love her, and whether you like it or not, she loves me, too."

"Kid, I assure you she doesn't love you. Now get away from me. You're bad for business."

"Okay, okay, I'll leave, but you can't keep us from being together. She loves me. You'll see."

Devin reached into his pocket and pulled out some money.

"Hey, Eddie, let me get a gram from ya?"

"What, are you crazy? Your money isn't any good here. Get lost, turd."

Devin shrugged his shoulders and headed back into the bar. Ed stood up to make sure that Devin actually left the bar. When he was gone, Ed continued and opened shop.

My eyes scanned the bar for any sign of Kitten. I wondered when she would arrive and if she would be able to feel me again. I heard a ruckus just outside, and apparently, Ed did too. It was Kitten and Devin. They were pushing one another around the boardwalk. I rushed outside to see if Kitten was okay. Ed was right behind me, and he snatched up Devin with one hand and tossed him over the fence onto the sand of the beach.

"Are you all right, Kitty? Did he hurt you?" Ed grabbed at her, body checking to see if she was all right.

Kitten laughed uncontrollably and fell to the ground. "Did you see Devin go flying over the fence? That was so funny. Ed, you're a pisser. Please, do that again."

Ed scooped up Kitten and carried her back into the bar.

"What happened out there, Kitty? Are you trying to get into trouble? Do you want the cops coming in here and taking all of us away?"

She continued to laugh. "Ed, you worry too much. Calm down! No one is going to get into trouble. Relax! Why don't you throw someone else, Ed? That was fucking funny as hell!"

"Listen, Kitty, you're all high on shrooms, and I think you should go home and relax until your high wears off."

She darted off to the restroom, and I just had to follow her. She stood there in front of the mirror and made funny faces at herself. I giggled and was thinking, *Why is she acting like this?* She washed her hands and brushed her hair. I enjoyed watching her apply her lipstick and how she licked her lips when she was finished.

She pushed the bathroom door open and headed to the bar. The bartender had drinks ready for her when she arrived.

"Thanks, Tiger!" Kitty said, as she picked up the shot glass and slammed down what was going to be the first of many drinks to follow.

"So, Kitty, how have you been? Devin didn't hurt you, did he?" he asked, grabbing her hand in his.

"Why is everyone always worried about me getting hurt? Don't you people know I can take care of myself? But did you see him go flying over the fence? That was so funny." She laughed and laughed, holding her stomach as tears trickled down her cheeks from the laughter.

"Listen, Kitty; don't get all mad at me. I was just making sure that you are okay. I care about you, don't you know that?"

"Yes, I'm sorry. I know you're my friend, and you care about me, but, man, just take it down, will you?" She hollered across the room, "Come on, Ed, throw someone else. Please!"

Kitten pulled herself up and waved goodbye to Ed. He rushed over to her.

"Where are you off to?"

"I'm going home, Ed. Jesus Christ, what are you, my mother?"

"Look, Kitty, you aren't in the right frame of mind to be gallivanting around the streets. I just want you to be safe. Let me take you home."

Kitty continued to giggle. "Okay, Ed, I'm going home, but I don't need an escort. Please don't treat me like a little kid. I'll be just fine."

She leaned in and gave him a kiss on the nose, messed up his hair, and gave him a light slap on the cheek. "I'll call you tomorrow. Try not to worry so much. I'll be fine. Trust me."

Ed pointed his finger at her and said in a stern voice, "You go straight home now. I'll call you later to check up on you."

She took some beer to go and headed out the door. I followed close behind. She headed down to the end of the beach near the sanctuary. I loved this place, and it was obvious that Kitten liked it, too. She slipped into someone's back yard and stole a blanket off of the washline, folded it up, and headed into another yard. There, she took a bucket candle and a cushion from a lounge chair. When she had gathered all the supplies she could carry, she headed to the watchtower. Quietly, she snuck past the guard and stayed low as she made her way through the dunes, being careful not to disturb the nests that were all around her. Looking around to be sure that she wasn't seen or followed, she began to ascend up the ladder to the lookout tower.

Kitten placed the large cushion on the floor of the tower and lit the candle. She reached into her purse, pulled out a joint, and lit it with the flickering flame of her lighter. I watched her closely, but she just sat there and stared out over the deep blue water of the Atlantic Ocean. She took a long pull off the joint and held it. As she exhaled, she said, "Why am I always alone? Wow, it's nice up here."

I could see her begin to cry, and she continued smoking to ease the pain. Why was Kitten in so much pain? I wanted to kiss her.

"When will I finally be happy? Show me something, anything, just give me a sign," she whispered.

I did not want to let her down, so I headed out to find her a gift with the hope that it would cheer her up. I saw a wild fox scavenging around a trampled nest full of eggs. The fox saw me and followed me as if he were begging for food. I knelt down and patted his head. This animal seemed to know me and had the ability to see me. I headed down to the waterline to find the gift. I was gone for a few minutes when the fox came back, but he was not alone. Kitten was right behind him. She called out to the fox and begged for him to stop, but he just kept running away from her.

"Why do you run from me? I won't hurt you, little fellow. I just want to be friends. Please come back."

She hung her head down low and mumbled something to herself. Falling to her knees, she reached out her arms and buried them in the sand. I watched as she rolled around, flinging sand about and kicking her feet into the air. She was very playful and full of energy. My smile was so wide I thought my face would crack. I knelt down to get a closer look at her. She laughed and rolled around in the sand.

"What are you doing here?"

Very much to my surprise, she was talking to me. I could not answer her. I just sat there amazed and confused. I could not say a thing. I just smiled.

"Didn't your mother teach you any manners? You shouldn't sneak up on people. What are you doing here?"

I was shocked and did not know what to say. The only thing that passed my lips was, "I like it out here at night, and it's very beautiful here. Don't you think?"

"I know. I come here all of the time. It is the only place that a person can go to figure out the little troubles in life, and it is so beautiful. Isn't it beautiful?"

"I think this is the only place in the world that you can come and see a wild fox on the beach. I love the wildlife here."

"Me too, but you have to be careful not to get caught. The game warden will run you into the jail if he finds you here, but I don't care, I come here all the time."

My knees were shaking; I was not sure how to act. I had waited so long to talk to her. I did not know quite what to say. Her talking to me was making me very nervous.

"I usually only come here late at night when there aren't any people around. I think we're safe." She smiled.

I smiled at her and said, "Would you like some company? My name is John, John Davis."

"I'm Kitty. Are you from around here?"

"Not really, I just hang around the beach, because I enjoy watching people. I'm an artist of sorts."

I could not think of anything else to say. I was no artist, but I did not want to seem like a wacko, and I did not want the conversation to end. I had waited so long to be able to talk to her, and I was not about to let this end.

"What are you doing here?" I asked.

"I'm just searching for answers that I know will never come, but the scenery is good."

I was in shock again; she was searching for the same thing that I had been searching for.

"How would you like to have a drink, John?"

"I would love one, thank you."

"Follow me."

She reached out to grab my hand, and I pulled away. I was afraid that if she touched me, this whole fantasy would come to an end.

She smiled, laughed, and said, "Don't worry, I won't bite you."

I laughed along and followed as she led me to the tower. I was in bliss, but was this all really happening to me? I just was not sure. I could not take my eyes off of her; the moonlight reflecting off of her beautiful face made her look like an angel.

"Where are we going?"

She whispered, "Be quiet. If you're too loud, you'll scare them away."

"Who?"

"The babies. Look, can't you see them?"

I hunched down to get a closer look. They were tiny little chicks in a nest. Kitten sat down beside them, and her eyes lit up.

"Aren't they the most beautiful things that you have ever seen before in your life?"

"I think you are."

She looked up at me, smiled, and shook her head. "You're sweet, but that's not me."

"Are you kidding me?"

I could not believe my ears. My Kitten had a very low opinion of herself. I reached out for her hand.

"Come on, I want you to see something," she said eagerly.

Kitten got up and began to jog. I followed close behind, and she pointed to the ladder of the tower. I followed her up to the observation deck, and we looked out over the dunes to the ocean.

"Isn't that the most beautiful sight?" she smiled.

I could not focus on anything but her face. "Oh yes, it's beautiful," I said, stumbling over my words.

"I like to sit here and think about the future. What will happen? Where will I be? Whom will I be with? I wonder if the world will still be here long after I'm gone, and what it would be like? Do you ever think about that sort of thing?"

I was not sure what to say. I knew the answer to that, but I did not dare tell her. I was so pleased to be spending this time with her, and I did not want to ruin a thing.

"I'm sure the world will be here for a very long time, forever, even after we are all gone."

Her smile was remarkable; it made my heart sing. I had never been so happy in all of my existence as the way I was feeling tonight. I began to think that I was mortal. I felt whole and alive.

"Do you think that we all have a purpose in life?" she asked.

"Oh, sure I do."

Her eyes began to swell up with tears. "I don't think that I have a purpose."

"Everyone has a purpose. You must have one, too."

I offered her a shoulder to lean on, and she accepted. The smell of her hair was like a dream, and this whole ordeal was just the same.

"What is your purpose, John?"

This question worried me. I was not sure how to answer. I wasn't sure what my purpose on this planet was, but I knew in my heart, she was definitely on the list.

"Well, I'm not sure what it is, but I believe if people in general are kind and good to one another, then the world would have to be a better place for everyone."

She looked up at me with wide eyes. I did not dare tell her that if you live the straight and narrow life and screw up once and only once, you could spend the rest of eternity paying off your debt.

"You won't find people like that around here. Everyone here is out to get something. There are so few genuine hearts; I don't think people like that come to the Jersey Shore."

"Don't be silly. You're here, and I think you are pretty terrific, Kitty."

"Thanks! You say such kind words."

I looked deep into her eyes. She had the most beautiful eyes. And then I got the nerve to ask her this question. "Kitten?"

"Yes, John?"

"Can I kiss you?" I whispered.

"You want to kiss me?"

"Yes, I would love to kiss you. May I?"

We leaned toward each other, and our lips met. I kissed her like before, but this time, she was kissing me and not Mother Nature. It was wonderful. I wished this night would never end. We kissed for what seemed like an eternity, and I did not want to let her go. The kiss ended, and she giggled.

"That was…" She hesitated.

I looked surprised. "Was what?"

She squinted her eyes and said, "Familiar. That kiss seemed familiar to me."

Every muscle in my body was alive and tingling. I knew exactly what she meant by familiar. I had kissed her twice before, and she remembered how those kisses felt. I was in her head and began to worry if I knew what I was setting myself up for.

"Would you like a beer?" she asked, handing one out for me to take.

Knowing that I could not physically drink with her, I said, "No, thank you, I've had enough to drink for one night."

She smiled and said, "Do you mind if I have one? I haven't had enough to drink yet."

"I don't mind. Drink up if you like. It's fine with me."

"John?" she whispered.

"Yes?" My heart was beating out of my chest from the excitement I felt. Just listening to her call out my name made me feel alive again.

"Will you stay with me tonight? It's nice to have someone to talk to. I don't want to be alone."

"Kitten, nothing could keep me from staying with you tonight."

I wanted so badly to give her something that no one else could give her.

"Kitty, look out there."

I pointed out over the ocean. "Can you see them?"

"What am I looking for? I don't see anything." Her eyes panned the open sea.

I rushed out over the ocean; my speed was so quick she did not notice that I had left her side. I pushed in the tide, forced a pod of dolphins toward the shore, and was back at her side in a flash.

"Straight out, do you see them now?"

"Oh, yes! I can see them. John, they're dolphins! Dolphins are swimming right before my very eyes; this is the best night of my life."

She jumped to her feet and began to hop up and down. "I have only seen them once before. I never thought that I would see them again."

I was very pleased with myself. She was happy, and I was at a total loss for words. The only thing I could say was, "They are beautiful, but not as beautiful as you."

"Oh yes, I think they are just about the most beautiful creatures that I have ever laid eyes on in my life. I'm so glad that you are here with me tonight. If you hadn't pointed them out to me, I would have missed them for sure."

"There isn't anyplace else that I could think of that could make me happier than being here with you, Kitten. Thank you for inviting me. I do enjoy your company."

The moon was getting higher in the sky. I pointed out the spectacular constellations and named them as she looked on. She seemed to enjoy my company, and I never wanted this night to end. She pointed out a tree frog that pounced onto the handrail of the tower. She reached out, and this tiny frog jumped straight to her. It clung to her wrist and crawled up her arm.

She smiled and said, "How are you tonight, little friend? Are you lonely?"

I laughed. "You seem to have made a friend."

"I think that animals sense how I feel, and sometimes, they come just when I need them the most. I love when they come into my life. It makes me feel so good inside."

"Do they talk to you, too?"

"No! Don't be silly. Animals can't speak English, but sometimes, I think they know what I am thinking. It's like they know when I need a friend."

"I'll be your friend, and if you ever need me, all you have to do is call out my name, and I promise you I will always be there."

She smiled. "How could you do that? You can't possibly be everyplace."

"Kitty, trust me, if you ever need a friend, I will always be there for you. You can just whisper my name, and I will be there."

I meant what I said, and I was hoping that she would call to me, but spending this time with her was just about the most wonderful thing that could have or has ever happened to me.

"That would be nice, just the thought of someone looking after me. Then I wouldn't have to be alone. I'm so glad that you are here with me tonight."

"I can be with you every night if you want me to."

"Yes, I want you to."

She took a pocketknife out of her purse and scratched our names into the wooden handrail. "I will never forget this night, and this will be our little secret to remind us."

I smiled at her and caressed her face with my fingertips.

She pressed her body against mine, and I covered her with the blanket that she took from the stranger's backyard. We looked out over the ocean, and with every breath she exhaled, I inhaled a bit of her soul. After I held her for few hours, she fell asleep. I did not move a muscle and cried until the sun came up. She had accepted me for who I was, and she wanted me around. My existence could not be more satisfying. The gulls were squawking as they feasted on breakfast, and the loud noise woke Kitten up. She looked around, and I smiled at her.

She stood up quickly and shouted, "John? Where are you, John?"

I was sitting right next to her, but again, she could not see me. How could I have her for my own? Would she ever be able to see me again? I watched as she shook her head.

"Where did he go? Why did he leave?"

I shouted to her, but she could not hear me.

"You said that you would never leave my side. John, where are you?"

I sat next to her the whole morning. She sat and sat. She was waiting for me to come back, but I had never left her side. The drugs had worn off, and she had lost the power of sight.

"Could it have just been a dream? Was it all just a part of the trip? If he went for breakfast, he would have been back by now."

She ran her fingers over the carving and began to cry.

"I thought I found him this time. Why is it that when I meet someone, they always end up being losers or figments of my imagination? Could I have just dreamed it all, or was he really real? Damn mushrooms, I'll never eat them again."

She gathered up her things and climbed down the ladder. I followed close behind, and as she headed toward the water, I dashed ahead to give her a gift. I rushed into the water and found her a beautiful snail shell. She stood at the edge of the water and called my name. I dropped the shell at her feet. She reached down to pick it up and began to cry.

"Why didn't you say goodbye to me before you left, John? If you were real or not, I'm still going to miss you."

She stood there for some time, and all I could do was look on as she continued to look out over the water in silence. What was she thinking? How would I ever be a part of her mortal life? I was becoming lost in all of the questions that I had and fear began to fill my body. Then I heard a shriek in the distance. Kitten heard it, too, and headed over to the disturbing sound. It was a woman. She was standing at the edge of the jetty calling out to anyone who could hear. I raced over to see what the problem was, and when I got there, I noticed that there was a child wedged in between the moss-filled rocks. The woman's frantic attempts to free the child were not working. She herself began to slip and slide into harm's way.

Kitten reached the jetty and climbed up onto the rocks to see if she could be of some assistance, but she too began to slip. That was when I saw it, the light; it was slowly moving toward the child. The waves began to crash all around her, and the tide was coming in quick. Kitten reached her hand out to retrieve the child, but she could not get close enough without putting herself in jeopardy.

"John!" Kitten shouted. "Help, please help us."

The woman shouted as she looked around for some assistance, but there was no one there.

"John Davis, I need you. Please help."

I blew past her, and the wind blew her hair around her face. I slipped in between the rocks around the child and attempted to free her leg from the tight grip it was caught in. Kitten and the woman lay on their stomachs making a chain to reach the child. When Kitten got her hands around the child's arms and pulled, she said, "It's no use; she is wedged in too tight. I can't get her out."

"You have to. You have to save my baby," the woman cried with grief.

"She is really stuck. I can't pull her out. Oh, I wish John were here. John, if you can hear me like you said, please help me save this child."

I pushed with all of my might. The waves continued to crash all around us, and with every blast of water, the child became more at risk of drowning.

"Grab on to me. You can do it. Take my hand!" Kitten yelled to the tiny victim.

The child reached as high as she could, and Kitten got a good hold of her. I waited for the next wave to crash, and I pushed the child again. She was free, and Kitten was scooping her up out of the deadly grasp of the rocks and dragging her out of harm's way. We did it! The child was saved.

"Oh my baby, are you okay?" the scared mother shouted.

"I'm okay, Mommy, I'm okay."

The child was crying and shaking with fear. Kitten and the woman carried the child back onto the beach and flopped down with exhaustion onto the sand.

"Someone call a doctor!" Kitten screamed.

"I think her leg is broken." The mother shouted, "She's not breathing!"

"You stay here, and I'll go get some help."

Kitten jumped to her feet and dashed up to the boardwalk to call for help, screaming bloody murder all the way. I pushed air into the child's lungs. As it passed through my lips, her chest rose up. I could see the hideous light creeping up in the distance. Her time was running out.

She returned with paramedics and looked on as they took the mother and child away in an ambulance. She didn't move a muscle and watched the vehicle until it was clear out of sight. Kitten headed back to the jetty with her head hanging low. She sat on the cool wet sand and looked out over the green rocks. She sifted her fingers through the sand and collected tiny pink stones until the pile spilled out over her fingers.

"Thank you, John, for your help. I don't think the child would have made it if it weren't for you. Was it you? I don't know what to think. Maybe I'm just going crazy. I hope the little girl is all right."

I desperately wanted to hold her in my arms again, like I did last night. I could not bear to be with her any longer. I had to get away. My heart was in utter torture. I headed to the bay.

Chapter Ten

*T*he sun was shining brightly, and the crowd was growing thick. As I reached the boardwalk, I looked out over the sand, and Kitten was still sitting where I had left her. My pace was slow, and I could not get her out of my mind. I continued to look back at her until she was completely out of sight. The night with her was so wonderful; I feared that it would never happen again. I would never again experience her sweet embrace.

I could hear a loud commotion coming from the amusement pier, so I headed over to see what was going on. On the way, I noticed a small dog tied up to the fence that separated the boardwalk from the beach. He was barking at the kids playing Frisbee on the sand below. I did not think much about it until I caught a glimpse of the dreadful light. It was directly below the fence where the dog was jumping. I hopped over to get a closer look, to see whom the light was coming for. Just then, one of the children overthrew the Frisbee, and the dog jumped up onto a bench and over the fence to retrieve it, unknowingly putting himself in harm's way. The children screamed in terror as the little dog swung back and forth, dangling from his noose-like collar.

Quickly, I reached, pulling as hard as I could to free the leash from its hold around the top of the fencepost. The dog dropped directly beside the glowing light and was clear from its deadly grasp. The light faded, and the dog was safe. The children all ran over to see if he was all right. They patted his little head and spoke comforting words of relief as he sniffed them all and wagged his tail.

I wondered how long this would go on, how long would I be bound to this job. My destiny, if that was really what it was, was really getting to me. I was beginning to think that maybe I would never pay my debt for the life that I took so long ago. I wondered how long I would have to wait. The loud commotion was still coming from the pier, and I continued on my way to see what the noise was all about.

There were men scrambling to place barricades, keeping the tourists off of the pier, and at least a dozen men rushing toward the far end of the pier where the roller coaster stood high above the boards. I followed close behind to see what was going on. There were security guards herding onlookers away from the scene, leading them off of the pier and out of harm's way.

One man shouted, "Grab that wench and hold tight."

Another hollered, "Where's the welder? I need him now!"

Racing like a bat out of hell came a bearded man driving a golf cart. He crashed straight into a dumpster and hopped off, gathering his equipment in a hurry, rushing to the man calling out to him.

"Sal, where the hell have you been? Get up here quick. I don't think this track will hold for much longer if you don't spot it now."

I looked up, and there was a large piece of fractured track being held only by a few steel cables attached to a wench. Sal was being hoisted up level to it in a bucket truck. He fired up his welding kit and began to bind the steel together.

"I need more tension on the line!" he shouted.

The men worked together, frantically trying to get the job done. They grunted and groaned, struggling, man against steel, bleeding and sweating through their strenuous task of mending the torn coaster rail. Fire and sparks filled the air, turning the jobsite into a cascade of heat and light. They all worked together to get the job done.

After an hour of fire, sparks, blood, and sweat, the job was complete. The men cheered and hollered, patting each other on the back shouting, "A job well done!" The mayhem was over, and the workers cleaned up their tools, leaving only a small trace of what had transpired. Small, dark burn marks where the hot steel fragments seared the wooden blanks below the coaster rail were all that remained of the work that had been done.

I looked on as the security guards began to remove the barricades allowing the tourists back onto the pier. That was one thing that I had noticed about people on vacation: They never cared what danger awaited them. They could bear witness to defective amusement rides and never think twice about purchasing a ticket for their children to ride what was certain to be an accident just waiting to happen. Just so long as the days away from the home and office were filled with pleasure and mayhem, nothing seemed to faze them. Silly how people are, they will subject themselves to just about anything if there is a slight chance to forget about the everyday, even if it is only for just a few moments. It is remarkable how people of today are selfish and disrespectful.

I looked out over the sea and watched as the light shone brightly while the gulls fed on a school of tiny fish. Then I began to think about Kitten and how I just left her sitting there on the beach all alone. She assisted in the rescue of the child wedged between the rocks, and I could tell that she was truly scared for the child in the way she just sat there looking out over the water. I wondered if she had gone home, or if she was still sitting on the shore pondering the reality of the night that we spent together; was it real or just a fantasy? I was wondering if we would ever have another night together.

My head was in a fog as I headed back to the boardwalk, watching the people spend and lose their money to the shifty carnies that manned the midway. Every year, it was the same as the last: Crackheads, junkies, and boozehounds manned their stands, doing their job of conning tourists out of their money and their innocence. There were clowns pumping balloons to make swords and hats for a small donation of only one dollar. There were balloon hats for as far as the eye could see. These guys must have made a fortune at a hundred balloons for ten dollars at the party store. You cannot go wrong with that kind of mark up. They did everything and all to get the money, and it was not hard to do. Mindless tourists were an easy mark.

I remembered how the beach was in my day: Miles of dunes filled with all sorts of wildlife, no such thing as vacationers then, only fishermen and local families having picnics together. The only woods you could see were the sun-bleached pieces of driftwood scattered around the shore right where the tide had left them. It was spectacular and pristine, free from all of the garbage you find today. Life was so much simpler back then. I was not really sure how the earth had held out this long, considering how it was raped and abused by everyone. But it still took my breath away every time I looked out over the ocean at the sunrise or watched as the sunset danced on the gentle waves of the bay. I knew in my heart that there was a God when I saw these things, just like I knew in my heart that Kitten and I were meant to be together. I was drawn to her, and she drove my ambition like fuel on a fire.

I headed down to the end of the boardwalk and figured that I would shoot over to Kitten's apartment to see if she had made it home and was okay. There were a lot of motorcycles entering town for the annual seaside equivalent of Daytona Beach. The loud pipes screamed through the streets, American flags waved proudly, and the theme bikes were in full force. Women dressed in leather shorts and bandanna tops straddled the hips of their knights as they cruised the main drag looking for the best place to park their awesome machines.

I loved bike week, catching rides on motorcycles was one of my most favorite rides of all.

I could hover in their wake of wind from one end of the island to the other. Many bikes meant many fights. Gang members and tribesmen killing each other over pool games or their present flop whores, this would keep me plenty busy for the next few days. Police would be out in full force, too, even before the sun went down tonight, and I could smell danger in the air.

The competition was hot and so was the tension. There were so many beautiful bikes. It was hard for anyone to choose the best from all the bikes that were there. The bars loved the action, being able to sell so much more liquor because there were fewer children and more drunks spending money. The poor tourists who didn't know that seaside held bike week would be in for more than they bargained for on this vacation. There were a lot more thefts going on due to the fact that bikers were more likely to pick pockets than the normal crowd that came down to the shore during the season. I could feel the air growing so thick with excitement you could cut it with a knife. I was going to be very busy tonight.

One of the cable stations' music clubs was setting up a big beach party to be televised live from the boardwalk beach house. I watched as the TV crew began to set up the equipment. There were seven guys unloading a large tractor-trailer full of speakers and cables. Cameras and banners were being hoisted atop of scaffolding in preparation for the broadcast.

The tourists began to gather around trying to get a free wristband so they could have their five minutes of fame and have their faces flashed across the country via satellite. The security guards were only passing out wristbands to young men and women with perfectly chiseled bodies. I watched as chubby girls and pimply-faced boys were turned away while only the beautiful were granted admission. There did not seem to be a higher standard when it came to TV. Beautiful people were number one.

I enjoyed watching the young ladies jumping up and down in their little bikinis trying to get the attention of anyone working the gate. It was like viewing the wiggly water balloons game. It was beautiful, but out of the corner of my eye, there it was, the hellish green light glowing for some unsuspecting victim.

The sound of twisting metal and the creak of over-weighted riggings became louder as I approached the end of the stage. Security had its hands full with all the young kids attempting to gain access to the site and was unable to prevent those who were climbing the camera scaffolding from doing so.

I could not believe my eyes. These kids were pushing the limit of weight the equipment could hold, and from the sound of it, it wouldn't be long before the inevitable would transpire.

There was not much that I could do to prevent the tragedy from happening. I darted over to the tower that was in trouble and harnessed one of the large banners around the back of it to support the weight, then rushed up to the extra police that were on staff to see if I could get some help.

I went over to a female patrolman and shouted into her ear as loudly as I could. "The tower is falling! Do something!" It took a few tries, but she finally looked up and witnessed the stress level on the overloaded scaffold and called to some other cops that were standing around to come and help her.

They rushed over to the scene and ordered the band to stop playing. One officer grabbed the microphone and demanded that people begin to file out of the stage area immediately, and the other cops worked the crowd that was on the beach, clearing the area just in case the equipment spilled out onto the beach.

The band was escorted off the stage and into the beach house, and the crowd became ruthless. Everyone started pushing toward the stage. I could hear the police radios calling out for backup, and you could see the fear beginning to show on the faces of everyone subject to the situation.

I prevented a fatality by pulling one teenager under the stage just before part of the support beam would have landed on her head. She would have been crushed for sure if I had not grabbed her leg when I did. I could see the light again, shining brightly over by the tower. As I approached the area, there were kids fighting and throwing pieces of the equipment into the crowd.

A large, middle-aged man was hanging onto the edge of the stage and leaning over to climb the handrail when it happened. The stage slipped off the support beam and slid directly into the tower, causing it to plummet onto the crowd. There was nothing that I could do to prevent it from crushing on the unsuspecting victims below. The light shone bright all around me. I could not do a thing to change what was happening; their fate was set.

The sand wafted up and around, filling the air with a manic hissing sound. The evidence was clear that many would die today. As the cloud settled, bodies were strewn, beaten and bloody. Crushed, unrecognizable mounds of flesh lay about the mangled bandstand as horrified onlookers wept with anguish.

Panicked parents began to gather around calling out to find their children, and slowly it became evident that some would not be going home today. Workers began to disassemble the blood-stained stressed metal, piece by piece as the paramedics scrambled to assist those who were still showing signs of life.

It was pure pandemonium. I looked around at the sad and sorry faces, and only one person came to mind after all of this chaos: Kitten. Where was she, was she okay? I looked around to see if my services were needed, but my work here was done. I needed a vacation from all this carnage. I was beginning to feel sick, and my head was spinning. I headed down to the bay.

I figured that I would walk past the old lady's house to see if Kitten was around, and when I got there, I could smell cakes and pies cooking in the kitchen. I walked over to the window and peered in hoping to see Kitten sitting at the table, but she was not there. I heard someone talking so I took a walk around back to see who it was. As I turned the corner, I couldn't believe my eyes. It was the most beautiful garden that I could have ever had the pleasure of being in. Sand pathways led to small sections, each with its own theme. I could hear the sound of running water, and large shadows of tall wildflowers cascaded over the sandy ground. It was absolutely spectacular.

I watched as the fish swam around in the pond, avoiding the rushing water that fell from the tall pedestal of rocks and seashells. It was so surreal I almost forgot where I was for a moment.

"So you came back?" a voice said, as food pellets fell into the pond with a "kerplunk," making tiny ripples in its cool water.

I turned my head, and there she was, the transparent woman who appeared to be happy at the fact that I knew she was addressing me.

"How is it possible? How do you see?"

"With my eyes, honey. Now, what are your intentions with Puss? She is a kind girl, but if she knew that you were following her around, I don't think she would approve. I'm not sure that I approve."

"She is wonderful. I love her. I did not mean for it to be this way. I can't help myself. She is everything that I could ever want in a wife."

"A wife? You forget where you are, John."

I looked at her and shook my head. "How do you know my name?"

"I know a lot of things; just because I'm old doesn't mean that I don't know what is going on, you know. I see the way you look at her. I can hear the blood pumping through your heart for her. I find that to be a dead giveaway, you know."

"What am I supposed to do? I am drawn to her. She is like my missing piece."

"Where do you come from, John? What is your full given name? It certainly isn't just John, now is it?"

The woman smiled at me with an inviting grin. I wasn't sure what to make of it. She reached for my arm, and before she could grab it, I pulled away.

"Do you know where Kitten is today?"

She smiled and motioned for me to follow her.

"If you want something from the world, then remember this: when you take something from this world, whatever it may be, you had better expect to have something taken from you in return. Nature has a real strange way of balancing out. How do you think you got yourself into this mess in the first place? Remember, you are here for her. Don't lose track of your work, though. You really need to concentrate; you're missing all of the signs."

"Is she really my soul mate?"

"Oh, I see that you were paying attention, good; I'm glad that someone is listening. I'm getting tired of people thinking that I'm off my rocker. I know what is going on in the world. You just look after her; she needs all the help she can get. Oh, watch out for Devin. He is a crafty one. She is always getting into trouble with that one. She seems to be in some sort of trouble as we speak. She needs you now more than ever before. Stay close to her; you may be her only chance." She was looking deeply into my eyes.

"What do you mean 'her only chance'? Chance at what? Why? What is going to happen?"

"Oh, sweetie, I never get the whole picture. I never see the whole picture, but I do know that there is trouble brewing, and it would be a shame to have Kitty be alone when it comes. Just be aware, things are never what they seem to be. Keep a watchful eye on her friends. I don't trust many of them around my Puss."

"I don't care much for most of the people Kitten consorts with. She deserves better. I'm not sure if I am even worthy to just be around her."

"You just do what you do best, and keep out of trouble, and everything will be fine. You will know what to do when the time is right. Now get going, she'll need you shortly, and you don't want to be late."

She smiled and pushed me toward the sandy path leading out of the yard. "Now don't you be a stranger. I want to see you again, you hear?"

I wandered out to the street pondering what just happened in there. The woman was a little scary. What was I supposed to do now? I headed over toward her house hoping to find her safe when I arrived. My hands were shaking; I wondered if Kitten was really in danger. The walk over to the apartment seemed to take forever, and the bustle of tourists packing up for the long ride home was becoming very distracting to me, not to mention the hellish glow of light directly ahead at the intersection.

I could hear the sound of hoof beats bounding so I rushed to see what could possibly be making such a sound. After hopping up onto a tree branch to get a better view, it all became quite clear what was going on. He seemed to be running for his life, chest heaving and legs moving just as fast as they could carry him. I could not make out his face; it was just a blur as he brushed the wind past me. Behind and gaining fast came a riled bunch trampling after the terrified boy, only a few strides away from the kill as they seemed to be gaining faster.

Filling the air behind me, I could hear the sound of screeching tires coming around the corner and down the block. As the boy headed toward the glowing light, I hurried to get to the spot before he did, but the car came to a halt directly in the light, and it disappeared.

"Hurry up and get in!" shouted the driver, waving him in.

The guy seemed to fly; he dove into the air and directly into the passenger window of the car, and it sped off leaving the hunters in a cloud of burnt rubber and asphalt. They choked and waved their arms frantically before them, attempting to muster up some clean air to breathe. But before the air could clear, the car was completely out of sight. I thought I would tag along for a ride on the back draft of the vehicle and see what the fuss was all about. I was curious to see just what was going on with this guy.

The window was down which made for easy entry to the back seat. As I slipped into the window, I recognized the face. It was Devin, that little rat. I wondered what he was up to now. The driver was not familiar to me. In fact, I knew I had never seen him before. His hair was long and stringy, and he had a few really bad tattoos on his bony, milk-white arms.

"Dude, that was awesome! I thought you were going to be killed."

"If they would have caught me, I would have been. What took you so long? You left me, you dink. What the fuck were you thinking?"

"I needed to get some papers, man. I was only gone for like a minute."

"I told you to stay put, asshole. That means don't go anyplace."

"Sorry, dude, that was cool how you jumped into the car. Where did you learn to do that shit?"

"Hey, when you're running for your life, you do what you gotta do. You know what I mean. Besides, if you would have just listened to me in the first place, this never would have happened. He sighed. "Take the next left, and slow down its coming up soon."

"Okay, man, I hear ya. Hey, is that hot piece of ass going to let us lay low at her place?"

"Yo, watch how you talk about her, man; she's my woman."

"Yeah, but she still has a hot ass."

All I could think about was the light and how I wished it would have caught Devin. I wondered if I would have known that it was Devin running and the light hadn't disappeared, if I would have had the power to intervene with his fate. Just another question I had no answer to.

"Don't be talking shit about my woman, fuck-head. I swear I'll kill you. The house is coming up. Turn off the radio, and shut the fuck up."

"You're the boss."

The rage began to build inside me. I imagined my fist crashing into his face, forcing the blood to flow. The feeling of complete and total release grew. The car came to a halt in the driveway.

"Now keep your mouth shut; don't let on that anything is wrong, and it will be cool. Understand?" He reached over and slapped him upside his head. "Do you understand what I'm saying? Don't fuck this up."

"When do we split the booty? You're not giving her any, are you?"

"That's my business, fucko; you only gave me a ride. You'll get yours; don't worry, but when I say so and no sooner. Ya got me?" Devin was grabbing at the guy and holding his shirt, shaking it back and forth stretching it out at the neck. "Ya got me?"

"Yeah, dude. I got you. It's cool. I'm cool."

"Okay, remember what I said. Now be cool." Devin looked at his reflection in the side-view mirror and pushed his hands across his head to fix his hair.

They gathered up their things and headed to the stairway. I was praying that Kitten was not home, but no sooner did I think it, the door swung open, and Kitty peeked her head out.

"Oh no, no way, Devin, you guys have to leave. Get the hell out of here."

She slammed the door and locked it just as he darted toward her. I was so proud of her. It made me laugh to see Devin standing there begging her to open up. She stood her ground and kept the locked door between them.

"Oh, come on, baby. I haven't seen you, and I miss you. Please open the door. Paulie needs to use the bathroom. Come on, baby; I've been in the car for like two hours. I have to use the bathroom, too."

"Let him piss behind the garage!" she shouted.

He frantically knocked on the door, begging and pleading for her to give in to him. I could hear her talking to someone, but I could not tell to whom.

"You better get the hell out of here if you know what's good for you. I mean it, Devin, go away."

"You wouldn't call the cops, baby. I know you too well. You don't want me to get locked up. Now please open the door."

Paulie went back to the car and grabbed a beer out of the back seat.

"Why do you bother with this chick, Devin? Let's go over to that girl Kathy's house. She's hot, and her best friend likes you. This ho isn't going to open the door."

"Don't fuckin' call her a ho, you asshole."

Devin headed toward him in a rage, and just as he was about to connect, Ed came tearing up the driveway. With screeching tires, the car came to a halt. Ed got out and smiled at the boys.

"Well, well, well, look what we have here. Hi guys, how ya doin'?"

"Listen, Ed, I don't want any trouble. I was just coming to see Kitty; that's all, man. I'm telling you."

Devin circled the car, and Ed was slowly following him. Paulie took a few steps back and leaned up against the fence. I could see Kitten peering out the widow of her apartment with a worried look on her face.

"I know. How do you think I got here so quick? Did you forget what I told you? You know all that dope you use is killing your brain, kid. Now get your friend and get the hell out of here before I do something to you that I'm probably going to regret letting Kitty witness. And don't let me catch you here again." You could hear his teeth grinding behind his words.

"Come on, Devin, she isn't worth it. Let's get the hell out of here."

"Get in the car numb nuts," he ordered.

Devin walked over to the house and looked up at the window. He opened up his arms and held them out for Kitty to see.

"Do you really want me to go? Because if you do, I'll leave now. I really don't want to leave without giving you a present."

"Get the hell out of here, kid. You have to the count of five to vanish, or I'm calling my buddies to come and take you where no one will ever find you. I'm moving my car. You had better be gone before I get back into the bottom of the driveway."

"Listen, baby, I'm going to put your present in the mailbox; just take it. You know that I love you. If you change your mind, you know where to find me, baby."

Kitten peeked out at the driveway, and Devin got into the car. She watched as it backed out of the driveway. Ed pulled back in, and Devin, as promised, placed something into the mailbox for her.

Ed got out of the car and shook his head at Kitty up in the window. She smiled at him and unlocked the door.

"Thanks for coming over so quick. I'm really sorry about that. I just didn't know what else to do."

"Listen, babe, I told you before, and I'll tell you again, I'm here for you whenever you need me. Call me anytime you need me. Now what's on your agenda for tonight?"

"Well, I thought I would go to the bar. Are you going out tonight?" She lifted one eyebrow.

"Yeah, I gotta make some money for my next pickup."

"Okay, then I'll see you later. Thanks again."

"Behave yourself, and I just might have a job for you."

She smiled at him and gave him a hug. I was so happy that she had Ed for a friend. He could help her in ways that I couldn't. He was a good ally to have. It made me feel more at ease knowing that he had her back.

"So, do you have anything on you? I'll pay you later tonight."

"No sweat, baby. I got something for you. Come on, I think you are going to like it."

Ed reached into his glove compartment and pulled out a package. He reached his hand into it and pulled out a few small packages, shook them in his hand as if they were dice, and smiled at her.

"Now take it easy, this shit is potent. Use it sparingly. You better have a lot of it left when I see you tonight." He got into his car and waved goodbye. "Are you going to be okay?"

"Yes, I'll be fine. Now go. I'll see you later."

Ed peeled out of the driveway and honked the horn as he sped down the block. She waved goodbye to him, and when his car was out of sight, she looked in her hand with a smile on her face. She seemed very excited as she trotted up the steps and back into her apartment. I hated how happy she would get whenever she got her hands on some drugs.

The apartment was a mess; it was evident that she had not done anything domestic in some time. After locking the door, she put her drugs on the nightstand and fell on the bed like a stone. She just lay there like a statue for over an hour staring up at the ceiling with a blank look on her face. I looked on in wonder. What could be going on inside her mind. As I stood there watching her, tears began to run from her eyes. She did not mutter a word; not a sound passed her lips.

Her breathing never changed its pace. What could be going through her mind? How strange it was to witness such a spectacle. I could see the pain in her eyes, far too much pain for such a beautiful young woman. I yearned to hold her in my arms, to let her know that I was here and had no intentions in leaving anytime soon.

I could not bear to watch her agony any longer. I concentrated on making her hear me, and when I felt the time was right, I hollered into her ear.

"Get up and clean!"

She popped her head up and looked around. "Who's there? What do you want?"

Kitten rubbed her head and put her feet on the floor. She reached into the nightstand, pulled out one of the packages, and searched her pockets for a bill to roll. I knew the drill and felt a tremendous amount of sadness come over me. She jammed the bill into the package and took a deep sniff, inhaling the drugs into her nose. She placed the package on the table and leaned back against the headboard. Kitten just sat there for a few minutes with her eyes closed.

"Well, I guess I should start cleaning."

With that, she worked hard for about two hours. She was like a blur before my very eyes. I had never seen a person clean up with such speed. She started with the garbage. By the time she was done, the large black bag was filled to capacity. Dusting would be the next task she would tackle, and in no time, the entire apartment was spick and span. The only thing that I can say about the use of drugs is that if you have a job to do, you get it done and you get it done quickly. It was incredible to watch; her eyes focused, and her mind was set. The filth and grime did not stand a chance.

Chapter Eleven

*S*he opened the door and called out. "Azreal! Here kitty, come on, baby!"

Azreal came running up the steps, stopping just at the open doorway.

"Where have you been all day?"

"Meow!"

The cat rubbed its body against her legs and purred loudly. They both made their way into the kitchen. Kitten prepared a feast fit for a cat. As she placed the bowl on the floor, I could see the look in the cat's eyes; someone was coming. No sooner did I notice the cat, then in came a serious-looking man. He was over six feet tall with the rugged looks of a blue-collar man. It was evident that this man wasn't there for a friendly visit.

"Who the hell are you?" Kitten screamed out and ran toward the bedroom. She slammed the door and began to fumble around in the closet.

"Open the door," the man demanded.

"No fucking way!"

"Let's go, girly. Open the door."

"No!"

I did not know what to do. Who was this guy, and what the hell was he going to do to Kitten? He reached into his shirt pocket and pulled out a slender rod of some type and slipped it into the keyhole. After a few jiggles, the lock clicked open, and he entered the room.

Kitten was nowhere in sight. I walked around the room searching for her, but I could not see where she was hiding.

The stranger opened the closet door and pushed the hanging clothes to one side. As the back of the closet was revealed, I could see my terrified girl, shaking like a leaf. She fell to her knees.

"Please don't hurt me! I'll do anything you want; just please don't hurt me."

She pleaded for her life, and the sweat began to bead up on her forehead. The man grabbed her by the arm and lifted her to her feet. I could see her squirming to get away, but this guy was just too big. He pinned her up against the wall, looked deeply into her eyes.

"You know why I'm here? Now why don't you just give me the keys, and I'll get the hell out of here."

"Keys, what keys? I don't know what you're talking about. I don't have any keys." She pulled a set of keys from her pocket.

"These are the only keys that I have. Who are you?"

The thug snatched the keys from her hand and smiled. "Now come with me," he ordered and pushed her toward the door.

She attempted to retrieve the keys, but she just was not big enough to match this man. He was very tall with muscles upon muscles as he led her down the stairs to the garage. He held her arm tightly, preventing her from getting away from his grasp.

"Now which one opens the door?" he snarled.

She pointed to the gold key, and her head hung low. She turned toward him with a cowed look.

"What do you want with my garage, asshole? You can't have my car! My car's not finished; it doesn't even run. Now let me go!"

"You know what I want. I came for the car. It had better be here."

"I don't know what you are talking about. What car?"

He swung open the garage door and demanded that she turn on the lights. When the lights went on, he looked around and shouted, "Where the fuck is the car? Oh, you put it someplace else, did you? Now tell me where it is. I want it now. Where is it? If you don't make with the car, I'm going to have to hurt you. I don't want to have to hurt you."

He pulled her close to him, and at this moment, all I could think of doing was jumping on his back and kicking the living hell out of him. It was times like these I wished that I was mortal. I stayed close to Kitten; if he had harmed her, I would have found a way to kill him. She shook her head.

"Look, I don't know what car you're talking about. It's obviously not here. What do you want from me? You obviously have the wrong garage. Sorry, but I can't help you. Now get the fuck off of me, you dirty bastard!"

"Oh no, sweetheart, you're gonna tell me where the Vet is, and then we're gonna go and get it. That's what you're going to do. You're gonna do exactly what I say."

"What Vet?"

I could tell that it was all coming back to her. I could see the look in her eyes. She knew just what he was talking about, and it showed on her face. Anyone could see that.

"I know that you know where it is, now take me to it."

"Okay, I know where I took it that night, but I'm not sure if it's gonna be there. I have to make a call first."

She reached into her pocket and pulled out the cell phone. "Ed, what's up? ...Hey, remember that Vet we picked up the other day?" There was silence. "What did you do with it? Yeah,...but where is it now?"

I could hear the fear in her voice. She was not getting the answer she wanted. The hostile man held his fist up and aimed it at Kitten.

"Listen, Ed, I really need to know where that car is...Okay, so bring it over here, or tell me where it is, and I'll go pick it up to save you the trip." She hung up the phone and looked at the man. "He said that he would call me back soon to let me know where the car was taken."

"You had better hope that he does, or I'm taking it out on that sweet ass of yours, honey."

They exited the garage and headed back up to the apartment. I was not sure what to do about the situation. All I really could do was sit idly by and see what happened next. He stared at her ass as he followed closely behind her.

"So if I get you the car, you'll leave?"

"Yep!"

"And you'll never come back?"

"Never."

"Hey, I was just doing my job. It's nothing personal; it's just business," she explained.

"So is what I do. It's just business," he agreed.

He looked at her with heartless eyes. I could see that he had more than the car on his mind. I thought Kitten was beginning to pick up on it as well, because she began to pull away from him. Her hands began to fidget, and she began to get a little jumpy. She smiled at him with those eager eyes that seemed to say, "take me." He stood up and looked at her, reaching out to her and pulling her close to him with brutal speed.

"Do you really have to stay here till I get the car?"

"Yes, I do."

"What if it takes all night, then what?"

"I guess we'll just have to see what happens, but I'm not going anywhere without that car."

She slid her arms up his chest and around his shoulders. Pressing her lips tightly against his, she kissed him long and hard. Leaning her body strongly against his, she continued to kiss him passionately with no concern of the consequences that lay ahead. I could not bear to watch Kitten working it with this thug. What a waste of good kisses! It should have been me on the receiving end of Kitten's kisses.

He lifted her up and carried her off to the bedroom. As the door closed, my heart sank, and I waited outside on the steps for over an hour. It was one of the longest hours that I had ever waited before. I could hear the screams coming from the window, and I held my hands over my ears to keep those dreadful sounds from entering. My heart was breaking, and if I were mortal, I would go in there and kick the living shit out of that guy. How could she let him take her like that? What was she thinking?

I heard a car pulling up to the house, and that was when I saw him. It was Ed; he had come to save the day again. Man, did I love this guy! He tiptoed up the steps and into the apartment. When he did not see anyone, he slowly headed toward the bedroom door. Standing there for a few seconds just listening, he reached into his pocket and pulled out a gun.

Throwing open the door, he hollered, "Freeze, nobody move!"

The two of them were like deer in the path of headlights, frozen with a petrified look in their eyes.

"What the fuck?

"Nice! Hey, Kitty, new look for you. Did you miss me?" Ed snarled.

"What took you so long?" she shouted.

"I can see you don't need me. Should I go?"

"What the fuck is going on around here? Who the hell are you?" the man said, surprised.

They both reached for their clothing. Kitten stumbled off of the bed and ran behind Ed. All of us looked on as her breasts were bouncing up and down. It was quite hypnotic, and they were beautiful.

"Well, kid, you still got it," Ed said with a smile on his face. "Why don't you ever get naked for me?"

"Oh, shut up! You know why I did this, stupid." She slapped his arm.

"Oh, just for me. You know that I love you even if you don't show me your tits. Now, as for you, Mister Naked, in my friend's bed, who do you think you are coming in here threatening a young woman in her home like this? I'll give you one minute to convince me not to kill you. If I like what I hear, you live. If not, you'll be eating lunch through a tube."

He pointed the gun at him, and Kitten got dressed and went into the living room to sit down.

"Look, dude, I was told to come to this apartment and pick up a Vet that was supposed to be in the garage. Cut and dry, that is it. How was I supposed to know that a hot sexpot like her would be here to fuck the shit out of me? She wanted me, dude. She wanted me."

Ed picked him up and slammed him against the wall with such force the mirror behind the door cracked. Large pulsating veins began to bulge out of Ed's neck and forearms. He snarled and snorted with flem flying, "I'll kill you, motherfucker!"

"Okay, okay! Tony G, that's the guy you want. He gave me two hundred bucks to pick up the Vet."

"What about the girl?" Ed squeezed a little harder.

"He said not to let her go. I was to bring her and the car back to the dock."

"Get your clothes on, scumbag; we have some details to go over." Ed waved the gun a little and pointed to his eye. "I'm watching you; don't even think about doing something stupid." Ed looked back at Kitten with the frightened brother face of concern. "What are you crazy? What the hell were you thinking anyway? This guy is a scumbag."

"Look, I knew it was going to take a few minutes for you to get over here, and I didn't want it to get ugly, so I figured consensual sex is much more enjoyable than rape. I chose to jump him before he could jump me. Why? Do you have a better solution as to what I should have done?"

"Girl, you need help!"

Ed smiled, and Kitten laughed out loud. She jumped on his lap and gave him a loving hug and kiss. She nuzzled her face close to him and whispered into his ear.

"You don't mind seeing me naked, so what's the problem?"

"No problem at all, baby. You can get naked in front of me anytime you like."

From out of the bedroom, the perpetrator remarked with snippiness in his tone, "Yeah, me too, foxy; anytime you want."

Ed moved Kitty aside and grabbed hold of the guy, pulled him out of the bedroom, and flung him onto the couch. "Now sit and stay! Tell me where this dock is you are supposed to deliver the girl to. I want to know how many people are going to be at this little party tonight and how heavy are they armed?"

"Look, dude, I don't know any of the details. All I know is that I'm supposed to meet them there at one AM in the back building. They didn't tell me anything else."

"Where is Tony now?" Ed asked.

"I don't know."

Ed leaned into him and jammed the gun hard into his ribs.

"The bar! Maybe at the bar, I'm telling you, I don't know anything."

Ed handed the gun to Kitten and looked deeply into her eyes very seriously. "Keep an eye on him. I'll be right back, but be careful, the safety is off."

"Where are you going?"

"I need to get some rope. We can't leave him here, and we can't take him with us."

"Wait here! Are you nuts?" she yelped. Kitten handed him back the gun and skipped off into the bedroom. "I got something better then rope, baby. Here, try these."

She skipped back out into the living room, swinging two pairs of shiny handcuffs between her fingers.

"I don't even want to know why you have those, honey," Ed laughed and motioned for the man to get up and come with him. "Now, where to put you?" Ed snarled.

"I know where we can put him. Come on." She motioned for him to follow.

Kitten ran down the steps to the garage, and Ed followed, dragging the man behind him by the scruff of his neck.

As Kitten opened the door, she said, "We can shackle him to this transmission. It's way too heavy for him to carry, and if we turn on the radio, no one will hear him calling for help."

The guy looked at her with a confused expression. Kitten hopped up and down, proud of her shackling idea. She giggled and shook her butt in his face. "Don't worry, we'll come back, and let you go. Just need to keep you on ice for a while. Besides you owe me."

She slipped her thumbs under the elastic of her underpants and pulled them up high on her hips. Ed clipped the cuffs around his wrists and just for giggles, hooked one to his ankle and tethered him to the red stack toolkit. The man was a sorry sight, but I was relieved that Kitten was okay.

"Don't go anywhere. We'll be back in a few hours."

Kitten turned on the radio and put a bottle of water on the floor next to him, reached into her pocket, and pulled out a small key.

She slipped it into the large toolbox and said, "Can't have you using my tools to escape, now can I?" Then she tossed a pack of cigarettes onto the counter and laughed.

"See ya later, alligator!"

They locked the door and walked arm in arm to the car, never saying a word to one another. I was amazed at the relationship they had. In fact, I was a bit jealous. I wanted to be the one who protected her. She didn't even call out my name. I told her that I would always be there, and she had forgotten all about it, but what good would it have done if she had called for me? I was there, and I couldn't do anything. She still slept with him. I longed to hear her call out my name again. She never gave it a second thought. I sat back in the large rear seat, looking up at the sky through the tinted glass as the trees zoomed by. I wondered just how bad this fiasco was going to get and if they knew what they were getting themselves into.

"I want more money for that job now, man." Kitten smiled and tapped Ed on the leg. He nodded and burst out into hysterics.

"I didn't tell you to go in that bar and let them see your face. You did that to yourself. All you had to do was hotwire it and that would have been that, but no, you had to show off your talents and be the pro by getting the keys. This is all on you, baby, all on you."

"Yeah, but why would she have me held at gunpoint for that stupid car? It doesn't make sense. Think about it. How much could she owe on the car? She probably paid that much for the guy we left in the garage. There has got to be something more to it."

"Maybe there is something in the car. I say we go and check it out."

"I thought you didn't know where the car was. What's the story?"

"I know where it is; I just didn't want to say anything over the phone, and I needed leverage for your body, honey."

"Nice. Now where are we going?" She pulled the hair from her face. "Where?"

"Sit back and relax. Here, smoke this. I'm sure it will calm you down a bit. It's kind of a ride to get there."

Kitten pushed it into the cigarette lighter and placed the joint between her lips, smiling as she slid into the seat. She stared out the window at the mile markers as her fingers fluttered through the wind from the car's motion. Her hair was floating on the same wind, and she was beautiful. I could not keep my eyes off of her. I thought about Beatrice and what she had told me. I had not assisted Kitten since

I accompanied her earlier, and I was sure that the worst was yet to come. My mind could only imagine what could possibly be waiting for us when we arrived.

We turned off a scarcely lit exit. The road was blanketed with large pine trees, and all we could see were the tiny reflectors that lined the center of the road. Kitten dozed off, and her chest was heaving with every breath she took. The bumps in the road made for quite a display. Again, I couldn't take my eyes off of her. I could see Ed rubbing his thigh as he stared at her breasts, watching them jiggle about. I could see him begin to salivate at the thought of having her for his own. I had to admit, they were spectacular, and the same thought went straight to my groin, as it did Ed's, because he was squeezing his stuff and undressing her with his eyes. Then, in a flash, Ed was slamming on the brakes and jerking the wheel hard to the left to make an emergency U-turn in the middle of the road. The jolt shook Kitten up pretty badly, and she had a frightened look on her face.

"What the fuck is going on? Is everyone okay? Did you hit something?"

She was panicked and began rubbing herself, checking to see if she herself had sustained any injuries.

"Sorry, babe, I missed the turnoff. We're okay, and no, I didn't hit anything."

"Where are we?" she demanded to know.

"We're almost there. I'm going in the back. I don't want them to know we are coming."

"I thought these guys were your friends. What's all the fuss about?"

"Look, honey, these guys are into a lot of shit I don't even want to know about. I would hate for us to walk in on something that is absolutely none of our business. It's just best to lay low for now. Don't you think?"

"Oh shit, Ed. What did you get me into with this damn car? I'm too young to die; I haven't even seen the Grand Canyon, not to mention Mount Rushmore. What about the redwood forests? I need to drive my car through a giant red tree, Ed. I have to do it before I die. I don't want to die."

"Listen, girl, you have nothing to worry about. Everything is going to be cool. Trust me."

"Yeah, I know, you're a trained professional."

Kitten giggled as she twisted her butt back and forth in her seat. Ed gave her a light shove. She rocked in her seat and grabbed hold of her breasts to keep them from bouncing about the car. Ed laughed and leered at her, watching as her grip cupped her luscious, jiggling breasts.

"Could you find a road with more bumps? I don't think this one has enough bumps in it, do you? What are you trying to do, kill me?"

"Please be quiet. We are almost there. I don't know who will be here. Just give me a minute."

Ed parked the car and headed into the woods.

"Not without me, you don't. I'm coming with you."

"Okay, but be quiet, and the next time I tell you to wait, you had better wait. Do you understand?"

"Yes, Daddy, I understand."

She looked at him with a fiendish grin, knowing that she was a spoiled brat who could have just about anything she wanted. There was a game path, and we followed it for about three hundred feet until we came to a tin garage. As we walked around to the front, there were rows of tin garages, and the surroundings were that of a junkyard. Stripped cars were everywhere, only they were not old junk cars; they were new cars. Ed pointed to the Vet parked beside one of the garages. Kitten smiled at him and headed toward the car.

Ed whispered, "Where are you going?"

Kitten crouched beside him and explained, "I'll get the car. You clear the path. They'll never know I was here. This car is quiet, and I can get out. I have to take the main road. Just make sure and keep them from seeing me."

Kitten tiptoed to the car, ducking behind a stack of tires. She was smiling to the point of fracture as she peeked around the tire stack. It was clear she was enjoying herself. You could tell this was one of the things that she did best. Danger seemed to enhance her beauty, and the excitement began to build low in my body.

Ed headed to the garage where there seemed to be some activity. It was the only one that had lights on. Peeking into one of the windows, he put up a hand warning Kitten to wait for his signal. Now Kitten did not usually follow instructions. She was a hardheaded girl who liked to have fun and get what she wanted, no matter what the consequences may be. Her feet were popping up and down. She was anxious. I kept a sharp eye out for danger; the light seemed to be at bay, but for how long? I wondered.

Ed moved slowly around the building, checking out every crack he could put his eye to. Kitten slid the metal rod between the window and the rubber weather stripping of the driver-side door. Looking around, she jiggled it back and forth, searching for the mechanism that would set the lock free. She looked over at Ed and raised an eyebrow. Ed shook his head and pointed a finger at her reminding her to stay put.

As she slid the rod, I heard it beginning to catch onto something, and so did she, because she grasped the rod tightly, and with a hard tug, she jerked that lock open. A look of utter bliss was painted all over her face with a smile that traveled ear to ear; she was glowing. She waved her arms in the air, doing the wave all by herself. She was looking very satisfied with herself. There was nothing that this woman could not do. She was marvelous, and I wanted her now more than ever before.

Ed looked at her display and laughed, body shaking from the pure hysteria of it all. Kitten slowly opened the shiny red door. She squinted her eyes as it opened one inch at a time. She slipped into the seat and under the steering wheel. Reaching up under the dashboard, she pulled out a roll of multicolored wires. Holding a small flashlight between her lips, she aimed it at the roll and fingered through the wires. She came to a red wire and then a black one, and she clipped them both in half with a nail clipper, exposing the shiny bare wires. As she struck the black wire to the red wire, the car's electrical system began to work, and with the final strike, the car was running. Kitten quickly sat up in the seat and looked around to see if anyone had heard what she had just done, but the coast was clear, and all seemed to be well.

Ed waved for Kitten to head out of the driveway. She smiled and waved to him as she rolled the car out of the parking space. She looked all around, out of every window and in every mirror to see if anyone had witnessed what she was doing. She pulled out to the end of the driveway and waved to Ed, letting him know she was okay. Ed waved back to her and headed out back to the trail. Kitten was long gone, so I hitched a ride back with Ed.

We got back to the car, and Ed urinated on a tree and belched. He walked around to the back of the car and opened the trunk. I walked around the back of him, and I could not believe my eyes when I saw what he had inside. There was an arsenal of firearms and a duffle bag. He reached in and pulled out the bag. As he got into the car, he lit a joint, put the key in the ignition, headed out, turning the car around, and peeled out, leaving a cloud of dust floating in the breeze. He raced down the road and pulled out onto the highway, tearing up the pavement with his screeching tires.

As we came to the intersection, there she was, parked in the gas station leaning into the car for something. Ed pulled in next to her and got out of the car.

"What the hell are you doing? Why did you stop?"

"The tank was empty, and I didn't want to run out of gas, and I have no money, or I would have left already. What took you so long?"

"I had to make a pit stop, baby. Now get in the car, we have to go. I'll meet you at the garage. Don't get pulled over. Stick to the back roads when we get back to town. I don't want anyone to see this car. We don't need any problems, honey. Just stick to the plan."

"You got it, baby, back roads, not a problem. I'll stick to the plan."

Kitten got into the car and tore out of the station while Ed paid for the gas. As he handed the attendant a ten-dollar bill, the man looked Ed in the eye and said, "That was a hot piece off ass; I would love to tap that shit, man. How do you do it? I'll give you one hundred bucks if you let me mount that little piece of ass. She is fine!"

"Watch your mouth, before I put a fist in it, punk."

Ed snarled at the guy and left him in a cloud of blacktop and smoke. My eyes were panning the area for the little red corvette. I was eager to see where Kitten was. I needed to know that she was all right. We drove for some time, and when we got back to town, Ed headed back to Kitten's house. Was this where they were going to meet? Why would they meet here? As we pulled into the driveway, I didn't see hide or hair of the Vet. Ed opened the garage door and smiled at the sight he saw. The captured assailant was still shackled to the transmission. He was sitting there looking as pathetic as ever. The scene was priceless. It was times like these I wished I could laugh and be heard.

"What the hell is going on? You can't keep me here, you know. If I don't call in soon, they will come looking for me. I wouldn't want to be you when they do come. Buddy, you are going to get yours."

"Shut the fuck up, asshole. You are the one who should be worried. I have you, remember? Now get your ass up, dickhead."

Ed unlocked his foot and pulled him to his feet, dragging him out of the garage and to the back of his car. Ed opened the rear door and pushed the man inside. He reached in and latched the handcuffs to the door handle.

"Now, don't fucking make a sound. If I hear one peep out of you, I'll cut your fucking tongue out, prick."

Ed pulled out of the driveway and drove slowly down the street. He pulled into the go-go bar parking lot and drove to the back of the bar and got out of the car. Reaching in and grabbing the frightened man, he pulled him with one hand and punched him in the face with the other, forcing the blood to flow from his nose. With another blow, the blood was forced from his cheekbone, and the man was out cold. Ed unlocked the man and tossed him out of the car onto the ground next to the dumpster. He laughed and looked around as he fled in his car out of the driveway. I looked behind to see if anyone had seen what just happened, but the coast again seemed to be clear. I sat back and enjoyed the ride, wondering if Kitten had made it to her destination safe and out of harm's way.

We came to an old row of garages; they looked condemned and seemed to be held together with cobwebs. This place was dilapidated. I could hear animals scattering in the distance, and as we turned the corner, there she was. She had all of the doors open, and she was lying on the seat with her feet hanging out of the car.

"That's a great look for you, baby."

I could see her head pop up from under the dashboard. She knelt on the front seat and smiled at him.

"What took you so long? Where the hell have you been?"

"I'm here now, baby. Why so uptight? You weren't followed, right?"

"No, I don't think so. Man, I love this car."

She got out of the car and walked around to the toolbox sitting on the ground. She wiped the sweat off of her forehead, reached into the toolbox, and began shoving tools into her pockets.

"We should have stopped at my house; I can't work with these tools. Dude, you really need to get a stack for this garage."

"Why do you need tools? What are you working on here, girl?"

"Well, I was thinking why Carla would want this car so bad. She has a lot of cars. What is so special about this one? And why would she send that goon over to my house just for a car? Don't you think she would just let it go or something?"

"I don't know, Kit. What do you think it is?"

"Well, call me crazy, but I'm willing to bet that there is something in this car just like you said, money or something. I'm going to go over every square inch of this car until I find it."

"Kitty, that is a complete waste of your time. Why would she hide money in her car? That doesn't make any sense. I was just kidding when I said there was probably something in this car."

"Yeah, but think about it. Why does she want this car so bad? There has to be more to it than just the car."

"How long is this going to take?" Ed sighed and rubbed his eyes.

"I'm not sure. I'm going to start with the easiest, most logical places. I don't know, maybe a few hours or so. Why?"

"Well, if this is what you are going to do, I'm going out for something to eat. Do you want me to pick you up something?"

"Yeah, I'll have whatever you are having, but bring some beer. I'm really thirsty."

"Is that all, Your Majesty? Or do you still require my services?"

"No, thank you, you are dismissed, for now." She laughed.

Ed scurried to his car. I thought it was cute, the power she had over him. She could do and say just about anything she wanted without a care in the world. I watched as she flipped her head down, shaking it to gather her hair so she could clip it into a ponytail. She pulled her hair tight against her head and slid a jack under the car so she could get a better look at what might be hiding underneath. I loved watching her work with tools; it was so sexy to see her getting all dirty, and I wondered when we would spend another night together.

She knocked and banged metal against metal, searching for the treasure she was sure was hiding just under the surface. She climbed out from under the car and pulled the front of her shirt up to her face to wipe the droplets of sweat that were collecting on her cheeks. The smell of her body became more intense as she worked her fingers to the bone. I wanted her so badly my insides began to tingle with excitement. I got really close to her face with mine and inhaled her essence as she worked. I fantasized about holding her in my arms and kissing her damp, salty skin. And the excitement of it all was evident in the seat of my pants. Just then, I could hear Ed pulling back into his parking space, and the excitement was gone, for the most part.

"Okay, sweetheart, you have a choice, a burger or chicken? I went to Berger Chef."

"I don't care; I'll have whatever you aren't going to have. Did you get the beer?"

"Yes, dear, I got your beer. Here, have one. So, did you find any buried treasure in that thing yet?"

"No, not yet, but I'm getting close; I can feel it. It's got to be here somewhere."

"You don't even know what you are looking for, or if there is anything to find for that matter. This is a complete waste of time."

Ed reached into the bag and pulled out a burger and handed Kitty a beer. She took a long slug and did not stop until the beer was empty.

"Damn, girl, you better slow down."

"They're only nips. I'm cool."

She buried her head behind the front seat and continued looking.

"I'm telling you, you're never going to find anything."

No sooner did Ed say those words than Kitten hollered, "I knew I would find it."

"What did you find?"

She just sat there dazed for a moment. She had a puzzled look on her face.

"Well, what did you find? Is it money, how much?"

"It's not money! Oh, man, this is bad, this is very bad."

Ed jumped to his feet and plunged his head into the passenger-side window.

"Let me see what you got here."

Kitten stepped out of the car and backed up against the workbench.

"It's in the back; there is a compartment in the floor between the seats. Do you see it?"

Ed reached into the back and pulled out the contents of the hidden compartment.

"Well, if it weren't you, I would have never believed it, but, baby, you have the worst luck of anyone I know, and, honey, this takes the cake."

"Is it what I think it is? Now what do we do?"

Ed grunted as he stood up, and in his hand was a large bag of white powder. Drugs. The car was loaded with drugs.

"What are we going to do with it?"

"With it? You mean with them?"

He reached into the car for a second time and pulled out two more bags of powder. There were three in all. He placed them on the workbench.

"You better get that car inside and close the door. I don't think it's a good idea that anyone knows this car is here."

"What are we going to do? Oh crap, Ed, they are going to kill me for sure. Thank God we still have the guy in the garage. We'll put the drugs back and bring the car back to my house. He can take the car to Carla and Tony G, and no one will have to know that we found them. I'll live and so will you."

"Well, babe, that would be a great plan, but I already cut the bum loose."

"What do you mean you cut him loose? Why did you let him go?"

"I didn't let him go. I smacked him around a little and dropped him in the garbage at the bar."

"You dropped him in the garbage? What did you do that for? They are going to think that we stole the drugs. Ed, they are going to kill me for sure."

"It's cool, baby. I have a plan."

"Well, it better be a good one. I'm too young to die."

"Don't worry, baby. I'll put you in a safe house. I won't let anything happen to you. You'll be safe. I'll fix everything."

They put the drugs back into their hiding place and sealed the garage up tight before they headed out. I jumped into the back seat and wondered what was next. How did Kitten get herself into these messes, and how could I help her get out of this one?

"What safe house? Ed, where are you taking me?"

"Don't worry, Kit; it's cool. I'll take you to the safe house, and then I'll go to the bar and talk to Tony. I'll explain what happened and then bring the car back to him. When the coast is clear, I'll call my buddy and tell him to cut you loose."

"Cut me loose? Why is he going to have to cut me loose? Where are we going?"

"Listen, honey, you aren't exactly disaster-proof, and I need you to stay put."

Kitty just looked at him with her mouth open wide. I could not help but look at that inviting pink tongue; the coarse dampness of it made my mouth water and my mind wander.

"I have seen some of the people with whom you are acquainted, and I'm not sure I like the sound of this. What? Is the guy going to keep me tied up in a shed or something?"

"A shed? That's not even close. Don't worry, I'll tell him not to tie you too tight."

"Ha, ha very funny, I'm not kidding, Ed, I don't want to go. Just drop me off at the beach or something."

"Can't do it, babe."

"Take me to a public place. What could happen?"

Ed just shook his head no. We pulled into Kitten's driveway, but before she could get out of the car, Ed reached over and grabbed her arm.

"Give me the keys. I'll get you a few things."

"Oh no! I'm getting my own things."

She jumped out of the car, and Ed shouted at her to stop. She gave him a smart-ass look and handed the keys out for him to take.

"After you, Captain, you're the boss. You are in control."

"Don't be a smartass."

He patted her on the rump, and she followed him up the stairs to her apartment. He motioned for her to be quiet, and he slid the key into the lock. Opening the door slowly, he reached his hand in, turned on the light, and walked inside. Kitten stuck her nose in and looked around the corner.

"Is it safe to come inside? Is anybody here?"

"Come on in, get your stuff, and let's go."

I followed her into the bedroom. She was rushing around like a chicken with its head cut off. Grabbing a bag out of the closet, she scrambled to the bathroom and grabbed a bottle of pink stuff, and then she ran to the dresser and pulled out some clothes. She dove into the closet and shoved a pair of shoes inside.

Ed screamed from the kitchen. "How old is this pasta?"

"I don't know. I think I got it like two days ago, maybe three."

She tossed the bag on the bed and opened the nightstand drawer. She looked around the door to see what Ed was up to and grabbed a little pouch from the back of the drawer and stuck it into the bag.

"Okay, it's time to go."

"I'm coming. I'm coming!"

She walked out of the bedroom with a smile on her face, bag in hand.

"Okay, I'm ready to be held hostage."

"Don't think of it as that. It's going to be cool, I promise. It's not what you think."

"I trust you, Ed. If you say it's cool, I'm sure it's even better than cool. Let's go."

They locked up the apartment and headed off to God knows where. The music was blasting out of the car stereo, and Kitten drank her beer as they cruised down the busy street. As I looked out the window, I could see the light in the distance not too far from my reach. I was tempted to assist, but remembering what the woman had said, I didn't dare leave Kitten's side, at least not until I knew she was safe.

Chapter Twelve

We drove for about an hour, and as we approached our destination, all was not what it seemed. The house looked old and drab. The bushes and grass surrounding it were overgrown, and the windows were hazy from years of grime. Why would he take my precious flower to such a horrible place?

Kitten had a worried look on her face, and I could not blame her, because I was beginning to get worried, too. As we reached the two-car garage, Ed tapped Kitten on the leg. She looked at him with eyes open wide.

"Now don't say anything until we get inside. It's a lot better than it looks, trust me."

"Dude, you suck."

Kitten just hung her head low with her chin to her chest. She sighed aloud as she opened the car door and reached into the back seat to get her bag. She reached through, and I could feel her energy diminish with every step she took. Ed smiled and put his arm around her. She closed her eyes as he whispered into her ear.

"You are going to love this, wait and see."

He opened the small entranceway on the side of the garage and led her in while holding her hand. He grabbed the bag from her just in time to catch it before it slipped through her fingers. She stood there in awe, mouth wide open and eyes as glassy as a porcelain doll's. She turned in a circle to see all that was around her. A smile began to grow on her face, as did one on mine. The place was splendid, green, bright, and alive.

"Wow! This place is great."

"I told you. It looks worse than it is."

"Wow!"

She followed Ed over rocks and through large palm-like trees. A butterfly fluttered past her face, and the light wind danced with her hair. She was pleased with her new surroundings; it was evident by the look on her face. It looked like a rain forest courtyard.

"Ed, this place is wonderful. Why haven't you ever brought me here before? God, I love this place."

"I haven't had the time, and besides, you are always running off to here and there. I can never get you to stay put for more than a couple of hours. Go, go, and go, that's the only thing that's ever on your agenda."

"Well, if you would have brought me here, I wouldn't have been in such a hurry to go anywhere. Man, this place is great!"

Ed smiled, and they walked hand in hand. He opened a door that led inside the house. Kitten's feet were tapping, and her hair was bouncing as they peered into all of the fish tanks and terrariums filled with exotic reptiles and amphibians. There were animals and plants for every inch of each room. Wicker cobra chairs lined the hall, and bamboo grew within the damp soil of the large ceramic pots that were in every corner.

"How big is this place? Who lives here?"

"So many questions! Didn't I ever tell you, never ask questions if you expect to get the truth? The less you know, the better. Now behave and keep quiet."

Kitten pulled her hand stiff to the top of her forehead and saluted him.

"Aye, aye, Captain, as you wish."

She puckered her lips and smiled at him with her eyes as she pretended to turn a key in front of her kisser suggesting not a peep. Reaching out, she grabbed the collar of his shirt and hopped up and down smiling ear to ear. She stopped for a moment and whispered into his ear.

"Can we see more? Please!"

She kissed his cheek and continued to hop up and down. Ed motioned for her to go ahead of him, and she clapped her hands quickly and quietly and headed through the room and out the next door. She darted across the room and flopped onto a giant beanbag chair that was directly next to a table with an exotic lamp on it. The wallpaper wasn't wallpaper at all; it was blue shag carpet. She reached her arms up over her head and brushed them against the soft furry surface.

"This place is so cool. Can I live here?"

Ed laughed at her and sat down in the beanbag across from her. He pointed across the room, and when she turned to look at what he was revealing, she laughed and said, "Is that what I think it is? Can we have some?"

Ed nodded, and she rose from her seat and seemed to float over to a tall electric green plant that was sitting quietly in the corner. I watched her caress the plant. She plucked a flower off of it and turned slowly around, smiling fiendishly at the task she had just completed.

"Stop being silly and get over here with that."

"Here I come! This is so cool!"

Ed reached his hand out to her. "Give me that and sit down."

He took the flower and pushed it into the top of the lamp. I did not know at the time, but it was not a lamp at all, it was a pipe, and the flower was marijuana. I should have known it was drugs; there were always drugs to the left and to the right of this girl. I was surprised that Kitten was not in more trouble than she usually was with all the illegal substances around her.

They smoked the pot until it was gone, and Ed helped her up off the floor.

"Let's go. Animal is waiting."

"Animal! Which animal is waiting?"

"Not which, whom. Animal is the guy that lives here."

"His name is Animal? That's not a name; it's a description."

"Look, it's fine, now come on."

They walked through the kitchen and through a door that led down to the basement. It was dark except for the dim red lights that shone from tiny holes in the ceiling. There was a large couch that looked more like a moonwalk than a couch, and directly in the middle of the couch lay a large man, face down and snoring loudly.

"Hey, Mal, wake up!"

"I think he's dead."

"Mal, get up, man."

The man rolled over and grunted as he lifted his head off of the cushion.

"Hey, dude, what's going on? You're early. I thought you weren't going to be here for a couple of hours."

"Get up. I want you to say hello to Kitty. I have to go, so do like I said."

The man coughed and rose to his feet, reaching out a hand for Ed to shake.

"I'll follow your instructions to the letter. No problem. The girl will be safe with me."

"Just don't let her out of your sight until I call. Kitty, this is Mal; Mal, this is Kitty. Now, Kit, you stay put and don't give Mal a hard time. Stay here until I call or come back to get you."

"Okay, okay, I'll stay put, Master. Just go do what you have to do to keep my ass alive."

She turned and smiled at Animal as Ed headed back through the house. "So what is this place? Some kind of pet shop or something?"

"Nope, it's my place. I just use the animals to get what I need through customs. I know a guy at the airport. He gets the animals in, and I get the drugs. The animals are just the couriers."

"What do you mean? You don't put the drugs inside them, do you?"

"No, no, the drugs are in the boxes with the animals. It's cool, no worries, little cricket."

"Cricket?"

"Why don't you go and make yourself a drink. There is a bar inside that big globe over there. Help yourself."

Kitten nodded. She walked over to the large globe and lifted the Northern Hemisphere, exposing the spirits within. She poured a glass of whisky and lifted the top off of the ice bucket. She reached in with her hand, pulled out a fistful of ice, and plopped it into her glass.

"Man, this place is great."

"Make yourself at home. I'm going to lock up. There is plenty of food in the icebox. Help yourself."

Kitten shook her shoulders from side to side, and her head bobbed back and forth as she whisked away to the kitchen. There were orchids growing on the counters and in the glass-boxed windows. It was remarkable how different each one looked; it was like viewing precious art in a museum, each piece more beautiful than the last.

She pressed her nose in the heart of each, nuzzling gently, making sure not to leave any of them wanting for affection. I loved the way her eyes smiled; they were like tiny rays of sunshine blinding my eyes and deafening my ears. I could hear my heart beating within my head. She took my breath away.

"Hey, Mal! Do you want something to eat? Do you have any eggs? I make a mean egg."

There wasn't a sound to be heard. She looked around the room and opened the refrigerator. Her eyebrows raised high, and she smiled when the light hit her face. Meat, beverages, vegetables, and desserts packed the icebox. She reached in uncontrollably grabbing whatever she laid her eyes on. A pepper rolled across the floor as she shuffled to the counter with a piece of celery between her teeth. She was so cute; watching her could never get boring.

I listened to her humming as she twirled around the kitchen, opening cupboards and peaking in drawers. She reached out and pushed the button on the radio, then frantically turned the dial to find a tune that she liked. Shaking and chopping, she reduced veggies and cheese to tiny edible pieces before she stirred them up in a bowl with some eggs.

The butter was sizzling in the pan, and when it was evenly heated, she poured the mixture into it, producing the most wonderful smell an egg could make. She popped some bread into the toaster and began to set the table. She folded the napkins into little boats and placed them on the table. She began to shake the pan, and with one quick flick of the wrist, she flipped the omelet over without a hitch.

"Hey, what is this awesome smell? Wow, this is great. I'm starving."

"Cool, I'm glad; I didn't want to have to eat yours, too. I hate to waste food; it's a sin, you know. What do you want to drink?"

"You sit down, little lady. I'll get you a drink. This all smells so great."

She doused her plate with salt and pepper, making sure not to miss a single inch, and she dug in. Mal was finished with his plate before you could blink, licking his fingers and hungry for more.

"Oh, baby, that was good!"

"Do you want another one? I can make it, no problem, if you want."

"Yeah, I'll take another if you don't mind making it."

"Do you think I can go back and hang out with the animals, maybe smoke another bong of that crazy shit?"

"Sure, make yourself at home."

She swallowed her last bite and whipped him up another. When she was through, she headed back to the room with the furry blue walls. She plucked another flower off of the plant and pushed it into the top of the lamp and smoked it up quick. Reaching into her bag, she pulled out something and put it into her mouth. She sipped a beer and put more of the substance into her mouth. I couldn't see what it was, but I was sure it wasn't a snack.

Smiling as she peered into the glass tanks, she looked around to see if she was being watched before reaching into one of them. She pulled out a frog.

"Do you like living here? Are you hungry? I know if I lived here, I would like it; this place is cool."

The frog just sat there in the palm of her hand. Slowly, she placed him back into his habitat and closed the lid. I followed her into the kitchen where I watched her drink another beer, and when she was finished, Mal came in with some strange contraption in his hands.

"Hey, baby, do you want to do one of these?"

He held it up in the air, and the look on Kitten's face was of shock.

"I think I'll stick to the bottle, thanks."

"Okay, suit yourself. Do you want to go swimming?"

"You have a swimming pool?"

"Yeah, it's in the back." Mal motioned with his head.

"But I don't have a suit."

"Swim in your birthday suit baby I won't look."

"No, that's okay, I'll pass."

"There are suits in the cabana. I'm sure you'll find something to wear."

We followed him out the back door. The yard was huge. There was a large pond surrounded with smooth flat rocks. She skipped over to the small building, entered, and closed the door. After a few moments, she was out, and man, did she look beautiful! The bathing suit was a little small, and her breasts were popping out of the sides and overflowing the top.

"Whose suit is this?" she asked, pulling at the back of the suit.

"I think it's my sister's kid's, why?"

"How old is your sister's kid?"

"Ten or eleven, the suit looks nice. Really nice!" he said rubbing his chin.

I have to admit, she really did look sexy. Her tan lines were mismatched to the suit, and it was hot.

"This pool has a black bottom. Is it dirty?"

"Nope, it's just made to look like a real pond. Be careful, though, you can't really tell where the bottom is, so only dive in over there by the waterfall. This end is only like three feet deep. It's over eight feet down there."

She dipped her toes into the water and a sneaky smile covered her face. She sat on the edge of the rocks and plunked her legs in. She held her body up with her arms and lowered herself into the pool, feeling for the bottom. I watched as the suit became transparent when the water hit it. Her skin was tight and bumpy from the cold water. She was hopping up and down hoping for warmth, but it was evident from the look of her bathing-suit top, she was not getting any warmer.

"Shit, it's cold in here!" she said as she rubbed her fingers up and down her arms trying to warm up.

Mal smiled and stroked his chin. As he looked her up and down, I began to get frightened. I could only imagine what was going through his mind. Kitten dunked her head under the water and pushed off the wall with her feet, forcing her body gently across to the other side.

Her hair floated gracefully, expanding around her head. When she reached the opposite wall, her head popped out from under the water, and she pushed water through her lips like a fountain onto the rocks. She was giggling and hopping up and down with excitement.

"Aren't you coming in for a dip? The water isn't that bad once you get in."

"No, I'll just watch you for a while."

"So, where is your girlfriend? You don't live here all by yourself, do you?"

"I have lots of women, but not when I'm working."

"What do you mean?"

"Ed said no parties while you're here. He made me get everyone out of the house before you came over."

"That's not fair; you should be able to have whoever you want over to your own house. Don't be ridiculous, call up your friends and have them come over if you want. Ed has no right to do that to you. Besides, it would be more fun if more people were here."

"Honey, for a thousand bucks, I'd throw my mother out of the house."

"He is giving you money to keep me here?"

"No offence, but you wouldn't be here if he didn't. I like you, but not just anyone comes to my house, honey. VIPs only."

"Oh, well then, I guess if you don't mind renting it out when I need a place to hide, I'm a VIP, too. What else ya got around here to do?"

"What do you mean?"

"Well, if you are charging Ed a grand, then I had better get his money's worth. Does that include the pot that I smoke, too? Would you mind rolling one for me? I don't really like smoking out of that bong you have in the blue room."

"Help yourself to any and all you see, but you're pushing your luck if you think I'm waiting on you. If you want to smoke, you'll have to get it yourself."

She smiled at him and swam under the waterfall. The water rushed over her head and into the pool, and she disappeared behind it. I peaked around the back of it, and there she was, mixing a drink at the hidden bar inside.

She hollered, "This place is awesome, dude, worth every penny!"

She got out of the pool and grabbed onto a chair to keep from falling. Then, when she collected herself, she wrapped a towel around her hips and headed to the house for some pot. There was a tray on the kitchen counter covered with the stuff, and she rolled about six joints and went to the freezer for some ice. She poured some into a bowl and headed back out to the pool. She laid the towel down on a lounge chair and pulled a book out of her bag.

"Hey, don't you have any floating lounge chairs for this pool?"

"In the shed, there are lots of floats in there."

As she opened the door, a cat ran out and startled her. She went in, and when she came out, she had a large alligator float in her hands. She tossed it into the pool and placed all of her stuff on the ground at the edge of the pool. She hopped in after it and made herself comfortable, floating around drinking and smoking, reading her book. I enjoyed every minute as she frolicked in the water for hours. I could see the white portions of her body that were not covered by the bathing suit beginning to turn red. She was headed for a burn, and it did not seem to bother her.

"Listen, I'm going to be in the study for a while. Just make yourself at home, and I'll be just inside if you need me."

"Okay, no problem. I'll be poolside."

Mal walked into the house and shut the door. I sat under the waterfall in the bar watching her every move. She was beautiful, and all I wanted to do was tell her just that. She played with little water toy animals that sprayed water like water guns. Singing and giggling, she paddled around the pool, back and forth, kicking and splashing about. She was talking to herself, saying how wonderful the drugs made her feel and how she wished she lived in this house.

Kitten looked under the waterfall straight toward me. It seemed as if she'd seen me. Just then, I knew it to be true.

"Hey, who's there? What are you doing in there?" She paddled closer to me. "How did you get in here? Are you a friend of Animal's?"

All were good questions that I could not answer. She came in closer, and when she saw me, she smiled. "You! What are you doing here? I thought you were just a dream. How did you get in here?"

I was amazed that she could see me. I realized that the things she had eaten from her bag before must have been mushrooms. How wonderful! I was going to be able to talk to her, she could see me, and I was very nervous about the guy in the house.

"I thought that I would never see you again. Where have you been? I didn't see you come in. Do you live here, too?"

I gasped and did not know what to say.

"Well?" she insisted.

"I don't live here, but I told you that I would stay close to you, so here I am."

"How did you get in?"

"Well, if I told you, I don't think that you would believe me."

"Listen, that guy, Mal, is inside. He owns the house. He said that he doesn't like just anyone to be here, so if he comes out, you will have to hide in the bar."

"I don't think that will be a problem."

"Do you want a drink or something? How about some smoke? There is plenty of that around here. Look, there is a tray of it on the table."

"No, thank you, I'm just fine."

"I can't believe you are here. I just can't believe it."

"I was talking to your friend, and she said that you would probably be needing me, so I followed you here."

"Who did you talk to? What friend?"

"The old woman with the beautiful garden."

"Beatrice? How do you know her?"

"I was walking past her house today, and she told me to go to you. I'm not sure why, but I figured it was a good idea to do what she said."

"She usually knows what she is talking about, but I'm very safe here. This is my safe house." She spun herself around in a circle, floating gently on the clear water.

"What are you running from, if you don't mind me asking?"

"Let's just say I'm staying out of trouble." She rolled her eyes.

I smiled at her and reached out to touch her face.

"It's funny how you are always showing up while I'm tripping."

She giggled and swam around the pool. I wanted to go in the water with her, but I wasn't sure how she would react to me not getting wet if I had, so I just hung out on a chair beside the pool.

"Why don't you come in? The water is very refreshing."

"No, thanks, I'm fine right here."

We talked and laughed for about an hour or so, and she got very nervous when Mal come outside.

"Who the hell are you talking to?"

"Mal, I can explain. This is John Davis. He wanted to hang out with me, and I said it was okay. Please don't be mad."

Mal looked around, and even though I was sitting directly in front of him, he never saw me. He looked at Kitten, puzzled. He rubbed his head and laughed at her.

"You said his name was John? Where's he at?" Mal said smiling.

"What do you mean? He is sitting right there."

She pointed toward the chair, and Mal just shook his head and walked away mumbling.

"Well, you two have a nice time together. Wacko!"

She looked at me with a confused look and said, "What the fuck is going on here? Why couldn't he see you?" She began to move farther away from me. "Are you a ghost or something?"

I didn't know what to say to her. I was afraid that if I told her the truth, she would freak out, but on the other hand, what could I possibly tell her besides the truth. So I just blurted it out.

"I'm technically dead, but I think and feel just like you. Don't worry, I won't hurt you. Don't be afraid."

"What the fuck is going on here? You're a ghost? You follow me around and you're, like, dead?" She rubbed her head. "How dare you! What are you doing talking to Beatrice? Did she put you up to this? That crazy woman, she should stop butting into my life."

"She cares about you, and she wanted me to look after you; that's all."

"You better go. Get out of here. I can't have you around me now. It's just too much. I swear to God I'm never taking drugs again; this time I mean it, no more mushrooms for me."

She closed her eyes tightly; I believe she was hoping that when she opened them, I would be gone. So I did like any gentleman would do, I left before she could open them. It killed me to walk away, but I was afraid that I would ruin everything if I didn't, so I did. The coast was clear when she opened her eyes, and I was left to sit in the driveway until Ed came back for her. It only took a few more hours for him to return, and when he did, Kitten was ready to go. She was wired for sound and couldn't sit still.

"Hey, baby, what the hell are you on? Did you take something?"

"Dude, your friend is a strange one. Did you know that he doesn't even like animals? He just uses them to smuggle drugs into the country."

"Listen, Kit, you don't want to go talking shit about the man's business. If he heard that you were, then I would have to be hiding you from him. Do you get me?"

"Yeah, dude, I get you. So is everything okay? Can I go home now?"

"Yeah, you're safe for now, but if you get into any more trouble, I'm going to have to start charging you by the hour."

"You came to me about that car. It's all your fault. Besides, at least you don't have dead guys following you around."

"What are you talking about, dead guys? What dead guys? How do dead guys follow you around?"

"Never mind the dead guys. All I want to do is take a nice, hot bath and relax in my own house. I'm really tired, and I think I got sunburned today. Damn little bathing suit, good for nothing."

"Okay, I'll take you home, but promise me you will stay there for the rest of the night. I'll be over to check on you in the morning."

"Okay, but only if you promise to bring me some bagels."

"Okay, baby, I promise."

The rest of the trip home, they hardly spoke to one another. I was afraid of her seeing me, so I rode on the bumper and listened in through the window. I figured I should keep away for a while just to make sure that the drugs wore off before I would show my face again. I didn't want to scare her, but I couldn't get myself to do it. I jumped off the car before we turned the corner on our way to her house. I peered through the bushes and watched as she kissed him goodbye and headed up the steps to her door. I looked on as the door closed, shutting her off from my world. It left me wondering if she was thinking about me and worried that she would be afraid of me, afraid of me haunting her mortal life. I hoped she would know that I would never harm her in any way, shape, or form. I loved her deeply and longed to knock on the door to tell her how I truly felt. I hung around outside her apartment fantasizing about the night we spent together and realized that it would only be a memory, never to repeat itself in the future.

I heard a car pull into the yard, and when I could see who it was, I did not like what I saw. It was Devin. How I hated him! He hopped up the stairs to her door and turned the knob. She had left it open, and he walked inside. I ran around to the back and up to the fire escape to get a look at what was going on inside the house.

"What the hell are you doing here? Get out of my house!" she shouted, waving her arms in the air pointing to the door.

"Come on, baby, please let me explain. I just need a place to lay low for a while."

"Lay low from what?"

"From some guys I owe a little money to. It was just a misunderstanding. I just need some time to sort it all out."

"No way, Devin, I don't want any trouble here. I have enough problems without you adding to them."

"Well, can I at least put my car in the garage for a little while?"

"No! What car?"

"Listen, baby, I know you don't have any reason to trust me, and I don't blame you, but this situation's got me by the balls here. I really need to hide out; it's a matter of life and death here."

Kitten went to say something, and with a loud crash, the door was busted in. There were three men standing in the living room, and they did not look happy. In fact, they looked horribly dangerous, and I began to worry about the situation. Devin ran behind Kitty and smiled as he spoke to the men.

"Hey, Al. What brings you here?"

181

"You know why I'm here, scumbag. Where's my package? You better give it here and now, or you aren't going to like what I'm going to do to you next."

Kitten pushed away from Devin and wrapped her arms around herself as she began to walk sideways toward the door, and one of the other men grabbed her.

"Not so fast, sweetheart. Where do you think you're going?"

"I was just on my way out for a bite to eat. Can I get you something?" She poked out her chest and smiled, flirting with the men.

"You're not going anywhere, doll face. Sit down!"

"Yeah, sit down!"

"Shut up, stupid! Now, Devin, you weren't going to steal from me, were you?"

"No, Al, of course not. In fact, I was just telling Kitty that I had to get going. I was just about to come and see you."

"Well, now, I guess we just saved you a trip. Hand over the goods."

Devin looked around with a scared look on his face.

"You better not tell me that you don't have my package. This would make me very angry. You don't want to see me angry now, do you? Remember the last guy that tried to fuck me up the ass."

"Yeah, I remember. I just have to go and pick it up. I hid it because I didn't want my girl to get any ideas that any of it would be hers."

"Any of what, Devin? Don't bring me into your bullshit. Listen, guys, I don't know what the hell he is talking about. He came here begging me to hide him. I didn't know why, but now I do. I have nothing to do with this asshole, believe me."

"Yeah, you dames are all alike; you lie just to hear yourselves talk. Why don't you just sit down and shut up? I need to have a little dance with your friend here."

The man motioned to one of his buddies with a nod of his head and that man approached Devin with a devastating blow to the stomach. As Devin buckled over in pain, the man followed in with a blast to his jaw, forcing Devin off his feet and onto his back. Kitten tried to make it to the door but was forced back into her seat by the other thug that was there. She looked over at Devin with hatred in her eyes.

"You're such an asshole!" She shook her head. "You suck!"

"Hey, Devin, your girlfriend doesn't like you very much. Looks to me like you don't have too many friends. Now, you and me are going to take a ride, and if I don't get what I want, your pretty little girl here is going to lose her good looks."

"I'll get your stuff, Al, just don't hurt me."

"Oh, you don't care what I do to the lady just so long as I don't hurt you? That's rich!" He looked over at Kitty. "Your boy here doesn't seem to think very highly of you, now does he, sweetheart? You should pick 'em a little better."

She just sat there sobbing on the couch.

"Santo, you stay here with the lady. Make sure not to let her out of your sight, and if she tries anything, make her bleed."

I could see her shaking. The entire couch was moving back and forth as the three of them headed out the door and down the steps. Kitten's eyes were filling up with tears, and Santo just laughed at her.

"You shouldn't cry, little chick. Just do what I say, and I promise I won't hurt you much."

I hated that she was so alone. Where was Ed when you needed him? How did she get herself into these messes? I needed to let her know that everything was going to be all right. I hopped into the window; she could see me out of the corner of her eye. She turned to look directly at me and stood up only to be knocked down flat on her back.

"Didn't I tell you not to get me mad? Now stay put, and you won't get hurt."

She pointed over to where I was standing.

"Don't you see him? He is right there. Don't you see him?"

"Honey, you must be on something, because there isn't anyone else here. Now be quiet."

I put my finger up to my lips as if to say be quiet. She just stared at me, and I watched the tears rolling down her cheek.

"It's too bad that you can't see him, because he is here, and he is going to kick your ass."

"Kick my ass! No one's going to be kicking my ass, honey. Now shut up, or I'll make you shut up!"

He slapped her across the face, and she flew off of the couch. I mustered up all of my strength and hit him with everything that I had in me, sending him flying into the bedroom doorway. Kitten took the opportunity to get out of the apartment and ran down the street ducking in bushes and hopping over fences to get away. I followed close behind her. I called out for her to stop, but she just kept running. She ran all the way to the lookout tower where we spent the night together, and when I got to the top, she was sitting there, running her finger over the carving in the wood.

"Why are you haunting me?"

I wasn't sure how to answer. "I'm not a ghost."

"What are you? Who are you? Is your name even John? How come I'm the only one who can see you?"

"You can only see me when you eat the mushrooms. I am not sure why it works that way. I was surprised that you can see me at all. Only animals and small children usually see me."

"What do you want?"

"I want to help."

"Help, help with what?"

"Help you stay out of trouble. It seems to find you a lot."

"What do you know about it? I don't appreciate being followed around by someone that I can see only if I'm tripping. How do I know you are even real? You could just be a figment of my imagination. You probably aren't even real, just in my mind. Are you like a pervert or something?"

"I'm real. I don't mean you any harm. I'm only here to help, and no, I'm not a pervert." I knew deep down I yearned for her.

"Well, I don't need your help; I was doing just fine until you showed up, thank you very much." She crossed her arms and pushed her chin in the air.

"I could see that. I just was making sure you were okay."

"How did you get here? I thought you left when I was at Mal's house. Where did you come from?"

"I was outside the window when that big jerk put his hands on you. If I could have, I would have killed that scumbag for what he did to you."

I reached out and slid my hand down the side of her face. "I think you are the most beautiful woman I have ever met in my life."

"Thanks, but I still don't know what to make of it all. It's creepy."

She pulled her cell phone from out of her pocket and dialed. "Bea,…can I come over?" There was a pause. "I'll see you in a few minutes." She hung up the phone. "Now you come with me. I'm going to take you over to Bea's house, and she is going to explain how this is at all possible."

We headed back to the apartment, and Ed was there. He had Santo by the neck and was putting him into the back seat of the car.

I could not argue with her. She was furious with me, and I couldn't have her anger on my conscience. She ran to the bedroom and grabbed another baggie of mushrooms.

"I'm not letting you out of my sight, even if I have to eat ten bags of these nasty things."

I just looked at her. I didn't know what to say, so I just allowed my lips to curl up at the corners, and I hung my head in shame.

"So, how long have you been following me?"

"Not very long."

"How long?" she demanded.

"Well, it wasn't Mother Nature who kissed you that night on the beach. It was me. Please don't be angry. I never meant you any harm. It's just that you are so beautiful, and you seem to be lonesome most of the time. I only wanted to watch over you. I never meant you any harm."

"Where else have you been? The bay?"

"Yes."

"The bar?"

"Yes."

"My apartment?! How many times have you been to my apartment?"

"A few times, I guess."

"When I'm in the shower? Are you watching me when I'm changing and showering?"

"Kitten, I assure you, I have been a complete gentleman. I meant you no harm. You have to know that."

"Listen, you can't be invading my privacy like this. I don't have to know anything. It's not fair. Just who do you think you are? Where did you come from? Why are you following me?"

"I only wanted to help. When I talked to Bea, she said that I should stay close to you. She said that you were in danger and that I needed to keep you safe. I never meant you any harm."

"I'm sorry if I don't seem grateful, it's just a little creepy, and how would you like it if I was to follow you around without your knowledge? I'm sure you would be just a little pissed off, and don't even try to deny it."

"I'm truly sorry. If you don't want me to hang around, I'll go back to my work and leave you alone, but it seems like you need my help."

"Work, what kind of work do you do?"

I explained to her what had happened to me, and she seemed a bit confused. I went on to tell her how it all worked, leaving out the gory details. She didn't say a word to me. She just looked at me with a blank stare. We walked to Bea's house with our heads down. She looked up once or twice to see if I was still there. I smiled at her. She half smiled back at me and began to mutter something to herself under her breath.

"Hello, Superman!" the boy shouted with a huge smile on his face as he waved his arms frantically in the air to get my attention.

"Hi!"

Timmy continued to smile and wave as we passed him. His mother tugged on his arm and looked back at Kitty with a puzzled expression.

"How, how did that boy see you? Why did he call you Superman? Who is he?"

"He is one that can see. I spoke to him a few times. He is a great kid. He thinks I'm Superman."

"Cute kid, why is it that I can only see you when I'm tripping?"

"Tripping?" *What in the hell is tripping?* I thought.

"Using mushrooms, why can I only see you when I'm using mushrooms?"

"I'm not sure, but I'm really glad that you can."

"I'm not sure if I like this at all. I'm still a little freaked about the whole thing."

She started walking ahead of me, just far enough ahead to be alone. I stayed back so she would be comfortable.

We made it to the house, and before Kitten could knock, Bea opened the door.

"Well, well, if it isn't Puss, and I see you brought your friend with you again." She motioned to me.

"You mean you can see him?"

"Of course I can see him, I'm old, but I'm not blind. Come in, come in. I'm sure you have some questions."

She led us into a seating area and told us to sit. Kitty sat in the chair next to the window, far away from me.

"Now is that a pleasant way to be seated when you have a guest, Puss? Don't you think you will be more comfortable here seated beside John on the couch?"

"No, I'm fine just where I am."

"She is angry with me," I said in a low tone of voice. "I don't think she wants me around anymore. Maybe I should go."

"Oh no, you aren't going any place. You just sit there, and, Puss, you come with me."

Kitten followed Bea out to the backyard. I couldn't follow without being seen, so I went to the kitchen where I could see and hear what was going on in the back, out of sight behind the curtain.

Bea sat Kitty down in the garden and placed her hands on her shoulders.

"He is here for you, Puss. Don't be afraid. Didn't he come in handy at all today?"

"Yes, but it's creepy. Why is a dead guy following me around?"

"Oh, Puss, he's harmless. He loves you, honey. I know that he would never do anything to hurt you. You are perfectly safe with him. Besides, he was meant to be here, watching over you."

"I don't need anyone watching over me. I can take care of myself."

"You told me so yourself, he helped you get out of a jam. Why don't you like him child?"

"I like him just fine. I just don't like people watching me while I'm in the shower, or while I'm getting dressed. It's creepy, Bea."

"I'm sure he gave you your privacy. He doesn't seem to be a scurvy character. I have a feeling that you two were meant to meet. The signs are all there, you only need to follow them. I'm sure he has some purpose to be around you; maybe you should keep an open mind. You know, Puss, if you didn't use those dreadful and dangerous substances, you probably wouldn't have known he was even around you. Maybe it's you who needs to change things a bit."

"So now what do I do? Do I tell him it's okay for him to follow me around, or do I just try to put the whole thing out of my mind? I'm confused, and how will I know if he respects my wishes if I can't see him?"

"You just do what your heart tells you to do."

The light was so bright I could hardly stand to look at it. The walls began to shake and the windows rattled. It was as if the ground was about to open up and suck us all in.

"I don't think we are alone." Bea said.

"What is it? Is it him? Why can't I see him?" kitty look around, confused.

"I believe they are coming for him."

Well, she was right. Before I could focus on their faces, they had scooped me up and whisked me away to a place that was very familiar to me. But why was I here, why had they brought me back to this terrible place?

I could see the footbridge just up ahead, and I could hear the laughter in the distance taunting me to look further, but I refused to look.

"Why, why have you brought me back to this horrible place? I don't want to be here." I shouted.

I couldn't make out the face from all of the bright orange light that was shining in my eyes, but the voice was familiar to me. It was she, the one who brought me into this life. Why would she come for me now? What did she want from me?

She spoke to me in a stern tone. "You have broken the rules, and because of your insolence, you shall be punished."

"Punished, why? I haven't done anything!" I pleaded.

"You have been told time and time again never to converse with the mortals, but you refuse to follow orders. Your job here on this earth was made clear, but you ignored the light and your work. You must pay for your mistakes."

She left me at the footbridge for I didn't know how long. I relived that dreadful day over and over, the pain, the torture, and every time the rope snapped, I awoke at the footbridge only to relive that horrible incident again. Why did she leave me here? Why didn't she stay and talk to me and explain what was expected of me and how long I would continue this drudgery?

Chapter Thirteen

*A*fter what seemed like a lifetime, the rope snapped, and I awoke on the beach beside the jetty as the waves crashed over the shore with a loud and thunderous roar. I looked around; there was not a soul in sight. The wind was cold and the sky was gray. The amusement pier was deserted. There were no lights, no whistles; even the music was nonexistent. There was only the sound of rusted signs swaying in the wind. Where had everybody gone? Why was I all alone? Was this my punishment? Was I destined to be all alone in a world with no one?

I headed over to Kitten's apartment to see if she was okay. When I got there, the garage was empty and the apartment over the garage was boarded up with large pieces of plywood. Where had she gone? Why was this happening? I headed straight for the church. Maybe if I went there, I could get some answers.

The streets were deserted. There was not a person or animal in sight, and I was beginning to feel frightened. The church was dark and smelled like mold; it did not look as if there had been anyone inside for quite some time. I headed in and sat in my usual seat. I looked around, but the glass was not bright and beautiful; it was dark and dingy. There was no sun and no hope in sight.

"WHY?" I shouted at the top of my lungs. "WHY?"

I could hear a voice, but it was faint. I could not pinpoint where it was coming from. I opened the large door and walked out to the street.

"John, come here, John!" the voice called out.

I headed down the road, following the voice; it did not call out my name again. It only laughed. It seemed to taunt me, forcing me to follow its unnerving chatter. Why was I being tormented? Where was everyone and who was laughing at me? I came upon the Water Park. It was desolate, not a soul in sight, only that horrible laughter, but where was it coming from?

I looked up, and as cool rain began to hit my face, I could see a small figure in the distance high atop one of the slides looking down at me and laughing that insatiable laugh. There was no wind, so I was forced to take the long climb up the wooden planked stairwell. I fixed my eyes on the figure, never changing my direction of sight. As I ascended, with each step, I could feel my anger growing, the laughter piercing my brain like a hot knife through butter. I could feel my throat closing up with every step, and as I reached the top, the figure was standing before me laughing and holding his belly struggling to stand.

"Why are you laughing at me?" I shouted.

"Boy, oh boy, you really screwed up. Man, I have seen a lot of dumbasses in my time, but you definitely take the cake, man."

"Who are you? What the hell is going on here?"

"I'm Frankie Parks, been here for over twenty years now, and you, pal, are the only one that they talk about."

"They, who are they? Why do they talk about me? I never get to talk to anyone. I thought I was alone here. Why haven't I seen you before?"

"Whoa, hang on a minute, buddy, too many questions at one time. Where the hell have you been? The world has been like this for a mortal year now. The people are gone and so is the wildlife. I have never seen anything like it before. Dude, you could fuck up a High Mass without even trying. Everyone was sent to God knows where, and I was left here to wait for you."

"Wait for me, to what?"

"You really don't know, do you?"

"What is it that I am supposed to know? Every time I see someone who might possibly answer my questions, they just yell at me and vanish without a trace."

"You don't enjoy your work, do you, John?"

"No, not lately, but what does that matter?"

"Don't you get it, if you don't do your job with a sincere heart, you will never be free. We all get tired of saving souls, but the only way to save yourself is to fulfill your destiny with a heavy heart."

"What does that mean?"

"It means, SUCK IT UP! Stop blubbering, and do what you are expected to do."

"Yeah, I know that, but after all of these years, I thought that I had. How long do I have to endure this curse before I'm able to be free from it?"

"As long as it takes!"

"What does that mean? Are you here to take me where everyone else is? Where did all the people go?" I looked him straight in the eye. "What the hell is going on here? Who the hell are you?"

"So many questions, John. Why do you ask so many questions? It's your fault that I'm here. When are you going to do what is expected and get us all out of this mess?"

I could not understand what he wanted from me. I was getting agitated by the way he was blaming me for all the trouble with the world at this time. What could I do about it? I wanted to search for Kitten, but I knew that no matter what I did or where I searched for her, I would never find her. I looked around at the silent and desolate space that was once filled with shouting kids and happy tourists, praying that if I had closed my eyes, I would open them to a new view, filled with the people and the noise that my ears longed to hear.

"Well, John, when are you going to stop all this garbage and do the right thing so we can all get out of this emptiness?"

"I'll do whatever needs to be done. Just tell me a few things first."

"Okay, what do you want to know? Make it quick, if you don't do it soon, we'll all be in deep."

I sat there for a minute thinking of the perfect questions to ask. Then I realized that when I began to ask questions of anyone, they only answered one of them, so I thought of the only question that truly mattered to me and said, "My question has two parts, maybe three, will you be able to answer them all for me or is this just a waste of my time?"

The man smiled at me and said, "It depends on the question, John."

"Okay, will I ever be able to live as a mortal man again?"

"Wrong question, John; ask me another one."

"Will I be able to live as a mortal with Kitty Morris?"

"Wrong question again, John. Come on, John, you can do better than that. Ask me something good."

"Okay, how long do we have to do this? Why are we here and when can we leave? All I want to know is how long do we have to intervene with death before we have satisfied our sentence? Who decides how long we do this?"

"Okay, now we're talking, I can answer a few of these. Well, for starters, you are here for as long as it takes, and no one knows how long the stay is, it just is what it is. Second, Moxie decides who stays and who goes, but you never know where you are going to end up. Most of us don't ask, I heard of a guy who asked the wrong questions, and no one knows what happened to him."

"Do you know what happens to others like us? Where do they go when their time is up? Do they become mortal?"

"Some become mortal, but some go to the bad place. Trust me, dude, you don't want to go to the bad place. It's not good, don't want to end up there."

"What is the bad place? Is it hell?"

"Hell? It puts Hell to shame. Just don't talk about it. I'm not allowed to talk about it, and frankly, I don't want to talk about it."

"Okay, I'm sorry. Can I become mortal again? What do I have to do to become mortal?"

He just sat there looking at me with a blank and saddened look on his face.

"Listen, John, you need to work, that is what it's all about, work, work, work. There isn't anything else, only work. Don't you get it? You did whatever you did to end up in this. Now is the time you pay. Trust me, you will pay. I have only been here for like twenty mortal years and to me it feels like an eternity."

"I have been here for a few hundred years, and I don't know as much about this place as you do. Why is that?"

"I didn't kill anyone with my bare hands, John. I only hit them with my car; you pounded the life out of another human being with your bare hands. What did you think was going to happen? Did you think you would repent and go to heaven for what you did? Let me tell you something, you are going to have to work hard to get what you want. They are all talking about you, and it doesn't sound good from where I'm standing. You should get to work and do what you were meant to do."

"I thought that was what I was doing? I have saved more people than there are days in a year, each year that has gone by. How many more do I need? Who is keeping score?"

"I told you it's Moxie. He is the only one who can set your future, and if you get him mad at you, you will never get out of here."

I wondered who Moxie was and why he had not spoken to me. "Who is Moxie anyway? How do I get to talk to him? When will he come to me, telling me my destiny?"

"Moxie can't be beckoned; he comes for you when it's your time."

"If that is true, how do you know so much about him, and everything else?"

"I don't know firsthand. I'm only telling you the things that I have heard. Moxie doesn't just talk to anyone."

He stood up, and as he did, the sky opened up with a loud, thunderous crash, and the rain came down in buckets. I could feel it stinging my body, making me wet, and that was something that I hadn't felt in quite some time. Just then, a lightning bolt crackled down, and the man that I was just speaking to disappeared in a cloud of fire and smoke. There was an electrical smell in the air and that was when I saw him.

He had a fiery red-hooded cape. I could not see his face, but I could sense that he was looking to talk to me. I could not move; my feet were planted in the ground. The hair on the back of my neck stood straight up, and I just knew that it wasn't going to be a good thing. The large figure moved as if it were floating directly toward me. I bowed my head in its presence, afraid to look upon it for fear that something terrible would happen if I did.

The figure did not have a face; I strained to look at it, but could not focus on any sort of features. I was blinded by this presence and feared what was about to happen to me. The sky closed in around me; echoing thunderclaps bellowed, surrounding me. As I fell to my knees, the figure reached out to me, and with a light touch to my cheek, I was whisked away to Kitten's apartment. I raced to the steps, and as I reached out to grab the handrail, I realized that the windows were still boarded up tight. Not wanting to turn my head, I clamped my teeth down tight and did the same with my grip on the handrail. I could feel the pull in my entire body, and I fought it for as long as I could.

As I turned in the direction of my captain, I could tell that he was beginning to disrobe and present himself to me, but as the robe was lifted, it would all become clear. She was breathtaking, even more beautiful than I remembered. She seemed to peer deep into my soul. Our eyes locked, and like a magnet, I was drawn to her. My feet never touched the ground; she pulled me to her without moving a muscle. Our faces were only a whisper away, and as we focused on one another's eyes, everything I ever wanted to know, every forgotten promise, all of my abilities and all of my deepest emotions were clear. Rebirth, I had been reborn; this would be my second chance to complete my destiny. The hope was overwhelming, more now than ever before, and as I gazed back at her breathtaking beauty, I suddenly felt bad for the way I had been conducting myself and hung my head in shame.

"What can I do to fix all of the mistakes I've made? I do not know what to say. I'm truly sorry for the way I have behaved. I can see it all very clear."

Her lips parted, and as they did, a wild flock of tiny seabirds created a thunderous clap as they flew in unison into the air behind her.

"How have you been, John? You look a little off." The voice was soft and soothing to my ears.

"I have waited for so long to have my questions answered, and after all this time, knowing all that I do now, well it's all just a little too much to absorb."

She smiled at me with such admiration. "John Davis, you have done everything right. The only conduct that you should be ashamed of is the lack of faith you have in yourself. There isn't a tasker out there that can match your skills, except for Frankie; he is your best student, the only one besides me who even comes close to your talents. But you already know that, don't you, John?"

She took a step back, flipping her shiny golden locks as she floated over to a patch of flowers. With a wave of her hand, they opened from their slumber, releasing their perfume in the breeze. She plucked one from the bunch and handed it to me.

"When you breathe in its fragrance, you have but only one time in your life, both mortal and from this plane of existence, to return to. Make your choice wisely; you will never have another chance."

"If I become mortal, can I still make a difference in the world?"

"You can do whatever you feel you have to do, John; your life will be your own. Your choices will be of your own free will, just like before."

"What if I don't make the right choices?"

"When you go back, you will not be able to be seen until the next full moon. You must reveal yourself to the one you love at midnight, at a place of significance. Then and only then, will you be free to make your choice."

I received her flower, and as I put it to my nose and inhaled its spectacular essence, the only love that I could picture was the love I had for Kitten, her smile, the way she looked at me. The sound of my name as it floated out of her precious lips filled my mind with love and devotion. She was the one. She was my only true love, and I would have the rest of my life to show her just that.

As I opened my eyes, I was still standing in Kitten's driveway, but the boards that covered her windows were gone and a warm pleasant glow of light shone in their place. As I pulled a deep and comforting breath into my lungs, it seemed like the first time I had ever done such a thing. I jumped up to the window to get a better look inside. My powers were strong enough that I could float without a breeze, and I moved in close to see if Kitten was inside. She was sitting on the couch.

I closed my eyes and pictured myself in the house sitting next to her, and when I opened them, there I was, seated in the very same place I had imagined myself to be. Opposite my Kitten on her living room couch, I could not think of a better place to spend my time. She was licking peanut butter off of her fingertips. In her lap lay a plate with the sandwich on it, and in between her knees was a tall glass of milk. She was reading a book about spirits and poltergeists with about five or six yellow markers stuck to various pages. Her hair was up in a ponytail, and she was wearing a pastel orange pair of short shorts and a small tight sports bra to match. Never knowing that I was seated directly beside her, she continued to read and drink her milk. As mesmerized as I was admiring her unprotected body, I could not help but wonder what other special abilities I was capable of.

The milk was cold; tiny droplets of condensation moistened the smooth tan skin just before it plummeted down her thigh to the end of its existence. She twisted in her seat from every cold stroke the cool water made. The cool ocean breeze made the clop-footed bird marionette dance against the hardwood floor, forcing Kitten's eyes to peer over her book.

She smiled and her nose crunched up. "Nice moves, baby. Are you having fun?" The bird continued his dance. "I'm too tired to dance. I'll sit this one out. I owe you one." I moved to the coffee table and watched as she chugged down her glass of milk. The white mustache lined her upper lip and glistened as the flickering flame from a tiny candle danced the light across her face. My feet began to tingle, and my legs trembled at the sight of her. As I leaned in to steal a kiss, the insufferable ringing of her telephone interrupted my heist.

"Hello," she said in a drowsy voice. There was silence for a moment. "I'm too tired; please leave me alone…I'm not in the mood for your crap tonight."

I knew that Devin was on the other end of that telephone line. He always popped up at the most undesirable times, which would include anytime his name was mentioned. This was one infection that Kitten couldn't fight off alone. She was going to need help from me to free her from his tethered grasp. I tuned in to her conversation and could hear her voice trembling.

"Just leave me alone…Okay, okay, I'll talk to you, but not tonight…I'll come over in the morning…No, don't come here, I'll come to you."

The conversation switched, and it got quiet again, but this time, the silence was extended a few more beats. Closing her eyes and shaking her head, she pursed her lips.

"I told you no. I'll meet you at the nook, and you better have money for breakfast…I'll see you at around ten thirty…Now, don't bother me again tonight. I'm going to sleep."

She slammed down the phone and headed straight for the fridge. My guess was beer, and I was right. Beer always followed in Devin's wake. Azreal was sitting on the balcony, and Kitten looked to him for comfort as she called out.

"Baby, we he the baby!" she said in a baby's voice.

The cat brushed up against her legs as she took a seat outside in the salty air. The night sounds were alive and floating up from the garden below. My senses were on overload. I could hear the voices from the boardwalk as vividly as if I was standing directly in the middle of it all. As I discovered yet another of my now enhanced abilities, it had become clear to me my services would be needed now more than ever.

Without thinking, I blasted off into the night sky, soaring as quickly as lightning, slightly overshooting my target when I landed. The light shone bright directly under the slow moving chair lift, and I willed myself to that exact spot. The young father, to irresponsible to know that alcohol and babysitting do not mix, was too busy rocking the chair back and forth to please his own childhood memories to realize that he was only a few short rocks from losing his precious cargo. I hovered directly in the path of that chair, and the boy began to wave at me. As the chair swung back, the boy slid forward, and I pushed with all of my might to keep him from plummeting to his death. I shoved the boy into his father and steadied the chair from all the rocking. I looked down where the light was shining, and as the chair passed over it, it disappeared into the night. I hung around for a few more minutes, making sure the two made it to the end of their journey.

I heard a loud shout and knew that it was Kitten's voice doing the shouting. I looked around to see where she was, but she was nowhere to be found. Could I be hearing her if she was still at home? I rode the salty air back to Kitten's apartment, and as I popped into the kitchen, I could see Kitten looking down into the garden, pouring splashes of beer on top of a voice that came from below.

"Hey, you're getting me wet."

"I told you not to come here tonight. Get the hell out of here!"

"Oh come on, baby, let me come up. I just want to talk to you. Please don't call Ed. I only want to talk."

"No, Devin, go home."

"Kitty, you know that I love you, baby. Come on, baby, remember the night that we went crabbing on my uncle's boat. You can't tell me that you didn't feel it, too. I love you, honey. You know that you are the only girl for me."

I could see that his words were wearing her down, and it would only be a matter of time before she would succumb to his woes and let him in. I hated this man with every ounce of my being, and I needed to nip this situation in the bud, but how? The commotion became disturbing, and Devin shouted in horror for Kitten to open the door. He ran up the stairs and began pounding on the door.

"Let me in, let me in! Kitty, you have to open the door!"

She opened the door, and Devin pushed her out of his way and slammed the door shut. He ran into the bedroom and begged her.

"Don't tell them that I'm here. Get rid of them."

"Get rid of who? Who is coming here, Devin? I told you not to come here."

I could hear the noise coming closer to the apartment; the voices began to get louder. Kitten ran to the window to see who was coming. She headed toward the door, and as she stepped in front of it, it crashed in on top of her, knocking her off of her feet and onto the floor.

"Well, well what do we have here?" the large man said.

He was dark and dangerous. I could see the bulge under his shirt, and I was sure that it was a weapon of some kind.

"It's a girl, Carmine. Haven't you ever seen a girl before?" The smaller of the two men laughed as he knelt down beside Kitty. "Excuse me, miss? Where is Devin?"

Kitten was shaken; she rubbed her hand across her forehead and began to sit up.

"Who?" she asked in a confused voice.

"Devin, where is he? I saw him come this way, and you are the only piece of ass that he hits on this block."

"Excuse me, just who do you think you are busting in my door. Get out of my house. You know you are going to have to pay for that."

"Oh, Carmine, pay the lady."

He pulled a large wad of cash from out of his pocket and peeled off two one hundred-dollar bills tossing them onto the floor beside her.

"Now where is he?"

"I don't know who you mean."

"Listen, honey, we don't care about you. All's we want is Devin. Now, if you tell me where he is, we'll leave and never come back, but if you lie we're gong to stay, and trust me, you will tell us where he is."

I could not bear to have these two men torturing my Kitten so I flashed to the bedroom where Devin was hiding and pushed a shelf full of books onto his head. They fell with a mighty crash, and the moans from his pain gave him away.

"Looks like he's in the bedroom, don't it, Carmine?"

Carmine lunged to the bedroom and hauled Devin out from under the pile of books by his ankle, dragging him out into the living room.

"Okay, okay, I give."

"You better give me my fucking money, you piece of shit."

"What do ya want me to do with this fucking guy, Leo? Are we doing it here or are we taking him elsewhere?"

Leo leaned down, grabbing Devin by the face. "You're not going to do anything stupid, now is you? It would be a shame for me to have to bring the pretty lady with us, now wouldn't it?" He pushed his face toward the floor. "Now, where is my fucking money?" He motioned for Carmine to get him to his feet.

"I have the money. I have the money." Devin pleaded, "Please don't hurt me."

"That's what I like to hear. Where is it?"

Devin looked over at Kitten, and her jaw opened and fell down to her chest.

"Oh no, you aren't going to put this on me." The men looked over at her. "I don't have any of your money, sirs. He just came in here begging for me to let him hide out for a while. I was telling him to leave when you broke down my door."

"Okay, Carmine, put him in the car."

Carmine hoisted Devin up and escorted him down the steps and into the trunk of a long black sedan. When the lid was closed, he waddled back up to the apartment and washed his hands in the kitchen sink.

"You should use antibacterial soap. Don't you have any antibacterial soap?"

Kitten just sat there petrified. She kept looking at the door, anticipating the arrival of her knight in shining armor. Realizing she never called for him, her expression seemed grim.

"Grab the girl," Leo instructed.

"No! I don't want to come with you. I want to stay here."

"Sorry, toots, no can do. You have to come with us. Now you can either come quietly or you could leave limp. You make the choice." Leo smiled with a crooked grin and turned toward the door. Carmine was holding onto her arm, and she shouted, "How much does he owe you?"

"What's it to you?" Carmine said as he squinted his eyes at her.

"If I pay you what he owes, you can bring me back the money that he gives you and I can stay home."

"If you pay, you get the money back yourself. I just want my money."

"How much money are we talking about?"

"Three thousand, can you come up with that, toots?"

"No, I only have about half of that."

"Sorry, no deal, I need my money."

Leo motioned again for Carmine to bring her to the car. Carmine snatched her up, and as he was headed toward the steps, I pushed him from behind, knocking Kitten from his grasp. Then I gave one last forceful shove toward the bedroom, and as they both fell onto the floor, I slammed the door shut behind them. As he reached for the knob, I pushed the folding chair against the door and raced to the window flinging it open for Kitten to escape. She looked at the open window and shouted, "John, is that you?" The men were frantically banging on the door. I knocked over the lamp to get Kitten's attention, and it worked because she was out the window and running across the neighbor's backyard before they figured out what had happened.

I followed close behind her, making sure she would be safe. She went around the block, and after about twenty minutes, she doubled back to see if they were gone. The coast was clear, and she darted into the kitchen to grab her money can and a beer. She stepped over the busted folding chair and into the bedroom, straight to the nightstand drawer for her contraband. She dialed the cell phone as she stuffed her purse and pockets with whatever she could think of, then she ran to the bathroom, grabbed her toothbrush, and darted out the door and down the stairs.

"Ed, it's Kitty, I'm in trouble, and I need a place to go. Meet me at the bar; I'll explain everything when I get there." She disconnected her call before listening to the reply on the other end of the line.

Fumbling with her keys, she almost dropped them, but when she gained control, the garage door was open. I watched her eyes light up as she headed for the Dodge. Reaching with one hand, she curled her fingers around the tarp and lifted it up with a strong and heavy heave ho. It lifted and slid off and to one side of the car. She hoisted the battery to its secure spot under the hood and grabbed a wrench from the workbench.

"Oh, baby, I hope you start. Please, God, let him start."

There was sweat dripping from her nose, and her face was set with determination as she mounted the power source to the metal beast.

"Oh please, baby, for me, start." The tears began to well up in her eyes, and her voice was cracking with fear.

She slipped herself behind the wheel and eased comfortably into the seat, closing her eyes as she pushed the shiny key into the chrome dashboard. As she turned it to the first stage, the dash lights became evident, the radio static sounded, and when she turned it just another notch further, it began to crank over. The engine whined. Shortly after the first few seconds of sound came from the engine, her face lit up. Pumping the gas ever so gently, she bit her lip in anticipation of the full turnover.

"Come on, come on, you can do it. I know you can." She begged and pleaded with her machine. She turned the ignition off and rested her head on the steering wheel. There were tears falling down from her eyes as she turned the switch again, and again, she bit her lip as she pumped the gas peddle harder to the floor forcing the fuel to pump into the engine. With a roar, the beast was growling and vibrating beneath her seat. A smile widened on her face, and as she took a deep breath, she let out a tremendous sigh and turned in her seat to get a look at what was behind her. Slowly, the vehicle rolled out of its womb, born to intimidate. Kitten put it in park and jumped out to shut the garage door. She locked it up tight and hopped back into the car.

She punched the gas pedal, and the monster took off, screaming down the driveway, into the street and out of sight. Never looking back, she turned on the radio and rubbed her hands along the steering wheel, smiling proudly at her accomplishment. As she reached Route 35, she stopped for a traffic light and adjusted the rearview mirror to apply some lipstick she pulled from her purse. Even in a crisis, she was concerned about her appearance. Man, I loved this woman. The sound of honking notified Kitten that the traffic light had changed, but she did not seem to care and took her time pulling away.

She called Ed back and explained that she wouldn't be able to meet him at the usual place and instructed him on where to meet her. She snapped the phone closed and tossed it onto the passenger seat letting out a heavy sigh. I sat there admiring her beautiful face as she drove down 35. Her smile continued with each mile she drove. She looked down at the gas gauge. "Shit, I'm gonna run out of gas!" She pulled into the very next station that she came upon and rolled up to the pumps and got out to pump her own gas.

The attendant approached. "Would you like me to fill it up, sexy?"

She smiled. "Sure, but only give me twenty."

The attendant punched in the dollar amount and pulled the nozzle from the pump. He looked around the car but could not find the gas tank door.

"Excuse me, where is your gas tank?"

Kitten laughed. "It's behind the license plate."

"Oh, I didn't know there were tanks there," he said, unsure that it was a fact.

"Yep, it's there," she said as she pulled the plate toward her, revealing the gas cap.

"Cool!" He pushed the nozzle into the tank and clicked it open. Looking at the car, he said, "Wow, this is a huge car."

Kitten paid the man and replaced the gas cap herself. "Thanks," she said, and got into the car and drove away. She pulled into the next store she came upon. All eyes were on her car, and I could swear there were some drooling in the bunch. I have to say the car was beautiful, and because Kitten was driving, it was even more beautiful than it would have been all by itself. As she stepped out of the car, all eyes switched from the car to Kitten. There were hoots and hollers coming from all directions as she walked into the store.

She approached the counter. "Let me have a pack of Marlboro Reds and a pint of blackberry brandy please. Oh and do you have any rolling papers?"

The cashier asked, "What kind would you like?"

"It doesn't really matter, but my favorite is Bambu, if you have them," she said smiling.

She paid for her order and headed back to her car. There were some men looking in the driver's side window. "Can I help you?" she asked abruptly.

"Nice car you have here. Would you like to sell it?"

Kitten laughed. "It took me a really long time to finish him; this is his first road trip. I'm not interested in selling him right away."

"I'll give you eight thousand for it right now, cash."

"Sorry, but like I said, it's not for sale. I really must get going. Excuse me, gentlemen." She pushed her way through the men, got into her car, and headed out to meet Ed.

She pulled her car into the parking lot of a little bar and parked in the back, rolled herself a joint, and locked the car up tight. As she waited for Ed, she smoked her joint and rubbed the car with a handkerchief that she pulled from her purse.

"You are so beautiful. I thought for sure you would be, but looking at you parked here like this I know, it to be true. You are my best work yet. I don't think I'll have the heart to let you go. I think you'll be mine and only mine. There isn't a soul on this earth that is worthy of having you, including myself. You are gorgeous."

Ed pulled his car beside hers. "You finished it? Wow, it looks great. How much do you want for her?"

"Him, it's a him, and you're not getting this one. In fact, no one is getting him. He's all mine."

"So, why did you call me to this dump? I have a lot of business to attend to you know; time is money, honey."

"They have Devin, and they tried to take me, too, but I got away. I don't think it'll be safe to go back to the apartment. I don't know what to do."

"Who has Devin? Where did they take him? Tell me what happened."

"Devin came over, and while I was telling him to leave, the men broke the door down and took him away. They tried to take me, too, but like I said, I got away. They put him in the trunk of their car, and when they came back for me, I locked them in my bedroom and got away."

"Why did they take Devin?"

"They said that he took their money, and when I offered to pay what he owed, they said that I didn't have enough money, and they were going to take me for collateral."

"Where do you think they took him?"

"I'm not sure, but we have to find him. I think they are going to kill him."

"Okay, but how are we going to find him if you don't know?"

"Maybe we can talk to Bea; she might know where to look."

"The psychic? You know that I don't believe in that crap."

"What other choice do we have?"

They agreed and drove off. Ed followed Kitten to Bea's house, and they parked in the driveway. They walked to the garden, and I followed close behind. Bea was grilling chicken and had the picnic table set for three.

"There are cold beers in the cooler under the bench, and the corn is almost ready. I'm glad you finally made it." she seemed to be expecting them.

Ed looked at Kitty. "How did she know we were coming? Did you call her from the car?"

"No, silly, she just knows things. I told you that. When are you going to listen to me when I talk to you."

Bea laughed. "Ed, you never trust, but someday you will, someday you will." She patted him on the back and tickled his neck with her fingertips.

"Then you know why we are here? Tell me why we are here," Ed said with a smile on his face.

"Ed, you are looking for someone. I believe it's someone who you don't care to help, but for Kitty, you'll do anything. This kid is in grave danger, and you only have about three hours to find him before it's too late."

"Do you know where he is? Is he okay?" Kitty asked with fear in her voice.

Bea served the chicken and corn to her guests and explained what was happening.

"Devin is okay now; he is being held in a warehouse in the Lakewood Industrial Park. There are lots of lights. You can see a baseball stadium from the side of the building, and there is a cement picnic bench in a fenced-in area. This is where he is being held. You must take care not to go through the front, use the bathroom window. It's on the south side of the building, and it's open. The men haven't told anyone about you, Kitty, so it's safe, but, Ed, I have to tell you one thing: You are going to be faced with an important decision tonight, and if you choose wrong, you will lose your life, so keep your wits about you."

"What's going to happen? What's the big decision, Bea?"

"Puss, you know that I don't see all of the details, I only tell you what I know. That's the best I can do. Now eat, you both need your strength. It's going to be a long night."

Ed stood up, pushing his plate away from him. "Now let me get this straight. Devin is locked in a warehouse in the Lakewood Industrial Park, and I'm in danger. I don't see how this could be. I don't give a shit what happens to that little piss ant. I'm not putting myself in danger for that stain."

Bea stood up and reached for Ed's hand. "Ed, if you don't go, Kitty will not make it. They will come for her, and when they do, it will be she who will lose the gift of life. These men have already been to her home. They know her, and she will never be safe. You must go, Ed; Kitty's life depends on it."

Kitty gasped. "Why me? What did I do?" She held her head in her hands and began to cry. "I'm never going to be able to drive through a tree, am I, Bea?"

Ed rubbed his head and pressed his lips tightly together. "God damn it, Kitty; I told you Devin was trouble. Why didn't you listen to me? Why did you let him back into your house? You never listen to a word I say; it's always, 'Yes, Ed,' and then you do what you want to anyway." He turned to Bea. "How long do we have?"

"You have a little over two hours. Don't go unarmed; you'll need protection," Bea explained.

"Don't worry, I have everything I need. Come on, Kitty, let's go."

Kitten wrapped her arms around Beatrice. "I love you!" She held on tight, not wanting to let go.

"Everything is going to be all right, Puss, I promise. Now go find Devin and finish this thing. Once you do this, everything will come together." Bea looked behind Kitten and smiled at me. "Watch over her, John; you still have work to do."

"John? Is he still hanging around here, Bea?" She looked around trying her hardest to see me.

"I told you he would be. Puss, he is here for you. You need to have an open mind. Ed's right, you never listen."

Ed laced onto the horn beckoning Kitty to get in the car. She hugged Bea again, lifted her purse off the bench, and headed to the car.

"Oh, Puss, by the way, the car sounds great. I knew you could do it."

Kitten smiled as she pressed the door handle, and as the door swung open, she turned and looked at Bea. "It's better than I expected; I like it, too." She sat in the driver's seat and backed out of the driveway.

"Ed, what are we going to do?"

"Listen, babe, you are going to stay in the car, and I'm going to handle it. First thing we do is drive to the stadium and find this warehouse. Now hit on this and relax, honey. It's going to be cool, I promise." He passed her a joint.

Chapter Fourteen

*T*hey drove to Lakewood Stadium without saying a word to one
another. Kitten shuffled through the radio stations stopping at an
all-eighties block. She glided her fingers in a circular motion around
the knob of the gear shift that was in the center console beside her
seat. There was a half smile barely visible on her face, and as I looked
into her eyes through the rearview mirror, I could see the slight signs
of happiness that she felt for her car.

As they approached the park, the lights were shining bright, Ed
shouted for Kitty to pull the car over. She did, and he got out of the
car.

"Now what do I do?" she asked.

"Go put the car in the lot across the street and meet me back
here."

Kitten drove to the parking lot and locked her car up tight. She
opened the trunk, stuffed a tire iron into her pants, and headed back
over to meet Ed. She jogged across the street, dodging a car that was
speeding, and tripped on the curb throwing her face first into a line
of bushes.

"Nice form!" Ed said laughing.

"Very funny, very funny, asshole, why is it that whenever we
have a job to do, you are always laughing at me and making me feel
like a fool?" she said as she brushed the dirt off of her clothes and
rose to her feet.

Ed continued to laugh. "Sorry, babe, it's just the way it is. You always make me laugh. Come on now, let's find this warehouse."

They walked through a dirt path that separated the roadway from the industrial park, and when they got to the end of the path, they stepped onto an empty parking lot.

"This can't be the one. I can't see the stadium from here. How are we ever going to find him? There was fear in her voice, and she began to shake.

"All we have to do is walk along this treeline here, and when we can see the stadium, we found it. Don't worry; we'll make it in time."

She hung her head down low and followed Ed. As they walked, she followed slowly, and when Ed found the place, she almost didn't believe it. She looked down the side of the large warehouse, and like Bea predicted, there was a cement picnic bench in a fenced-in area.

"Do you think this is it?" Ed asked.

"It has to be; there's the bench Bea talked about." She pointed to the bench and started to run, heading straight toward it.

"Kitty, get back here. I have to check the place out first." He chased after her and scooped her up in his arms, pulling her off to the side out of the bright lights that shone on the driveway. "Are you crazy? We have to do this right, or we'll both get caught."

Ed put her down and headed to the south side of the building to look for the bathroom window. They weaved in and out of bushes, shrubs, and trees, and when they reached the halfway point, there it was, the bathroom window, unlocked and open just as Bea said it would be.

Kitten scurried up a tree, and as she began to reach for the window, Ed grabbed a hold of her foot. "What the fuck do you think you're doing?" he whispered.

"I'm going in. What does it look like?" she whispered back to him.

"You stay here, I'm going in." He tugged a little harder on her leg, and she slid down the trunk of the tree and onto the ground.

"What did you do that for? I'm going with you, Ed, and there's nothing that you can do to stop me." Kitty put her hands on her hips and looked at him with a straight, stern face.

"Listen, babe, this here is dangerous business. You could get us all killed. You stay here." He stomped his foot and pointed to the ground.

"What if someone comes, and I'm out here all alone, and then what do I do?"

Ed reached into his pocket and pulled out a small handgun. "If anyone comes but the police, you shove this in their face and hightail it out of here. Don't try to be a hero, just run." He placed the gun in her hand and kissed her on the cheek. "Don't worry, everything is going to be all right, I promise. Now stay put."

Ed struggled to get himself up the tree and into the open window. He fell to the bathroom floor with a loud thud. Kitten giggled down below and covered her mouth to keep her voice from carrying. Ed popped his head out the window and looked down on her with squinted eyes. She bent over and giggled some more. When she looked up, Ed was out of sight.

I flew through the warehouse looking for Devin and whoever else was there. It was some kind of processing plant. There were tanks filled with liquids, and smoke lifted above the tanks, dissipating into the air before it rose too high. The smell was strong and harsh on the eyes. When I came to the entrance of the offices, I could hear people talking. I looked back to see where Ed was, and he had just come around the corner into the tank room. I watched as he held his nose and blinked his eyes continuously from the fumes of the harmful liquids.

I followed the voices to a large office. When I entered the room, I could see Devin. He was tied to a chair and being brutally beaten by the two men. His face was pummeled to a bloody mess, and his right arm was broken. His shirt was ripped, and his chest had large slices all over it. He was bleeding profusely and was obviously in a lot of pain.

I could hear Ed coming around the office door, and in the distance, I could hear Kitten spilling onto the floor from the bathroom window. Ed was right, she never listened. I headed over to her, making sure that she would be safe. She was fixing her hair in the mirror when I arrived, then she fumbled in her bag for some lipstick. I took a deep breath and admired her for a moment. She heard Ed's voice and ran toward the tank room. I followed closely and pushed the air to force the harmful vapors away from her as she headed toward the office. When we arrived, Ed was pointing a machine gun at the men.

"Now, everyone just stay where they are and nobody gets hurt." He pointed the barrel of the gun switching from one man to the next with a sinister half smile on his face. "Don't move!"

Kitty got a look at Devin and screeched, "Oh my God, Devin, are you all right?" She ran over to him and pushed the men out of her way. "How could you do this to him, you animals?" Frantically, she tugged at the ropes that held him to the chair.

Devin let out a loud shriek, "Ahhhh, my arm, I think it's broken." He squirmed in his chair writhing in pain.

"Sit still so I can get these ropes untied. Moving isn't going to help." She pulled a knife from her purse and cut the ropes, freeing him from the chair. He fell to his knees and went limp on the floor. "Oh, Ed, we need to get him to a doctor quick."

"Okay you, slowly put your hands up, and don't make any sudden moves. I'm locked on you, and I'm not afraid to blast your guts all over the wall behind you either." The man put his hands up over his head. Ed motioned to Kitten. "Okay, Babe, get the gun from his belt. Now it's your turn." Ed pointed to the other man. "Put your hands over your head, and if either of you move, I'll blast you both sky high." He motioned again to Kitty, and she took his gun, too.

She emptied the bullets of both guns onto the floor and heaved the guns out into one of the tanks just outside the door. "Let's see you get them now, dirtbag."

She raced over to Devin and helped him to his feet leading him out the side door to the parking lot. She placed him on the bench and ran through the woods to get her car. Devin lay on the bench bleeding from all over. His face was swollen and almost unrecognizable. He looked up at me with little hope left in his eyes. The light shone bright around the corner as Kitten's car roared up the driveway. Its deadly glow followed her vehicle, and when the car stopped, so did the light. She ran around the car and opened the door.

She ran over to Devin. "It's going to be okay; we're going to get you to the hospital, and they're going to fix you up real good. Don't worry; you're going to be just fine." The rear seat was brightly lit with its rays of death waiting for its victim to be placed inside. She tried to lift him, but she could not do it alone. "I can't get you up, Devin. You have to help me. Get up! Get up!" She pulled and tugged, but she could not do it.

I heard shots, so I went inside to see what Ed was doing, and when I got there, one of the men was dead on the floor in a pool of blood, and the other man was hanging from a chain hovering inches from one of the poisonous liquid-filled tanks.

"Please! I'll do anything, just let me go!" the man pleaded.

"Oh anything huh, what will you give to me if I let you go? What do you have to offer me?" Ed laughed.

"The car, you can have the car."

"What would I want with a Guido's car? What else do you got?"

"It's in the car, there's X in the trunk and enough money to buy just about anything you could possibly want," the man pleaded.

"Oh really, and why should I believe you? I know you'll say just about anything to save yourself." The light shone brightly at the bottom of the tank, and with a heavy sigh, Ed pushed the green button that controlled the chain, and it lowered the man into the tank with a splash. After a minute of floundering, the water went still. Ed walked up to the man lying on the ground and checked to see if he was still breathing. The light had already gone dim, and just for good measure, he pressed the gun barrel onto the man's forehead and pulled the trigger. I closed my eyes, and my throat clenched tight as I heard Kitten's footsteps approaching. Ed heard them, too, because he darted over to her before she could witness the carnage that was just around the corner of the tank.

"What happened? Where did they go?" Kitten said out of breath with her chest heaving, as she pulled her shirt collar up to her face to wipe the sweat away from her eyes. "I can't get Devin into the car. I need your help. Should I call the police? What did you do with those two men?"

Ed just led her out toward the door. "We can't call the police; the men are dead. It was them or us, and I chose to save us. They were bad men, and we don't need any of them following us around. I'll help you get Devin into the car, and you can drop me off before you get to the hospital."

I raced out to the car and pushed it forward down to the end of the driveway so the light would go away, and Devin's transport would be safe for travel. When Ed and Kitten got outside, Ed picked up Devin.

"Kitty, would you like to tell me why you parked so fucking far away?"

"Ed, the car was over here just a few minutes ago. I didn't park it there." She looked around in mass confusion. "I know I parked it over here." She ran to the car and helped Ed guide Devin comfortably into the back seat. "You're going to be okay, just like I said. We'll be at the hospital in like, not even ten minutes from here. You're going to be fine."

They both got into the car and simultaneously closed the doors. Kitten raced to the hospital, making sure to watch out for patrolmen in the area. Looking in her mirrors, hands shaking, she made it to Route 37. As they approached the emergency room entrance, Ed hopped out of the car.

"Kitty, just drop him off; don't talk to the cops and make sure he doesn't mention my name to anyone. Do you hear that, Devin, my friend? I saved your ass, and this will be the last time. If my name comes up at all, I'm coming after you, and I won't be bringing Kitty along to drive you to the hospital. Where I'll take you, only you and God will know where you are."

Kitty grimaced at Ed and proceeded up the driveway to the emergency room. As she pulled up to the ambulance doors, she shouted, "He needs a doctor; he has lost a lot of blood. I think he is going to die!" Two paramedics threw down their cigarettes and ran over to the car. When they saw Devin's condition, they sucked in air through their teeth and narrowed their eyes at one another. "Is he going to be okay?" she cried.

"We need a gurney out here!" one of the men screamed.

A nurse came out with the gurney, and the two men hauled Devin out of the car and hoisted him up onto the bed, making sure not to jostle him around too much. A security guard came out of his little booth and instructed Kitty to park her car in the lot. This was the opportunity for Kitten to get away. Instead of parking, she raced out of the driveway and headed down Route 37 toward the beach. She dialed someone on her cell phone, but they didn't answer. She threw the phone down on the passenger seat and cranked up the radio.

Her eyes were filled with tears. As she reached into her pocket and pulled out a joint, she swerved and almost hit the bridge wall, but she regained control of the car and proceeded on her way. She took the turnoff toward her apartment, and when she pulled into the driveway, Ed's car was parked in front of the garage. She parked and headed up the steps, finding Ed reattaching her door.

"Listen, kid, this is the last time I get your friends out of a jam. This one was big, and I don't have it in me to do it again," Ed said in a low voice. "He's lucky I didn't let them kill him."

"I understand, thank you for everything. How can I ever repay you for all you have done?"

"Just keep yourself out of trouble. I would hate to see anything happen to you, Kitty, you mean too much to me. With everything that has happened, am I able to trust you to do the smart thing and stay away from that loser?"

"Yes, Ed, I promise, I will not see him ever again."

"What happened at the hospital? Did you talk to the cops?"

"No, the security guard told me to move my car, and then I just came here."

"Good girl, you did the right thing, but I'm telling you, if Devin mentions my name, I'm coming after him, and there is nothing you can do to stop me."

"Trust me, I won't be seeing him again. Thanks for fixing my door."

"No problem, sweetheart, you should know by now that I'll do whatever I can for you. Just don't get into any more trouble. And to make sure that you don't, here, I have something for you. It's a little gift from the guys who broke your door. They insisted that you have it." He tossed a sack at her, and she caught it.

"What is it? What's inside?"

"Just open it."

"Oh my God, Ed, where did you get this?"

"I told you, it was a gift from the thugs that broke down your door. Now you don't have to heist cars or sell drugs or whatever else you do that could get you into trouble. Just put it away and use it sparingly."

"Can I give you some for your trouble?"

"I have already taken my cut; this is all yours, honey."

"Okay then, can I get a few bundles from you? I have money to pay."

"I left some on the nightstand for you; spread it out, it's really potent shit. I'm going out of town for a few days, but I'll call to see how you are doing. Just don't go see that Devin. Stay the hell away from him, you hear me?"

"Yes, Ed, I hear you."

Ed hugged her and kissed her on the cheek before he headed down the steps to his car. Kitten ran outside and smiled. "How are you going to leave if I'm blocking you in?" she shouted.

"Please move your beast for me." Ed laughed.

"I'll talk to you in a couple of days!" Kitty shouted as she pulled into the street.

"You just keep your half of the deal, and I'll be happy. See you in about a week."

Ed sped off down the street, and Kitty pulled her car back into the driveway, making sure to lock it up tight before she went up to her apartment. As she walked through the door, Azreal came running into the house rubbing against her legs and purring at the same time, meowing for her attention.

"Hey, pussycat, how was your day? Boy, wait till I tell you about my day. This was one for the record books, but I won't bother you with that right now. I think I'm going to take a nice hot bath and relax. I'm bushed from all the excitement."

She trotted off to the bathroom and disrobed. I gave her some privacy and sat in the living room thinking about how I was going to get her in a place of significance under the next full moon. I only had a few days, and I still didn't know where I was supposed to take her.

The radio was playing, and Azreal pushed the bathroom door open with his nose just enough for me to see her sitting in the tub.

She was rubbing her body with a washcloth, singing to the music. She dried off her hands and pulled the hamper basket over to where she could reach it. She had a few lines of cocaine waiting to be inhaled. She pulled them in with a large sniff and rested her head on the back of the tub. About an hour went by before she opened her eyes again. I was beginning to worry about her. She never acted like this. What was going on in her head? Why was she doing this to herself? I watched as she rose from the bath and blotted the droplets of water from her body. She was a vision to behold.

She padded to her bedroom and rummaged through her closet searching for something to wear. Smiling, she pulled out a tiny schoolgirl's uniform and a shiny pair of patent leather shoes to match. Giggling to herself, she got into her cute suit and smiled as she admired herself in the closet mirror. She glided her hand across her chest firmly, gripping one of her breasts. The left side of her lip rose as she puckered at herself with gleaming eyes into the image she saw in the mirror. Reaching down with her free hand, she grabbed hold of her left ankle and slid her fingers up along her inner thigh. When she reached her short hemline, she cocked her head up, looked with pride into the mirror, and laughed out loud.

"Wait till they get a load of me." Her voice was confident. She was preparing for something, and I was almost afraid to imagine what the night was going to be like.

"Damn, I look sexy; the boys aren't going to know what hit them when they see me tonight. What do you think, Azreal? Do you think Mommy is going to knock 'em dead tonight or what?"

She gathered up her drugs and placed them into her purse, grabbed a beer from the refrigerator, and trotted down to her car. I knew that she was going to that shitty pub, and I hated that she was dressed like this, but what could I do? I needed to talk to Beatrice and fast. I took the ride to the bar with Kitten, making sure that was where she was going. When I saw her enter the bar, I zoomed over to Bea's house for a little chat. I had some questions and needed answers.

When she saw me, she said, "Did everything go okay? Is the boy all right?"

"Yes, he is at the hospital. He got beat pretty bad, but I think he'll be okay."

"Good, I knew they would make it. Has Ed gone already?"

"How did you know he was going?"

"I told you before, I know a lot of things. I just don't see it complete. Now what brings you here?"

"I was just wondering if you knew where I was supposed to take Kitty during the full moon. I was told to reveal myself to her, but I'm not sure of where I'm supposed to do it. Do you know?"

"Sorry, I do not. I wish I could help you, but I can't. You are going to have to figure this out for yourself. Don't worry, you'll manage." She smiled gently at me and motioned for me to leave.

"Thank you anyway. I hope to see you again."

"You will, son, you will."

I headed back to the bar, taking my time to think about where I would take her. The only place I could think of was the lookout tower on the beach where we spent our first night together. That was the only place that really mattered to me. I knew that she had a good time there, and there was not another place of significance that crossed my mind. Besides, the carving was there; it was our place. It had to be it.

The boardwalk was hopping, and there was a wave of bodies coming and going, talking and eating, playing and fighting. I could not wait for the summer to be over, and the vacationers to be on their merry little way. As I approached the bar, I noticed that Kitty was dancing with a girl. All the men were focusing on her tight ass as the skirt lifted up when she twirled around. She was wearing a white thong, and just a hint of a tan line showed from her bathing suit, being only a tiny bit larger than her undergarments. She was beautiful. The bartender was clearly getting pissed off and so were the people waiting for their drinks to be served. Tiger was neglecting his customers because he was too busy keeping his eyes on Kitty. I could tell that she was making him crazy the way that she was carrying on. There was fire in his eyes. One of the bouncers saw what was going on and approached Tiger.

"Hey, Bobby, what are you letting her get you all pissed off for? Let it go, man; she's not with you. You can't tame that one. You know how she is."

"Stay out of it, Eli, you don't know what the fuck you are talking about. I'm gonna marry that girl. Mark my words, by the end of the summer, she'll be mine."

He pushed passed Eli and snuck up behind Kitty. Wrapping his arms around her waist, he lifted her off of her feet, spun her around, and planted a passionate kiss upon her lips. She didn't resist him; she kissed him back, gently caressing the sides of his head and the back of his neck with her fingertips.

My heart was pounding; I hated to see her doing this with other men. The more I thought about it, the more it became clear Kitty was damaged goods. Why did I feel the need to spend time with such a popular woman? How could I expect her to be mine, to fall in love with me? I was not sure what to think of my newly found emotion. I had had just about all of them when it came to Kitty Morris, but this one was not pleasant. Could I be the one to tame her? Would she love me and only me? I hated feeling this way; I was ashamed to have these feelings of such jealousy and resentment for her. I kept telling myself, "She is a lonely women; she needs someone to love her. She just hasn't found the right man to keep her happy." I knew that I could be that man. If she could love me in that way, then I would become mortal and our lives would be perfect.

I looked back at Bobby and Kitten; their bodies were still intertwined with passion. My heart was breaking, and I knew that the few days that I had left were going to have to count for something other than my own agenda, so I left my love at the bar so I could attend to my work. I looked back for one last time as I stepped out onto the boardwalk and could not help but feel empty inside. Would she be with me and only me? I needed it to be that way. I did not want a repeat of my first life. I was not able to control myself then. Why would I think that I could control myself now? I needed to clear my head, and being a protector of life, I knew of only one way to do it, my way, safety first. I headed over to the amusement pier to see what was going on. There were voices carrying over to me that seemed to need some attention.

"Why don't you just leave me alone?" a young woman shouted.

"Oh come on, let's just go back to the room and go for a swim. I don't understand what the problem is."

"You're the problem, Alex. Who was that girl, huh? Why, did she mistake you for someone else?"

"I'm telling you, baby, I don't know who she was. You know something, I bet she did think I was someone else. Now let's go swimming, honey."

The girl stormed off heading down the ramp leading off of the boards and down to the street. Alex wasn't far behind her, and when she realized that he was close, she darted out into traffic, and the light showed itself. It sat waiting for her arrival.

I rushed out, but before I could divert the automobile, it struck the girl sending her flying into the air. The light moved down the street, and onto the hood of another automobile, but there was nothing that I could do to soften the blow, so I threw myself onto the car directly in the center of the light. I cradled the girl in my arms for safety. A feeling of control suddenly came over me, my teeth chattered together, and the girl let out a painstaking groan.

"Help me please!" she gurgled, staring directly into my eyes. But what could I do? "Please help me." There was blood trickling from out of her ears and nose. Her legs were shattered and her collarbone was poking out from under the skin. I held her in my arms to bring her whatever comfort I could provide. I looked into the car, and the man driving showed a face of disbelief. He was mortified at what had just taken place. Fumbling for the key, he turned off his engine and got out of the car dialing his cell phone for the EMS.

"There was an accident. A young woman landed on my car. She needs an ambulance right away." His hands were shaking, and he began to cry. "Help is on the way."

Alex came running over to us. He took one look at her and began to cry. "Someone call nine one one, help! Someone help! Marsha, talk to me. Can you hear me?" He pulled his shirt off and gently placed it under her head.

"I don't think you should be moving her! The police and ambulance are on their way," the man said with a look of concern.

Marsha didn't take her eyes off of me. "Thank you! Thank you!" she said in a low tone of voice.

I could hear the sirens in the distance. "See, they are coming," I told her. "Everything is going to be all right." She tried to smile but the agony of her injuries was unbearable.

There was a crowd of people beginning to swarm, and a few bike patrolmen arrived to begin the crowd control. One of the very first to arrive was a young man, and when he saw the victim, he ran to her side. "Marsha, it's going to be okay. Help is on the way. They should be here in less than two minutes." He looked over at Alex and said, "Sir, I need you to please stand back. Give the girl some air." Then he shouted, "Everyone please stand back, please get back onto the sidewalk!"

A patrol car pulled up and then another. Two more arrived, and the police were ushering the traffic down the side street and away from the scene of the accident. There were people still trickling out into the street, and the police were ushering them back to the sidewalk. "Please remain on the sidewalk, people, so we can do our jobs."

The public voices overlapped. "What happened?" "Did you see that?" "Holy shit, she went flying onto that car over there." "I can't see!" "Is she dead?" "She was running from someone." "Oh, that poor girl!" "Where is the ambulance?" "They should really have stop signs on this street." "Dude, that was freaky, I need a drink." The masses were out, and it seemed that when tragedy struck, they came from out of the woodwork.

Alex sat on the curb with his head in his hands. The police were questioning him and the two drivers that were involved in the accident. All faces were somber with disbelief at the present events that had taken place.

The crowd parted for more patrolmen, and one of them raced over to the girl. "Marsha! Oh my God! Marsha, are you okay?"

The officer that was questioning Alex saw the patrolman with Marsha, and he ran over to his side. "Shawn, before you find out from someone else, I have to tell you that Alex is over there." Shawn had hatred in his eyes and lunged toward Alex. The other officer grabbed hold of him. "Hold up, Shawn, you can't freak out; there are a lot of people around."

"Alex! Did you have something to do with this? I'll kill you, you bastard!" Three more officers assisted in holding Shawn back, keeping him away from Alex. "Well, did you? I told you to stay away from my sister, and damn it, if I find out that you were the reason for this happening, I promise I'll kill you myself."

"Shawn, see to your sister. The paramedics are here; go with her to the hospital. Someone will take your bike back to the station, and I'll call your mother and tell her what happened. We'll take Alex in for questioning and sort this mess out. Just stay with your sister." He patted Shawn on the back and nodded his head. "Come on, man, she needs you now." He ushered Shawn over to the ambulance.

"We got the victim and one passenger, and we are en route requesting a police escort," the EMT said into the radio microphone as the siren wailed ordering traffic to pull over to the right. "Shawn, we have an escort and all green lights directly to the ER. The trauma unit is ready and waiting for our arrival." The rear doors closed, and they were off to the hospital.

Alex was arguing with one of the cops, and they placed him in handcuffs and stuffed him into the back of one of the patrol cars. The crowd began to disperse as the tow trucks went about their business dragging the blood-soaked cars up onto the flatbeds and off to wherever it was that they took them. I wondered if Kitten was still sucking face with the jungle creature. The thought created discomfort in the pit of my stomach. I was hesitant to find out for sure, but being that there was nothing more that I could do here and I longed to be near her, I flashed myself back to the bar.

Dark and smoky, a sticky film of tar covered the entire bar from the windows to the plastic palm trees; it was dank and disgusting. I could never comprehend how Kitty Morris could be associated with scum like this. Then I considered her profession and had to be honest with myself. She stole cars for a living; she was a repo man. You could glorify it any way you liked; she was still a professional car thief.

It was wall-to-wall bodies and scented with the usual urine aroma. Kitten was sitting at the corner of the bar, and Bobby was down the other end earning a living, keeping one eye on the bar and one eye on Kitty. She was talking with a beer in one hand and a cigarette in the other to some guy covered in tattoos.

"So are you racking or am I?" she smiled.

"I'll break, you rack. I like to watch your rack!" He grinned.

"Don't you mean watch me rack?"

"Nope, I meant exactly what I said. You have a great rack, baby!" he leaned in and tried to kiss her.

She pushed her hands up against his chest, forcing him away from her. "Wait a minute; I said I would shoot a game of pool with you. That don't mean that we are going on a date here, honey. You need to just evacuate my personal space. If I find the need to rub up against something, it'll be the jukebox not you." She pushed him away and gently but firmly slapped his face. I had never seen it done in such a fashion that it would actually be a turn-on, but it was, and I thought her Tiger felt the same way, because when he saw her do it, he was on the move to be by her side. "What?" she asked.

He was looking at her with puzzlement. "What? How can you ask me that? What are you doing with this guy, Kitty? I thought we were going to be together tonight."

"Yeah, but you don't get off till like twelve, and I wanted to shoot some pool. It's cool; this guy is just being cute. I can handle him. I can handle myself!" She was getting perturbed at the entire conversation. Her eyes glared with fire at the accusations. "What is wrong with you, Bobby? We aren't together. You have no right to act like this. I thought you understood that I wasn't going to be getting serious with anyone. I just got released from that prison system, and I want to live free for a while. I need to find myself."

"I know, baby, but when I see you with other guys, it makes me crazy. I just want to hit someone." He rubbed his fingers against her hand and smiled at her.

"I'm not with other guys, Bobby. I'm sitting in a bar drinking and shooting pool. Christ, I can go to another bar if you like. I wouldn't want you to be distracted while you were working," she said in a very sarcastic tone.

"No! You don't have to go, honey. I've been a complete idiot. Go ahead; shoot pool with your friend. I'm cool!" He tried to say it in a convincing voice, but I sure wasn't convinced, and neither was

Kitty because she gathered up her things and headed toward the door. "Kitty, where are you going? You don't have to leave. Get back over here."

"I'm out of here. I'll come back after you get off. Don't follow me. I have some things to do, and you have to work. See you around twelve thirty." She walked out the door while she was still talking and bumped right into some young man. When she turned to apologize, her eyes widened, and she yelped, "Oh my God, if it isn't Joey! What the hell are you doing here?"

"Hey, babe, how the hell have you been? What are you doing here at the beach? Where are you staying?" He hugged her tight and kissed her on the cheek. "What have you been up to, girl?"

"Nothing much, you know, same shit just a bigger pile of it. What are you doing here?"

"I came down with my wife and kids, promised them a nice summer vacation."

"Then why did you come here? You should be in Orlando or something."

"Can't afford Orlando, dear. The pier is the best I could come up with. Where are you staying?"

"I'm actually living here. I got myself a little place not to far from here, and I'm working on cars and stuff."

"You're not still working with Eddie, are you?"

"Oh yeah, Ed and I are still partners in crime. But enough about that, what is this? You have a kid?"

"Not a kid, three kids: Mike, Carol, and Donna, three, two, and five months."

"Well now, I know what you have been up to lately. Dude, you need to get cable or something. Who did you marry?"

"You don't know her. I met her at a gig in Philly. You would like her. Had to knock her up to keep her around, but it worked out. I have the kids, and I'm really happy. You should come and meet them later. They are over at her uncle's house in Point. Do you want to come over for dinner tomorrow night?"

"I'll try, but I can't promise you anything. I have been really busy. I'm never sure what is going to come up." She reached into her purse and pulled out a business card. "Call me tomorrow. I'll let you know what I'm doing. Sorry, but I got to run. Call me!"

"Okay, Kitty, I'll call you tomorrow. It was great seeing you again. Try to come!"

"I will! Bye!"

She trotted down the boardwalk heading toward the southern end of the pier. There were a lot of people on the boardwalk, and she was getting irritated by the mob and cut off down to the beach. She walked along the coast carrying her shoes in her hand and walking with her feet in the water. There were some teenagers sitting in a circle laughing and having fun. Kitten stopped when she heard her name being called out.

"Hey, Kitty, where are you going in such a hurry?" It was Devin's sister. She ran over to Kitten and hugged her. "What are you doing? Have you seen my brother? He hasn't come home for a couple of days. Mom is really starting to worry about him."

Kitten looked at her, not exactly knowing what to say to her about Devin. "I think he came by the other night, but I was sleeping and didn't want to deal with him so I didn't answer the door. I'll call you if anything..." She bit her lip, and her head hung low.

"Kitty, what's wrong? Listen, come here and meet my friends. They are smoking a blunt, and you are more than welcome to join us. It's good shit, too. Frankie got it from some guy in Freehold. It's like primo or something."

Kitten looked as though she was going to resist the offer, but when drugs were involved, Kitten usually never said no. She accepted and sat on the sand in a circle with the other kids. "What's up, people?" she said smiling.

"Hello! Who is this?" one of the guys said smiling.

"This is my brother's ex-girlfriend, Kitty; try to act like a normal person, please."

"Here, take a hit from this bad boy. I bet you haven't smoked anything like this before."

"Thanks! Don't mind if I do," Kitty said as she plucked the large cigar from his fingers. She placed it between her lips and inhaled, steadily pulling the smoke deep into her lungs. She exhaled an enormous cloud and fell back on the blanket.

"Man, this shit is good! Can I get some off of you?" She reached into her pocket and pulled out some money. "What can I get for like sixty bucks?"

"I can't do sixty, but I'll do a forty." The guy reached into his pocket and pulled out a bag. "Do you have anything to put it in?" He passed a large pinch of the marijuana over to her, and she opened her hand to accept it.

"I don't have anything to put it in." She rooted through her bag looking but came up with nothing. "Wait, I have something." She pulled a cigarette pack from out of her pocket and slipped off the clear cellophane wrapper. "This will work. I got this shit, baby. Thanks a lot. I'm sorry that I can't stay, but I have a lot of shit to do. I'll see you around." She stood up and waved as she headed down the beach. "Thanks again!" she shouted.

They waved back to her and talked amongst themselves as she headed out to God knows where.

Chapter Fifteen

I followed close making sure to keep a close eye for the light and my duties at the same time. Kitten was so cute the way she made her way down the beach talking to the seagulls. She was stoned on marijuana and laughing at just about everything she saw. There were some men fishing on the beach, and she stopped to look at their catch bucket.

"How you guys doing? Catch anything?" She peered into the bucket with a big smile on her face.

"Yeah, we caught a few skates and a couple of stripers. Do you fish?" one of the men asked as he nudged his buddy's arm. "Would you like to have a beer with us? Help yourself to the cooler behind you."

"I sure would like a cold one if you wouldn't mind." The man reached into the cooler and pulled out a beer. Kitten reached out to grab it, and he pulled it away, just far enough out of her reach.

"What's the big idea?" she whined.

"I'm just messing with you, cutie; here you go." He opened it and passed it back over to her, but this time, he let her have it.

"Thanks a lot; this was very nice of you. I had, like, mad cottonmouth. You saved me." She chugged down the beer quickly. "Wow, that hit the spot! See you guys."

"Where are you going so quickly? Don't you want to have another beer?"

"Yeah, hang out and fish with us?" The shorter or stockier of the men pleaded.

"Sorry, I have other plans, but thank you for the beer. Bye!" She trotted on her way down the beach, leaving the men standing there scratching their heads.

I tell you, she was the only person who could walk fifty yards and get every thing from pot to beer without even looking for it. What was it about this woman that made me want her? She was so complex and needy. How would she be able to be with only me? Would she even consider having only one man in her life? I thought about how crazy Bobby the Tiger was when it came to seeing her with other men, and I knew in my heart that I would be just as jealous if we were to be together. But I was drawn to Kitten and desperately wanted her to be by my side for all of eternity.

As she approached the last amusement pier, she headed up the steps leading to a bar. It had a large deck that wrapped around the entire outside, and there were a lot of people drinking and having a good time. I followed her inside, and from ceiling to floor, the bar was covered in nautical décor. The walls were painted the color of the sea with scenes of bright-colored sea creatures frolicking about. There were fishing nets hanging from the ceiling with large plastic crabs all tangled up in them. She bellied up to the bar and ordered a shot and a beer then took a seat outside. She drank her drinks staring out over the water. I could only imagine what she was thinking, but she looked beautiful, her hair gently blowing in the breeze and her eyes wide open with excitement. I couldn't imagine what she was thinking about, but I was sure that it wasn't me.

She pulled out her cell phone and dialed. "May I have patient information, please… Emergency room, please…Yes, my name is Detective Swanson, and I'm calling about the young man that was brought in a few hours ago, beaten up pretty bad…What is his status?" She smiled at her reflection in the large bay window of the bar. "Who is the ER doctor for this patient?…Please have him call me if there are any changes in his patient's condition…Thank you very much for your time." She hung up the phone and went back inside the bar to order herself another drink.

"Are you okay, Kitty?" the bartender asked with a concerned look on her face.

"Oh yeah, Susan, I'm fine. You better give me another shot, though."

"Are you sure you're okay? You don't look okay." She poured her another shot but wouldn't take any of her money. "You know your money isn't good here. My car never ran this good before. You are the only mechanic that I know who charges next to nothing and fixes the actual problem. As long as that is a fact, you will never have to pay for your liquor when I'm tending bar."

"Your car is a pussycat. I love working on that baby. Just make sure you change the oil every three thousand miles; he's old and needs the clean oil. Just call me, and I'll make time. You'll probably be needing brakes soon, too, so don't wait too long." She chugged down the shot and took a long pull from her beer. "Keep it lubed!" She winked and headed back to her seat on the deck. "Nice to have a fan of my work," she said aloud.

The deck was filled with people, and Kitten's seat was taken. She sat down on the stairs and sipped her beer. The sun was going down, and I was one day closer to my destiny. Would I be able to pull it off when the moon shone brightly overhead? I wasn't sure. All I knew was I needed to have her for myself, and there was not anything more I wanted in the world.

A crew of guys was heading up the beach to the stairs where Kitty was sitting, and she smiled at them as they passed her. One of the men stopped and sat down next to her.

"Nice night, huh?" the tall stranger said as he eyed her up and down.

"Yeah, it's beautiful here? I love the beach."

"What's your name?" he asked with a lusty smile.

"Kitty, and you are?"

"I'm Judd. My friends and I are on vacation down here for a few days. We're staying at my parents' house down the other end of the boardwalk. There's gonna be a party later. Would you like to come?"

"Oh I don't think so, but thank you for asking. I have plans for later."

"A date?"

"Yeah."

"You can bring him with you. There is going to be a lot of people there, a few more wouldn't matter. Sure, bring him with you. It's the big house down on Dune. Just follow the music."

"Thanks a lot. I'll try and make it."

Judd got up and went inside to join his friends. He wrote something down on a piece of paper and brought it back out to Kitten. "Here is the address, and I put my cell number on it, too, just in case. I hope I'll see you there."

"Thanks, I'll really try."

He walked back into the bar, and Kitten finished her beer and looked in at them as they laughed and drank. She raised an eyebrow and smiled to herself. I watched her go back into the bar and right over to Judd.

"Hi!"

"Hi. Guys, this is Kitty. Kitty, these are the guys."

The voices overlapped. "Nice to see ya!" "Hey!" "How ya doin?" "Well H-E-L-L-O!"

"Would you like to have a drink with us?"

"No, I just wanted to thank you for inviting me to your party. I'll bring some wine or something."

"Bring the 'or something.' We don't have any connections down here, and it's a bitch to get shit when you don't know anyone," one of Judd's friends said.

"Okay, I'll see what I can do, maybe I'll see you guys later."

She walked out onto the boardwalk and looked behind at the group of men. Rubbing her head, she pulled out her cell phone and called Ed.

"Ed, it's Kitty…Could you drop by the house in a few and drop me off some stuff? I'm gonna need thirty."

"Thirty? What, are you running away or something?" I heard Ed yelling.

"Can you do it? Please! I really need it, Ed."

"Okay, I'll be there in about ten minutes, babe. Your lucky you caught me I was just leaving town."

"Thanks, Ed, you're the best."

She snapped the phone closed and gripped it tightly in her fist. "YES!" She stood there just looking out over the water letting out a huge sigh. She closed her eyes as the last bit of air expelled from her lungs and slid her cell phone into her bag.

I could hear hoots and hollers coming from across the way, and Kitty did, too, because she cut a sly grin and glanced over to the direction of the beckoning voices.

"Oh, baby, you are so fine. Let me take you out." The man was large, his hair was high and tight, and his arms bore many tattoos.

"No, baby, you don't want him. He doesn't even have a car. I drive a nice Mustang convertible. My front seat would look so hot with you in it. Let me take you for a ride." This young man was well groomed, his clothing was clean and neat, and his shoes were polished to perfection.

"Yeah, what color is it?" Kitten shouted across the crowd.

She could not be serious. Why would she even ask about the car? A man who shouts at a woman from over a crowd cannot be worthy of conversation. Why was she starting a conversation with this clown?

He ran over to her, tugging on his belt with every step as if to say, "I have a lot under my belt." She smiled and took a step back.

"Really, let me take you for a ride. My car is just around the corner." He smiled and shot her a romantic look.

"No, thank you, I wouldn't be caught dead in a Ford." She giggled and began to walk away.

"What the fuck you dissin' my car for, bitch? I oughta slap you, you fucking cunt!"

Kitten reached into her bag, grabbed something, and with her fist balled up, she socked the bastard right in the jaw. His feet flew up over his head, and he was laid out flat on his back.

"That's what you get for even suggesting the fact that you would like to put your fucking hands on me, you piece of shit. If you know what's good for ya, you'll stay the hell where you are and think about why you're there." She spit on the boardwalk and headed into the crowd.

"Holy shit, dude, she fucked you up. Man, I never saw any shit like that in my life."

"Shut the fuck up, jerk." The man staggered to his feet. His friend tried to assist, but he just pulled away from him.

"Well, I guess not having a car isn't such a bad thing after all." He laughed and ducked from a swing that nearly missed the back of his head.

"Shut the fuck up, Chris."

"Dude, she laid you out with one punch. That was no chick; that was a dude. It had to be."

They walked off, and I caught up to Kitty. She still had her fist balled up tight. The sound of music was getting closer as she pushed her way through the crowd, and I knew she would be making a beer stop just as soon as she came to the first bar.

When she sat down on the rickety stool, she placed her bag on the bar and opened her fist. Quarters, a roll of quarters was what gave her the power to knock him on his ass. What a woman! She really could take care of herself when she wasn't up against a handgun. I couldn't help but smile at her. Everything about her fascinated me. Her strength and her intelligence fed the magnitude of my love for her. She was unique, and I needed her to be mine. But I began to doubt my ability to make that so. How, if ever, could I tame her spirit? She was a wild woman. What made me think that when the moon was full, I would become mortal and spend the rest of my life with Kitty Morris?

I breathed her fragrance in and looked deeply into her eyes. She was all that I wanted. I just knew that it could work. It had to work. She chugged her beer, and just as she was setting down the empty bottle, the bartender brought her over another one.

"This one is on me," he said with a smile on his face. "I get off in a half hour. What do you say we go and get a bite to eat?" Who was this guy?

"Oh, Tommy, that's sweet, but I can't tonight. I have a ton of things to do. I don't really even have time for this beer." She put the bottle to her lips and never put it down until it was reduced to nothing but foam. "Thanks for the beer, but I really have to go." She grabbed her bag, threw a few singles down on the bar, and trotted out the door onto the street.

Just as she stepped off of the curb, Ed's car pulled to a screeching halt. "Get in!" Kitten just looked at him. He shouted again. "Get in the car!" He reached across the seat and opened the door. "What are you waiting for? Get in!"

She slid quietly into the seat, and Ed reached over her and slammed the door closed.

"What's the big hurry, Ed? Where are we going?"

"Where are you going tonight? And why do you need so much shit?"

"The house is down by the dunes past the batting cages and behind the empty lot. That's all I know. I haven't been there. I was going to check it out later when the party was well underway. I could make a lot of money in a house full of rich kids. Besides, I was invited. It's not like I'm crashing it or anything."

A police officer pulled up in his patrol car next to them in the opposing traffic. "Let's get a move on, sir, you're blocking traffic."

"Sorry, Officer, I was just picking up my girl; we were just leaving." Ed put on his blinker and pulled off slowly looking in his side-view mirror, checking on the cop as he rolled away. "I can't take this shit!"

"Ed, what is going on?"

"Kitty, I just have to be extra careful about cops after the Devin incident, now more than ever before."

"Why won't you tell me? And why can't I go and see him? Can I at least talk to his sister? I have to know if he is okay."

"I already found out for you. I sent one of my people in, and his chart was cool. No major injuries, a knife wound, lots of contusions a broken arm, and maybe he'll walk with a limp for a while, but other than that, he'll be fine."

"Nothing major, he'll be fine. What kind of bullshit is that? The guy is totally fucked up!" Her eyes filled with tears.

"Look, sweetheart, the kid is lucky he isn't dead. Those guys in there, they were gonna kill him. He is just lucky those guys didn't work for someone else."

"What if they come looking for him? Don't you think they will?" Kitty's voice began to crack.

Ed looked at Kitty with an, it-could-never-happen look and shook his head. "They aren't going anywhere, honey. Devin will be safe."

"Oh, Ed, what have I done?" Kitten's head hung low, and tears began to swell up in her eyes splashing onto the seat between her legs. "I didn't mean to get you involved in this. Oh God, this is entirely my fault. What is gonna happen now? Will they find out that we were there? I don't want to go to jail, Eddie; I don't think I could have a full-time girlfriend. I only like kissing beautiful women, Eddie; I can't do the hardcore dyke thing. I'm only into cuddling with girls. I can't go south pal. I don't want to go to prison."

Ed laughed at her. "This is why I love you so much. I never know what is going to come out of your mouth. Don't worry about the cops, honey; they will never know you were there. It's fine. I just don't want to get pulled over. There is always a chance something could go wrong. But you don't have anything to worry about, so relax." He patted her on the back and pinched her cheek. "I'll always take care of you, honey."

Kitten smiled and wiped the tears from her cheeks. "Ed, I don't think I can take this life anymore. Strange men are coming into my house and threatening my life. I don't think I can take another relationship. Everywhere I go, bad things are always happening to me. Now you go and save Devin and the terrible thing you've done, it's my fault. I'm the reason. It's just too much. Please take me home."

She stared blankly out the window watching the world go by on fast forward. I wanted so bad to hold her and tell her that everything was going to be all right. Her tears continued to fall as we pulled into the driveway.

"I'm walking you up. I'll check the apartment for you, and I'll stay until you fall asleep. I'll park across the street and keep an eye on you tonight. Then I'll have someone take the second shift, so don't be surprised when you see a car following you. I don't want you to be alone. I'll have someone on you wherever you go, so don't go trying to shake their tail on you. Just let them do their job."

"Ed, I don't need a babysitter. Just let me get some of those bullets from the trunk. My ammo is old and will probably backfire in my face, and I need the coke for that party tonight."

They got out of the car and walked around to the trunk. "When did you get a gun?" Ed asked. I was just thinking the same thing to myself when he said that. What was Kitten doing with a gun?

"What are you looking for, honey? What kind of gun you packing?"

"Do you have any .38 wad cutters? If not I'll take some .357s. They pack a bigger punch."

"Girl, where did you get a gun like that?" Ed said in a surprised tone of voice.

"It was a gift I bought myself a couple of years back, when I was working at the Navel Base. That place got rough at times, and I didn't like walking to my car at night. The bouncers were drunk half the time, and a girl's got to protect herself."

"Do you know how to use it?"

"I took second place sharpshooter three years in a row at my shooting range holster finals. I was great back then."

They entered the apartment, and Kitten went straight to a lockbox in her bedroom closet. She placed it on the end of the bed and opened it with a key. There was a shiny silver hand cannon resting on a cushion of rippled foam. The trigger had a lock on it, and she slid another key to release it. She pulled it apart and tossed it onto the bed. Holding the gun firmly in her hand, she motioned to Ed. "Nice, huh?" She pushed the barrel release and swung it open, exposing the oxidized bullets that were loaded in the gun. "Damn, look at these things. The copper is turning green."

She scrambled to the kitchen and opened the cupboard under the sink. "I have everything I need right here. She pulled out a black box and placed it on the table, grabbed a thick hunk of newspaper, and made a placemat for herself and began to clean her gun. "What should I do with these bullets? I can't just throw them away, can I? I never had to throw away bullets before."

"What difference does it make? Chuck them in the garbage. What could happen?" Ed gave the entire apartment the once-over and then went down to check the garage. He rigged the fire escape to make a lot of noise if someone tried to climb up to her apartment, and he replaced the broken floodlight on the side of the house.

"I checked the entire yard and rigged the fire escape; the floodlight is fixed, and if you don't mind taking a shower, I'll be on my way."

"Ed, a shower? You don't have to stick around while I shower. I'll be fine. Where did you get the floodlight?"

"I would feel more comfortable if I was here while you showered. I'll leave when you are in bed sleeping. This is just a security precaution. I'll clean your gun, and you go clean yourself."

"Okay, okay, I'll take a shower, but I can't be living like this. I need my privacy." She got herself a beer to take into the shower with her and closed the bathroom door.

When I heard the water go on, I could picture in my mind her beautiful body and imagined the bubbles of shampoo cascading down her luscious breasts and behind. She was my every desire, and I had to drag myself back to reality as I listened in on Ed's telephone conversations with his people.

The first call was made to a man named Johnny. Ed instructed him to be at Kitty's house at three o'clock and not to let her out of his sight. The second call was to a man named Vinny. He told this man to park on the block behind Kitty's apartment and make sure no one went in or out through the fire escape. And the third and final call was to a man named Tino. This call made me wonder; he instructed Tino to follow her, and when she least expected it, make contact and attempt to pursue her as a love interest. He offered him five thousand dollars to hit on Kitty, and the man apparently accepted because he gave him the address and told him that the money would be left with the bartender at the beach. I couldn't believe it. What was going to happen next?

Kitten came out of the bathroom in a small, fluffy pink towel. She padded her little feet into the bedroom and got dressed in a big, baggie T-shirt and came out brushing her hair. "So how's my baby, all clean and loaded?"

"Oh yeah, baby, clean as a whistle and ready to kill. I put it back in the box. I have people on the job. You don't need this gun. And next time you put your gun in hibernation, please take it out like once a month and clean it. It's too beautiful to leave to the elements. It needs to be cleaned." He shook his finger, tapping her nose with the tip. "Now get in that bed."

"Ed, are you telling me what to do? Is this something that I should get used to? I don't think I like this very much. I think it's going to get very boring very quick. I need my privacy, Ed."

"You'll have it, don't worry. It will be like every day. You won't even know that you are being followed."

"Where is the coke? You left it for me, didn't you?"

"Yes, I put it in the cupboard next to your coffee can, but I don't want you going to that party tonight, okay?"

He locked her door behind him and headed across the street with his car.

She watched him from the front window and pinched her lips together tightly. "I hate this shit. Who does he think he is anyway? I don't need a babysitter. I have a magnum." She batted the ashtray and trinkets off of the table by the window, sending them smashing against the door. "I don't want any of his psycho minions following me around. I need my privacy. I don't want anyone knowing my business."

She retrieved the cocaine from the cupboard and stuffed it into her purse, grabbed a beer out of the refrigerator, cracked it open, and slugged down almost the entire bottle and flopped on the couch. "Fuck this shit! I'm not having anyone following me around. I need to get out of here." She picked up the phone and told the other party to pick her up at the end of the block. "Be sure that you call before you reach Center Street…Give me about twenty minutes to get ready…I don't want anyone to see your face when you pull up…I'll be ready when you get here. Just don't forget to call, okay?" She snapped the phone closed and hopped to her feet, dashing to the bathroom, rushing to blow-dry her hair.

I sat quietly on her bed and began to root through her nightstand. There was a Stephanie Plum novel, a pair of handcuffs, traces of powder, remnants of marijuana, and what looked like some sort of jewelry box. She flew into the bedroom shaking her head around to fluff up the strands and fumbled in the closet for the night's wardrobe. When she was finished, she hustled a pair of shoes onto her feet and retrieved her jewel box from the nightstand, shoving it into an oversized carry bag. She grabbed her book, darted into the kitchen, and plucked the coffee can from the shelf, grabbing a tidy sum of cash and crammed that into the purse as well.

I watched her trot to the hallway closet, and as she reached up to retrieve a box on the top shelf, her skirt hiked up and I could see her pink lace panties. She had the most incredible ass, one worthy of being carved in stone on display in a museum. She carried the box to the bathroom and pulled out some hair clips and a red wig. "This could work. I don't think they will know it's me," she said to herself as she pinned down her hair and pulled the wig tight to her head. Appearing satisfied, she slid her fingers between the outer edges of the wig, camouflaging the strands of hair that were left behind. Giving her new red hair one last tug, checking its security, she smiled at herself and gave a turn around in front of the mirror checking out her new look. It was hot! She looked like a sex goddess; she looked like a hooker. What was she planning? I did not like it. I didn't like it one bit.

She closed up the box and tossed it on top of the hamper and headed back into the kitchen. "I'm cool now. Here kitty, kitty, kitty, come and get it." She opened the window and took a good look through her back yard and in between the houses at the street behind her apartment. "I see you, fucker! You think you're going to follow me, do you? Well, not tonight, buddy, not tonight," she snarled. Azreal jumped into the window and meowed at her. "Mommy's going out. Be a good boy. There is food out and fresh water. I'll be home later. Don't wait up." With that, she grabbed a beer and just as she cracked it, her phone rang. "Hello! I'm ready…Come and get me." Kitten left all of the lights in the house on and turned the volume on the television up a bit higher than usual.

She looked carefully out the front window and noticed that the man watching her apartment in the car across the street was not in the car across the street. "Where did he go? I know he was here just a minute ago. Fuck it, I'm out of here." She crept out of her apartment and lurched through the shadows all the way to the end of the block. A car began to pull up slowly and Kitten quickly opened the car door and hopped in. "Go, go, go!" The car sped off, and Kitten was laughing as she watched out the back window.

"Kitty, what the hell is going on? Who is that guy running to his car? Are you okay?"

"Kelly, I'm fine; it's cool, just drive."

"Why is your hair red? Is that a wig?" Kelly flicked the tips of her hair. "Where the hell am I driving to?"

"Head down to the boards and drop me off by the pavilion."

"Hey, I thought we were going to hang out tonight. Where are you going? Can I come?" Her face was hopeful.

Kitty shook her head. "Sorry, babe, I can't take you with me. Tonight, I'm going to be nothing but trouble, and you know what that means."

"I know, I know, I can't come." Kelly's head hung low, and she began to pout. "I promise that if it gets too scary, I'll go straight home. You don't have to worry, I'll be good."

"You know that I can't take you to the bar with me. You don't have a passable ID, and you know they won't let you drink with the one that you have. I promise to take you clubbing in Point next week. We'll go wherever you want."

Kelly smiled. "Anywhere I want? I'm holding you to that, you know."

"I said I promise, didn't I? Any place you want to go."

They pulled up to the boardwalk, and Kitten leaned over giving Kelly a kiss on the cheek. "You're the best. Thanks for the ride." She bounced out of the car, pulling at her skirt to keep it from rising, and trotted up the ramp. As she reached the top of the ramp, she began checking out her new hair in the reflection of the bar entrance. She walked slowly inside and went around to the side of the bar out of sight of her normal seat. She reached in her purse and placed a twenty-dollar bill on the bar.

"What is your pleasure, young lady?" Tiger asked.

"I would like to have a light beer please."

"Coming right up, beautiful." He looked at her as though he knew her, and as he headed over to the beer tap, he turned his head and stared at her, ignoring the foam that cascaded over the rim of the glass. He laid down a coaster, and as he placed the beer on top of it, he moved in close and asked, "Kitty, is that you?"

"No, I'm sorry, my name isn't Kitty," she said, shaking her head trying to change the sound of her voice so the ruse could continue.

"Kitty, I know it's you. What are you doing in this get up? Is it Halloween or something?" He giggled aloud and caressed her red hair with his fingers. "Nice color, though, very sexy."

"Oh shut up, Tiger. I don't want anyone to know it's me. I'm on the lamb."

"You're on the lamb? That's funny, you kind of look like a lamb, but with red hair."

"How could you tell it was me? Don't I look a little different? I thought I could get away with it."

"Babe, you can't hide from me. I'm probably the only one who has studied you from head to toe. If you colored your skin, I would know that it was you," he said smiling from ear to ear.

"Damn, if you know it's me, then everyone is going to know it's me. Fuck! I can't stay here."

"You know, I kind of like the red thing you got going on here; it's really a turn on. Stay for a while, and I'll take you to dinner. Then you can get out of here and not be noticed."

"Bobby, I can't go to dinner with you. I have a lot of drinking to do, and later, I have a party to go to."

"Why won't you let me take you out? I'm not going to bite you. Well, maybe a little, but I promise that you wouldn't mind it when it happens. Every time I want to do something nice, you won't let me. Why?"

"Tiger, you're a nice guy and all, but you are my bartender. You know the rule. I never date my bartender."

"What about the night by the pinball machine and all of those other times when you kissed me? It was hot between us; at least I thought it was hot. Don't you like me? Why is it okay for us to kiss, but not okay for us to eat together? Kitty, I just don't get you."

"Honey, nobody gets me, and I kissed you because I thought you were cute at the time. I didn't think you minded me kissing you."

"I'm cute at the time? What am I a piece of meat to be kissed at your leisure? Don't you even like me?"

"I love you, but not in the way you love someone that you have a relationship with. You know that I could never stay faithful to you, and you are jealous now and we aren't even dating. Imagine how it would be if we were. I don't want to lose you as a friend. That is why I won't go out with you. That's the only reason."

"I think if you and I were together you would stay faithful to me. I would make you happy, and you wouldn't have to work for Ed anymore doing God knows what. I could take care of you."

"See, this is what I'm talking about. I like working for Ed, and I enjoy my lifestyle just the way it is, thank you very much. I don't think having you trying to change it would make me happy at all, and then we wouldn't be friends."

"You're right, Kitty. I don't understand you." He frowned and walked away.

Kitten guzzled down her beer and headed down the bar to the restroom. She looked at herself in the mirror. "I have got to stop hanging out at this place." She fixed her hair and reapplied her lipstick then went into one of the stalls and snorted some cocaine. Flipping open her phone, she dialed and waited for an answer. "Yes, I need a taxi to pick me up at the corner of Sheridan and Ocean Terrace in Seaside Heights please...I'm not sure where I'm going yet...Thank you." She clicked her phone closed and did a last once-over of her body before she headed out.

"Excuse me, miss," Tiger said.

Kitten shot him a dirty look. "What?"

"I love what you've done to your hair." He laughed.

"Jerk!" she shouted and darted out the door. "What an asshole," she said, mumbling to herself. She walked around to the corner of Ocean Terrace and waited for her taxi in the shadows of the parking garage. Her feet were tapping, and she began pacing back and forth growing impatient with every second that passed. "Where is this stupid cab? How fucking long does it take to drive three blocks for Christ sake?"

Ed's car pulled around the corner. Kitten noticed him, too, and took a few more steps back so he would not see her. He pulled into a parking space and got out of his car. She watched as he put change in the parking meter and did not come out from the shadows until she was sure he was long gone. Just then, the taxi pulled up, and she hopped into the back seat and shut the door.

"Where are we going?" the driver asked as he jotted down something on a clipboard.

"Just drive, please; I'll let you know when we get there."

"Miss, I really need to call this fare into my dispatcher; they require a destination upon pickup."

"Okay, first take me to the liquor store on the corner of Grant Avenue and Boulevard, then we can head over to Dune Terrace."

The driver smiled and clicked the button on his radio. "Dispatch, this is car twenty-two. I have the fare and am in transit."

"What's your destination, twenty-two?" a voice spoke back.

"First, a quick stop on Grant and Boulevard, destination Dune Terrace," he responded.

"Twenty-two, the fare rate is nine."

"Copy that, Dispatch. I'm out." He latched the handset back onto the dashboard and circled the block heading down Boulevard toward Grant.

When the cab stopped at the liquor store, Kitten rushed in and grabbed a bottle of champagne. She asked the clerk for a pack of rolling papers and cigarettes, paid what she owed, and was back to the car in no time.

"Okay, I'm good. We can go to Dune now," Kitten said.

"Yes, Miss."

The driver tried to make small talk, but Kitten just stared out the window not muttering a word. As they approached Dune Terrace, you could hear the music from the party. The street was scarcely lined with mammoth rich homes, and all of the vehicles parked on the street were high-end top-of-the-line money cars.

"Wow, this is some party. Friends of yours?" the driver continued to attempt conversation.

"You can stop here. This is fine; how much for the ride?" Kitten said.

"The fare is nine dollars, please."

Kitten pulled some money out of her bag. "Here, keep it," she said and exited the car, shutting the door as the driver again tried to converse with her. "I don't have time for this crap."

She walked slowly toward the house; it was at the very end of Holiday Road where Dune Terrace began. Her mouth opened wide as she looked up at the balconies of the beautiful homes. "This is the life; it must be nice to have money." The party was loud, and there were people congregating in the front and at the sides of the house.

"Hey, baby, welcome to the party," one man said.

The voices began to overlap. "Oh, hot momma on the move... Hello, sweet cheeks...Will you have my baby?"

Kitty smiled politely and walked around to the back of the house. The yard was surrounded by a large fence. She opened the gate, revealing a huge yard with a swimming pool, hot tub, and a bar. There were people everywhere, and all eyes, both male and female, were on her as she made her way to the sliding-glass doors that led to the kitchen with champagne bottle in hand.

"There she is," a voice called out over the crowd. "I didn't think you were going to make it, but I'm glad that you did." He parted the crowd and made his way toward Kitty. "Come in, come in, my house is your house. Make yourself at home."

"Hi, Judd, this is some party. Thanks for inviting me. This house is great." Kitten leaned in and kissed him on the cheek. "I brought some champagne, but I know it's not enough for everyone." She laughed and looked around with eyes wide open. "I don't think the liquor store has enough booze for all the people at this party. You sure know how to put together a big bash."

"Oh, this is nothing; you should have been here last year. The cops couldn't even get past the gate there were so many people. They had to let the party continue till the next morning because they were afraid they might have a riot on their hands." He laughed and took Kitty by the arm. "Let's go someplace where we can drink this champagne without sharing." He guided her through the house, giving her the tour.

The place was a mansion with Italian marble floors and large overstuffed couches and chairs. There was a pond at the bottom of the stairs with fish in it and large potted trees throughout every room. The artwork that adorned the walls looked very old and expensive. I think one was a Monet, but I never went for that artsy stuff so I was not sure. He led her up to the second floor.

"Why are we going up here away from your party? Shouldn't you be with your guests?" Kitten said with a bit of unease in her voice.

"Oh, honey, don't worry; it's cool. I just want to take you up and let you see the beautiful view. If you want to go back downstairs, you can, but trust me, you are going to love it."

She shook her head no and followed him up the stairs. They walked down a long hall that led to a balcony and stepped out onto it.

"Wow, this is beautiful," she said. "The view is spectacular. Ocean front property definitely has its advantages."

You could see all the way down to the Boardwalk and all the way out to the sea. As I looked up at the beautiful night sky, I could see that my time was running out. I only had one more day to figure out what I was going to do about my destiny, and my stomach churned thinking about it.

They sat at a large glass table. There was an oversized umbrella canopy covering them that was lined with multicolored twinkling lights. I have to say I was very impressed with everything so far, but I still was not sure about her being up here alone with Judd. There was something about him I did not particularly care for.

"Wow, this is beautiful."

"I told you, you wouldn't be sorry if you came. Would you like me to open the champagne? Can I offer you some recreational party favors? I have lots." He smiled and motioned for her to follow him inside to another room on the second floor.

"Where are we going now?"

"Just in here, away from prying eyes. Trust me, I like you; I'm not going to hurt you. I just want to get to know you; that's all." He led her into a library.

When she entered, she gasped. "Wow, you sure have a lot of books. This house just keeps getting better and better."

"If you think this is great, wait till you see this." Judd picked up a remote control and began pushing buttons. At first, the lights went dim. "Oh sorry, wrong button." With the next click of the buttons, a cabinet opened up from behind one of the bookcases revealing a small room. "What do you think about this?" He smiled as she peered inside.

"Holy crap, this is so fucking cool," she said standing there with her mouth gaping open and eyes as wide as saucers.

The room was awesome; it had a bar, stereo equipment, television, and a spiral staircase leading up through the ceiling. It was quite impressive. Kitten thought so too, because her mouth never closed. Judd took his finger and pushed her chin up, closing her mouth.

She laughed. "Sorry, I have never been in such a beautiful house before; it's just a lot to take in all at once. Where does that go?" She pointed to the circular staircase.

"That? Well, that's the best part of all, my favorite part actually. Would you like to see?"

"Sure, I've never climbed up a round set of stairs before. You first." She glided her hands around the banister the entire way up. When they reached the top, he told her to close her eyes.

She seemed frightened, but she complied, and they emerged from the exit onto a small platform crow's nest on the roof. He settled her in and told her to open her eyes.

"WOW! This is just about as high as you can get without drugs," she said with laughter in her voice. "This is so cool. I would give anything to live in a house like this. You have got to be the luckiest man on earth."

"No, it's my parents' house. I come here every year, and you are the first person I ever brought up here. I'm glad you like it?" He leaned in to kiss her, and she didn't resist. "That was nice," he said. "May I do it again?"

She nodded her head yes, and they began to kiss, the sight of which made me insane with jealousy. I hated how flirtatious she was and how freely she kissed men she did not know anything about. I wanted to throw him off of the roof and take her in my arms, but I knew that wasn't an option.

I could not take it any longer. I had to get away, so I whisked down to see what the commotion downstairs was all about. I could hear women laughing, and it seemed that the hot tub was the place to be. There were naked women drinking and laughing. They did not seem to be of the legal drinking age. In fact, the more I looked around, the more I realized how many underage drinkers were at this party.

I heard a terrified voice in the distance, and that was when the hideous light showed its ugliness. I hovered over to the dunes where

I could hear the voice was coming from, and when I arrived, I wasn't surprised at what I found.

There was a young girl; the straps to her top were ripped, and a much older fellow was pawing her breasts. His hand hiked up her skirt roughly, and he plunged his fingers into her lace panties. She tried to scream, but as she did, he covered her mouth with his hand to muffle the sound. The light grew closer to the two of them. I was not sure for whom the light was coming, but I knew that it wouldn't be long before it made it to the spot where they were.

The music from the party was loud enough to mask the muffled screams of the poor child being taken by force. I was not sure what to do. I flashed back to the party and tried to get someone to hear the calls for help, but everyone was so drunk they would not here me. I raced back to the scene of the crime, and now the man was readying himself for penetration. The young girl seemed to be out of strength to fight, and her assailant was eager to complete what he had started.

She pleaded with him to stop, and he ignored her cries. As he was about to plunge his manhood deep into her virgin flesh, the police came rushing from the waterline to break up the party. It was a good thing, because they too noticed what was happening and arrived just in the nick of time to prevent the rape from going any farther.

I went back to see what Kitten was up to, and she was gone. I searched the house inside and out but couldn't find her anywhere. The police were finishing up their little disturbing-the-peace call, and I headed over to Kitty's apartment to wait for her.

Azreal was curled up on the couch, and when I entered through the window, he ran outside. I did not think he liked me very much. I sat on the couch until the sun came up, and Kitty still had not returned. I wondered where she could be.

A few hours later, Ed began banging on the door. When Kitty did not answer, he took out his spare key and let himself in.

"Kitty, are you here? I'm sorry that I had the boys watch the house last night...Kitty? Oh that girl!" He sat down on the couch and made a few phone calls demanding to know why she was not being followed. "I'll find her myself. What the hell am I paying these guys for? They can't even keep an eye on one girl, not one girl!" he shouted and nosed through her apartment.

He looked through her bedroom and gave the bathroom a once-over. I watched him lock the door behind him as he left in search of the illusive Kitty Morris. I did not know why he thought he could find her. I had no idea where she was. I closed my eyes and wished my way to the bay, but she was not there. I continued to look for her all day and into the night, but she was nowhere to be found.

When I looked up at the sky, there it was, the full moon, the moon of my destiny. How was I supposed to reveal myself to my one true love if I could not find her to tell her how I felt about her? I could see the light glowing for some victim but could not get myself to do a thing. I just stood there and let it happen. I looked on as a drunken teenager out night swimming was pulled in by the undertow of the strong ocean current and did nothing to save him.

I began to feel ill and ran down the beach to get away from all of the noise. As the music and laughter of the boardwalk faded into the night, I found myself at the very spot where Kitten and I had our first conversation. I stood there in the tall beach grass looking out over the sea, thinking about Kitty and what I would say to her if she were here. I could picture her beautiful face and sparkling smile as if she were standing before me. There was not a freckle on her body that I hadn't memorized; her image was engraved in my heart forever. I could even smell the sweet smell of her perfume.

I was beginning to realize what little time I had to find her and fulfill my destiny of becoming mortal again. The more I thought, the more I realized that no matter what I said or did, she would always be the person she was. I could never change her. Ed was her best friend, and he could not reason with her. Tiger was madly in love with her, and he could not tame her. What in the name of all that is holy made me think that I could have her for my own?

I headed to the tower where we spent our first night together. The wind was picking up, and I could smell her perfume even more strongly now. I looked up at the tower, and as I reached the ladder, the scent was stronger. Kitty was here. She was sleeping in the tower. I knew it was her. I flashed myself to the top and sat on the railing. She was lying down on the makeshift bed she had made from the stolen items, motionless. I looked at her for a few moments and tried to gather my thoughts on what to say to her. Midnight was only a few minutes away, and the excitement was growing inside me.

I went over it again and again in my mind. As the moon reached its highest point in the sky and the hour of truth was upon me, I leaned in and shook her shoulder to wake her from her peaceful slumber. Something was wrong. She did not budge. I gave a hard tug, rolling her over to her back. I gasped for air. I could not breathe. My heart sank deep into my chest; my tongue retracted into the back of my throat. I swallowed hard to choke back the tears and fell to my knees. "WHY!" I screamed with anger. I cradled her in my arms trying to revive her lifeless body, breathing air into her lungs that she could not for herself. "Kitty, you have to breathe. Come on, baby, you can do it, breathe!" Her body was cold, and her eyes blank and hazy. She was dead. My love was dead. I looked at her face and her body. She had been strangled to death and placed facedown on the floor of the tower, left like a sack of garbage. Her purse was gone, and in her hand was a perfect clear stone. I held her for a while asking why this had to happen. Why did she have to die? But there was no response. I could not get myself to leave her side. I did not want this to be happening. I wanted to spend the rest of my life with this woman, to be there for her, to love her for all of eternity. All my dreams were shattered. The beautiful Kitten lay quietly in my arms, cold and hollow, no life, no soul, just hollow.

Her blank eyes stared up at me, and I looked deep into them. "I love you, Kitty Morris, with all of my heart." Just then, a gust of wind came over me and lifted me up into the air spinning me around and placing me back down on the tower. When I landed, I hit hard and felt pain for the first time. I didn't understand it. I pushed my hand down on a nail that was sticking out of the handrail, and it pierced my skin. I began to bleed. I was mortal.

I had revealed myself to my Kitten, and even though she was dead, I had become mortal. I screamed in pain for the loss of my one and only true love. I was destined to live out the remainder of my mortal life without her. I cradled her in my arms till the sun came up over the Atlantic and viewed the beautiful sunrise for the first time as a mortal. I gently placed her down and covered her in the blanket, giving her lips one last kiss goodbye before I left to do what I had to do.

I crept quietly into the house on Dune Terrace, and while Judd lay sleeping, I took a knife and held it up to his throat. He awoke in fear.

"What the fuck?! Who are you?" he shouted.

"I'm the last person you will ever see," I said and slit his throat.

I went to the library and took one of the guns out of a trophy case, loaded it, and put the cold barrel to my head, pulling the trigger without hesitation. When I awoke, there she was, the beauty who came for me that day in the meadow so long ago.

"Oh, John, why, why did you do it?" she asked.

I did not say a word. She led me through the mirror image, and like before, my mortal life was over and my new existence had begun.

THE END